I0621877

www.pagebacon.com

L.B. SISK

ACKNOWLEDGMENTS

For my friends and family ... and my cat. All of them have contributed to my life in ways that I could never truly repay. I love you all.

For the great authors and artists who have inspired me. And, needless to say, a big shout out to Science Fiction, Fantasy, Graphic Novels, and all the bad late night movies that I endured because I couldn't get enough of the cheap props and even worse special effects.

For PageBacon who gave me the opportunity to see my work in print.

For anyone who has purchased this book. Thank you.

Contents

PREFACE...1

BEGINNINGS..4

CHAPTER ONE...50

CHAPTER TWO...116

CHAPTER THREE...153

CHAPTER FOUR...183

CHAPTER FIVE...231

CHAPTER SIX...246

EPILOGUE..291

PREFACE

*If mankind had wished for what is right,
they might have had it long ago.*
(The Pleasure of Hating)
—**William Hazlitt, English
essayist, critic (1826 A.D.)**

War. The Beast is at home here. How many battles has it fought already? No. It doesn't care. It doesn't matter. This is where it lives. This is the only time it is free.

"We have a tank group coming into Sector Four," Commander McNeil says, offering up potential targets. "They have reinforcements moving in from Sector Eight. Also, a jet is coming in low and fast. It looks like they got you on target. Do you mind keeping your package together in one piece?"

"I didn't feel like hiding today," it whispers a low, almost guttural reply. It seldom talks—smiles less. But today it's doing both. "Don't worry, Commander. I'll bring him back in one piece."

They are talking about *me.*

"You do that."

"Okeydokey," it chuckles while knocking down a hunter-bot with a severed armored head at the end of the spine—using it like a club before tossing it aside like trash.

The *Beast* is a nickname like *monster, demon and death*. The *package* is the human body that it inhabits at the moment. The man's name—*mine*—is Jim St. John. It's a symbiotic relationship. I see things—what it does. But I do not have any control of my body and I'm just along for the ride. I would call it a dream, but I feel it when it gets hit with a nuke. And the horrors that it unleashes on this world are real. The best way to describe it is that it is the personification of rage, something like a creature in an ancient comic book. Whatever we are together, however, is a debate for future psychologists.

The Heads-Up Display in our helmet highlights where the tank group is, along with another hundred possible targets. It jumps four miles to the tank group first, punches through force-fields as if they weren't even there, and tears the diamond-hard vehicles to pieces. In a flash, it slaughters the forty armored soldiers coming from Sector Eight. Then it takes a mobile gun unit into its hands and actually hammers others into oblivion with it.

It's relentless—a hunger, a thirst drives it. It loves the bloodshed. It loathes the enemy. It hates it.

It scours the battlefield, looking for anything that needs killing. A BLIP from its helmet reminds it of the fighter craft that is accelerating toward it. Because of the electromagnetic chaos, the pilot hasn't shot yet, actually needing visual confirmation with a targeting sight.

The monster smiles and jumps four hundred feet up into the air and tears that flying bitch to pieces. Quickly landing back on the ground, it lets its battlesuit—a simple, mirror-like mesh of nanobots and carbon nanotubes—extinguish the flames.

"I'm God here!" it shouts on all channels. "You defy us? You bring ruin upon you all!" It seldom feels giddy, but I can sense its enthusiasm—

"Jim! Jim!" Lisa shouts over our private channel. "My God, they're storming the medical lines. They have Torsons! How the hell did they—"

"Forget it, slut!"—it shakes its head, disbelieving she would bother us now—"He's ocupado."

A scream and violent blast cut the channel; however, before the Beast can gloat, a sudden feeling of nausea flashes through the demon's guts as I claw myself awake. It's literally like kicking him in the nuts.

"No, forget that pious bitch!" it shouts, trying to suppress my consciousness. "It's too fucking soon!"

<u>BEGINNINGS</u>

Societies and communities create laws. People must decide if the same are truths.

(About the Neo-Holocaust, from a televised speech)
—Albert Vlokvo, President of United Europe (2226 A.D.)

J im St. John woke up groggy and dehydrated. Common, yes, but things seemed different. For one, he hadn't woken up in Medical. The other, he was actually standing in mud—
KA-BOOM!

Beside him, a main battle tank exploded, showering out thick sheets of armor and pieces of bodies. Out of reflex, he caught the 20-ton turret. He threw it at the rest of the hovertank as it floated toward him, and it bounced off in another direction.

"Commander McNeil." He opened up a channel, just as he caught an eye full of someone being split open from balls to neck by a hunter-bot. "What the hell? Why am I up already?"

"Sorry about the rude awakening, bud. But your friend seems

to have left you holding the bag." His commanding officer has always been a smartass—the plus side of being named after the savior of mankind. "Looks like you are going to have to do things the hard way."

"I don't understand." Confusion and cobwebs from the reawakening has always slowed him down. "Why did I wake up? What happened?"

He remembered a scream, but there were lots of scream— hell, that was just one band member of this Mötley War tour: *Let's Kill Some Rebel Scum*. This conflict was some nine hundred miles north of Toldeclevchikee, and was therefore relatively safe from prying eyes. So there was going to be a lot of people dying today.

"No time. You can't think about that now ..." McNeil paused, something was up but the man wasn't talking. "They have our encryption pegged and are starting to jam our channels. We'll lose communications until we recode, so our people will be fighting blind for a bit. Until I can reestablish a secure line, you are going to have to kill as many of them as you can."

"OK"—he knew his job with or without the Beast—"but give me a minute. I just need to—"

"Jim ... can't ... Lisa now. You got to—" Static suddenly replaced the conversation, but what had he said about Lisa?

He then remembered the fucking scream, and he wondered if his heart stopped. Hoping it was only a nightmare and fighting his better judgment, he keyed the helmet to replay the last few minutes. And then his world collapsed.

Lisa?

Panicked, he opened his comlink and asked, "Commander, do you know where Scarlet Angel is?"

STATIC.

Plink! BOOM!

An explosive round bounced off of him and hit some poor bastard beside him. He flicked off the pieces of the resulting carnage. Heavily armored or not, that guy didn't have a chance. No chance at all.

Jim slid his hand over his thick, self-repairing bodysuit. His only armor was an invulnerable helmet, which matched the quicksilver-like look of the suit. He only needed the helmet to locate targets and communicate with his fellow soldiers. Otherwise, his skull was as hard if not harder.

"Hmm, maybe one day I'll find out how invulnerable I am?" he asked as his heart pounded in his chest, worrying about Lisa. There were other soldiers like him that didn't need armor. Lisa and many others required lots of it, but she was in Medical, usually far enough away and sometimes didn't—

Lisa, where are you? He couldn't find her homing beacon because of electromagnetic jamming, and the battlefield was so big she might have been too far away for his lifeforce detection power to sense her.

He looked for higher ground and jumped onto a nearby hovertank to get a better view. He soon noticed a colleague standing below him who was awestruck.

Jim smirked and waved. Compared to the rest of his troops, he didn't consider himself all that tall, only about seven-foot-two from head to toe without helmet and boots. Hell, he'd just met Cartwright the other day, and both of them had laughed about her powersuit, which had to be built by hand to accommodate her twelve-foot frame.

"Bank left. Take that trench," someone shouted in an open channel in Grid Fourteen. "Corporal, take a squad and make those *STIGS* pay."

Total carnage, this war had to be relentless, and no side ever kept prisoners unless for a brief interrogation.

Not finding her anywhere, he jumped away and left the tank in the distance.

Stigs. It was simply short for *Instigators*; however, because of overwhelming patriotism, it was used as an ugly stigma for the Rebels they fought. Its derogatory use almost seemed to trigger his rage again.

Almost?

He felt it obviously—the terrible hunger. He knew that it was mocking him now, trying to claw its way back out so that he wouldn't find Lisa until she was long dead.

"Yeah, fuck you," he snarled despite himself, but it was the howl of a man, not a Beast. He was remembering more of what had happened just before her medical team had been hit. To be fair, it only liked to kill, so it didn't like distractions. The laughing in the deep corner of his brain could be taken at face value.

"Lisa? Lisa?" he shouted over their private channel.

"Die! You sonaof—!" A stig suddenly jumped up in front of him, and took aim with a handheld cannon.

"Leave me alone!" Jim kicked the villain in the ribs. Armored plates cracked and electronics sparked, and the rebel was knocked a mile back into the darkness. Or out to orbit, Jim could never tell.

"TAKE *HIM* OUT!" Seeing his position, rounds from e-machineguns—AKA fast-recovering portable rail guns—flashed against Jim's skin and tried to hammer him back. He ignored them, disappeared by blending in with the world around him, and jumped to a totally different sector. Behind him, a small nuke flared, even though that wouldn't have killed him.

"Captain St. John? Jim? Where the Hell are you going?" the Field Commander, Colonel Carlos Jackson McNeil, his longtime friend, shouted and pleaded when he got a better channel. "The Medics can take care of it.

"Don't you understand? The Night Rangers suckered us here. They outnumber us four to one. You need to start killing these motherfuckers."

Jim almost turned, but he shook his head in defiance, even though his blood seemed to be boiling in frustration. He managed to cool it, but he refused to answer, fearing an argument would make him abandon his search. He couldn't think of anything else besides her.

"What are you doing?" He imagined his teachers, generals, the Panterian Guard—everyone!—standing like gods all around and shouting at him. Since being a vessel for the Beast, during war he always questioned his sanity. "It's too late for her. You can only avenge her death now. Follow your orders! Use your blades."

His blades *hissssssed.*

He dared not look down at the weapons, knowing he was insane for even imagining that they had desires of their own. Their bloodlust, an ache in the pit of his stomach, was an integral part of his rage. It churned his gut now, an unyielding thirst from the six weapons hanging between the knuckles of his hands.

"They plead to you, but you ignore them? You sick, fuck," another voice spoke in a hellish whisper. It was something that he knew was actually his own wild conscience and inner voice, the Beast itself.

"And how can you let your friends suffer?" it asked loudly, even though he was never sure if anyone else had ever heard it speak. "Avenge their senseless slaughter. You know that the forged adamant will slay them all."

He grinned despite himself, knowing a great deal about the weapons' history. They were named after a man named Kurgon, who'd developed the blades centuries ago. Some legends said that they'd been inspired by childhood comics; others, from nightmares. Regardless, each of Jim's 15-inch-long crystal blades was a perfect, implacable tool for what he'd been trained and created for.

Orders, directives, commands—Blast it, I can't now. Not yet! He was getting overwhelmed by all the requests, all the priorities. He wondered if he should just let the Beast take hold to save the rest of his friends. Lisa could be dead already—

"Nooooo!" he shouted, and jumped another ten miles to another sector.

"Damn you, let that bitch die," the Beast howled as it watched a series of full-sized nazer rockets strike into one of their platoons.

"Go back to hell. I'm going to find her," St. John shouted on all channels. "Then later, I'll kill them all later."

"Fine," the monster grunted and stopped pushing.

He climbed to the top of an embankment and looked around. He found a patch of land near a burning tank. He let his natural cloak subside, and he stood at the mouth of another huge crater. He took a calming breath, thereby giving his life detection power a chance to—

There!

He saw a flicker at the very edge of his perception, but it was enough.

"Lisa, hold on," he shouted into their private channel when he zeroed in on her location. He jumped and landed near what was left of her transport.

"Medics, I need you here now," he screamed, after opening a channel to the nearest medical team. The area was emitting gamma and x-rays, remnants of Torson grenades. Sometimes tanks and other armored carriers could withstand a couple of such explosions, but Lisa and her own med-unit hadn't been so lucky.

"Damn it. They can't hold 'em. Those … Stigs are …" Shouts from Jackson continued to trumpet in his ears over the comlink in his helmet. "Where … fuck … are …? We … eed … yo … now!"

"Lisa," he whispered. She was the only one left of her team that hadn't been vaporized. Her body … the little directional pocket nukes had worked their mischief, and had pealed through what little armor she had been wearing.

She managed a smile, but was shaking terribly.

He clenched his fists. The Stigs would pay for this.

"Lisa, I'm here—HERE!"

He quickly had to suppress the rage, when it realized that she'd probably be dead soon, and it could finally get back to work. Naturally, the Beast wouldn't be able to listen in this type of situation. It only understood orders to kill and survive. It would never be able to comfort Lisa, and he would never ask it to. That asshole's bedside manner for the soon-to-be dead was a pillow. Pressed over their faces.

Jim blinked and dropped to his knees then carefully, very carefully, reached out to her. For some reason, obviously the Beast's doing, he couldn't retract his blades. He got confirmation of that when he heard its laughing.

"Try not to speak," he said. His fingers brushed her right cheek, which was covered with tears.

He shuddered despite himself. He couldn't believe his own strength by staying by her side.

"So noble. Yit, I mus, m'love," she said in Neo-classic, which was a weird mix of Modern and 13th Century English. It was the language of the First Generation of AOM soldiers, and her pain must have been too much for her to mask it. "For if here I fault, yur eyes may ne'r see this visage crafted for our kind. The truth then woulthne'r b'told.

"Jim …" she paused or possibly just lost her voice. He never fully understood why she and the first group of their kind had been forced to speak that odd language. Because of that and the once semi-steady glimmer of her lifeforce, he knew Lisa was much older than her mid-twenties appearance.

You do like that old dried out pussy, don't you? the Beast poked from inside his mind, while Jim pictured daggers thrown at it—It easily deflected them with its blades.

"Jim, it's time," she coughed out, composed herself and subdued the old speech. "It's time I tell you the truth." Blood stained her face, and her lifeforce, her bio-energy, once so vibrant and steady, was flickering erratically. He also noticed the tiredness in her eyes, but also the strength she mustered to stay with him.

"Incoming!" his helmet sounded.

The war, in obvious protest, immediately hammered the ground with three heavy explosions. It had a point—a pair of lovers in the midst of this?

"Incoming! Incoming! Incoming! Incoming!"

"Hold on!" He sent out a distress beacon and threw himself over her again as another series of explosions pounded his back, while bullets ricocheted off his shoulders and neck. The onslaught seemed never-ending and he hoped that nothing was getting through his defenses.

"Mark! Launching!" a voice rang out in his helmet. Then a friendly nazer rocket, launched miles away, ended the assault. A bubble of calm seemed to envelop them again.

"Easy, Lisa. I will listen, but try not to move. It will do more harm than good," he said soothingly and then eased her back down, while applying pressure to the wounds he'd just reopened.

Come on, fucktard, the demon grumbled. *Let's get this* over *with. I need to slice me off some heads.*

Fuck, man, Jim lashed back. *If you do not shut the fuck up, I won't let you out, and I will simply kill these shit-stains myself.*

Ugh. Fine, the Beast grumbled and seemed to sulk.

"Jim, it doesn't matter." She shook her head, a wistful smile on her lips, possibly seeing, or at least picking up on his internal struggles. "You know it's too late. Death is near, and his touch is cold, colder than I could have ever imagined.

"But what did I ever know?" She crossed her heart in prayer —an ancient gesture she said that she'd learned on her own— and looked to the sky. "I don't know how to say what I need to —what I should have told you long ago. All I can hope for is that you can forgive me." Even while she spoke, her voice seemed to change and seemed to fill with uncertainty. She wasn't making much sense at all.

She paused, eyes drifting down. His hands were keeping her wounds closed, but she pushed herself free. Then she grabbed his right forearm with both hands. Surprisingly, even through the thick mirror-like material covering his arm, he felt a ring—a symbol—he'd given her months ago. Thereby making this all the worse.

Following her gaze, he grimaced when he saw a brilliant glare from things other than a ring. Forgotten briefly, his crystalline blades were still extracted, reminding him of where they were and what he was.

"Jim, listen," she implored. He looked back into her eyes, seeing fear that wasn't there before. "Jim, I'm sorry, but I've lied to you. You don't know how much we've all been manipulated."

Shaking her head, she clenched her teeth and shut her eyes. "Just before I met you, I was given my mission. I was to become your confidant. Help you adjust to a life in the FGGO. Aid and prepare you for your transformation—the Re-forge.

"And, become, if need be, your whore." Tears flowed and she shuddered and began to sob. He tried to reach out to her again, console her.

"No, stop. I'm OK. Just listen," she said, glancing away shamefully. "After I met you, got to know … fell in love. Jim, the lie became too much, too terrible.

"Sweetie, you're not going to like what I tell you, but there is nothing here worth fighting for. There's nothing noble gained by fighting these pointless wars, and there's certainly no honor for us here."

Jim heard the words, but he was too caught up with her injuries and pain. He knew she was having difficulty saying these things, as if something was actually holding her tongue.

"It's OK," he told her, not really knowing what to say. "It's the past. Besides, you've always told me to look toward the future," he babbled, speaking nonsense, and decided to shut the hell up and simply gaze into her eyes.

How did I meet someone so kind? His heart pounded like it did the first time they kissed—

A powerful sense of joy suddenly radiated from her, as she looked up to him. It was as if she could see his amber eyes through the thick visor of his round, mirrored helmet. In truth, he knew that she could see so much more.

"Yah, it-it's their fault," she said. "Their mistake was putting us together.

"Jim, listen," she continued, knowing she had his full attention now. "This-this cause you align yourself with is flawed—absurd."

What? He winced. *How dare*—His blood all but boiled when he heard her words, because of something that could only be described as PATRIOTISM.

No, let her speak, he warned the Beast when it stirred.

"Lisa, that's T-T-TR-TREASON," he stammered, not wanting to believe she was serious. "How can you say that after all these years, after all the things they did to me? The things you told me were OK?"

He remembered all the years of mental and physical preparation; remembered the procedure that had taken—even for him—over a month to heal; and remembered all the battles that had taken place since then.

Has she gone crazy? It seemed plausible. Otherwise, it nullified everything she had ever said to justify his role here, and confirmed everything he had always feared.

He looked in her sky-blue eyes, the tale-tale scrunching of her eyebrows as she sought his trust. He saw the tears covering her face, and he knew a lie would've been so much easier for her to tell.

"Honey," she said quickly. "I understand. I know. I know and if I had more-more time ..." Her voice softened. "You need not fear. Your heart has always been kind. Remember that. Remember how you loved me."

He touched her cheek. It was getting colder. "No. No. I can't. I can't let you go," he confessed the obvious. "Mock that cold touch. Fight for me. Fight for us!"

"Jim, the awareness of dying for something great and noble strips death of its absurd character, not only for those who die, but those who survive ..." She smiled weakly, quoting a phrase like he did so often when teaching new recruits. "Lepp, a French priest, once said that. Can't you understand that you have given me so much?"

"I don't care." He fought with her. Love, the culprit. "Don't leave me. There is so much—"

"Shhhh," she said, and her hand reached up—her fingers gently touched the ultra-hard plate of his helmet, which only hid his face from her. "Jim, it's too late."

Seeing her desperate stare of hope and submission, he resolved his heart. "Lisa," he moaned, "what will I do now?"

"For one, s-stop this nonsense," she demanded. "You can't keep working for these people. Promise me that. Don't let me die without you telling me—" She coughed, began to shake and couldn't continue.

He bit his lip. He didn't know what to do, couldn't imagine saying, let alone doing, what she so desperately needed to hear. Surprisingly, the Beast said nothing.

"Promise me," she repeated and hammered his arm with her hands. "Don't let them—"

McNeil broke in: "I'm going ... kill you ... this, St. John! You hear me? I swear ... God."

His commander's jumbled screams. Such poignant words!

Lisa grabbed his arm with both hands, jolting him back to this hellish reality when he felt the ring.

"I prom—" His throat squeezed shut before he could finish. Was the Beast so angry with Lisa now that it actually controlled him without becoming fully conscious? No, there was something else he couldn't fathom, couldn't understand.

Frustrated, unable to even breathe, he looked at what the grenades had done. She was half buried in the mud, wounds so deep, and her legs—

HER LEGS!

POP!

Something inside him snapped or exploded or burnt out. He simply, calmly pressed the release trigger of his helmet. The lower section of the faceplate flipped up and rolled back, thereby allowing him to take it off.

He set the helmet down, took off the red sunglasses he wore beneath it, and pulled back the tight-fitting hood of the bodysuit.

He then took a deep breath, defying whatever it was that had kept him from speaking.

"I'm sorry. I don't understand, Lisa," he consoled her, his words now spilling out. "I don't understand why it was so hard. But I promise, I promise, I give my word that I'll never be part of such massacre again. It is you, not the FGGO"—he looked deep into her blue eyes—"who holds my leash."

Lisa smiled. His eyes pictured her suffering and a strange sense of reprisal and satisfaction. "Thank you. I love you."

Their eyes locked again. He was speechless and nearly out of breath. And despite the apathy the Beast always showed toward death, he noticed that a single, lone tear had rolled down his cheek. Foolishly, he thought more would come, but should have known better.

"Lisa, I …" Carefully, he brushed his left hand through her remaining red hair, which had been scorched and burned by the grenades. Then he stroked her chin. She was so beautiful. "My Love, I'll never forget you."

Lisa was crying, her body still shaking. "Jim, I hope I can remember you."

"Shhhh," he whispered and lowered his lips to hers. Hands near each other's faces, eyes closed, they kissed.

HOPE.

"Alert! Alert!" the helmet sounded from the ground and Jim covered Lisa again when the war mocked them with another series of explosions.

Moments later, he finally dared to move.

"It's alright, honey. It's over now," he reassured her when the missiles stopped.

She didn't say anything.

"Lisa …" he trailed off, realizing she wasn't breathing. "Lisa? Lisa!" he shouted and tried to shake her awake, tried to make her open her eyes, but she wouldn't. She couldn't!

Another nazer rocket flew by, nearly hitting him. He watched it zip up and explode a sector away. E-rifle fire pulsed all around him. Explosions. Screams—

He remembered her scream.

"You died here," he choked out the words. "You died because of this? This took you away from me?" Unable to shed any tears or even grieve properly, Jim became enraged. "You never killed anyone. You never fired a shot. How many lives had you saved over the years? Even of the enemy?" His muscles tensed, his teeth clenched in silent anger.

"They took you away from me. They need to pay for what they've done." Suddenly he remembered another promise, one he'd made earlier. He could morn her death at least in one way. "It's LATER."

Savoring the thought of killing everyone—EVERYONE— around him, he tried to stand—but lifeless hands were somehow clenched around his wrists, and her eyes still seemed to plead to him.

He gasped and his anger immediately disappeared.

"No, right, right," he said, gently caressed Lisa's delicate fingers, and remembered what she had asked. "I'm sorry. I know. I promised."

He brushed a finger along her cheek. He just wanted to hold her anyway, hold her in his arms and keep her safe.

"Lisa, they'll never find you. I'll make sure of that," Jim moaned softly, soon moving her into the crook of his left arm.

"And I'll never be part of this again," he reaffirmed his promise. Then he grabbed his helmet, and put it on with his free hand.

He took a moment to gauge his surroundings with the HUD in his helmet, and then he looked for locations too. He knew that he needed to take her away from here and bury her in a safe place. He, however, looked at the lifeless form resting along his left arm. Emotions swirled inside him and the shock—

Jump, you fucking idiot, a voice shouted in his head, and he crouched down—

Three years ago because of a dare, he had jumped over a hundred miles. Now, controlled by a surge of madness and a BRAND NEW power, Jim leapt up into the sky—

Ka-crack! Ka-crack! Ka-crack!

His helmet picked up sonic booms from comlinks far behind him.

"St. John, I don't know what the fuck, but snap out of it!" Only McNeil would have had the balls to say such a thing, especially after hearing what had just happened. "Am I getting through to you? We need help here and now. They're flanking to our left and will surround us. We need your help, man. Come on, bud. Listen to me!"

Jackson's protests and orders only enraged Jim more, and simply increased his speed of flight. Not wanting to hear any more of that bullshit, Jim wanted to throw the helmet away, but he needed to know if anyone would try to stop his DESERTION

—

Desertion. He contemplated that, but this time there wasn't the electric jolt when he thought of his escape. He just looked down at the lifeless body of the one that he once and would forever love. Nothing else mattered now except for his promise.

"Jim, my God, do you hear me? Are you OK? Where are you going? DON'T LEAVE US!" McNeil still screamed for support.

Jim shook his head and scanned the world far below him. Naturally, regardless of the distance, the orders still came to him. They begged him to use his skill, his training, and his expertise. However, noticing that his blades had retracted back into his arms, he knew that their words no longer compelled him the way they once had.

And the Beast said nothing, not a word. Maybe it understood that Jim St. John had made his vow and that was that. Or maybe, possibly, it understood that this event would lead to a much more optimistic future.

The Kurgon Beast was now free. Truly free.

"General, we understand that you did everything in your power to try to prevent it," his boss of bosses said, while Jeff McDonald readied himself for the "but". He stared at the hooded figure, who was dressed in a blood-red robe. The High Priest—although Jeff never understood "of what"—sat in front of eleven others who wore robes of various colors of Cabinet. All of them together were the Panterian Council. Since they seldom used this Panterian Chamber of Council, which was located in the heart of the world's capital, Phijeyoton, Jeff doubted that this was going to be a good meeting.

"But, General McDonald, you let another go free."

Jeff grimaced. "Your Highness, the mind-controlling and behavior-modifying hormones, neural nets and drugs you've authorized me to use no longer work. I've requested time and time again to use alternative methods but have been ignored."

"I see." The blood-red hood hid the man's face. It was meant for intimidation, but the General had seen much scarier things in his life. "Perhaps it's time we suggest alternatives?"

He smiled at the Third Level Priest and hid his impatience. There were too many things Jeff could have been doing right now; however, considering the pomp and circumstance with the meeting in this building today, a feeling of unease began to creep into his thoughts. But he forced it down.

"Absolutely," he said. "If you approve my recommendations, I can begin implementation of them right away."

"Yes. Yes. We have considered them, General McDonald," the Guard said dismissively. "However, with the loss of the last sixteen Naturally Augmented Genetic Individuals—with one being particularly important—we have decided to go in another direction."

"Shit," despite himself, Jeff let out a curse. "Sir, what does that mean?"

The dark red hood partially hid a smile, while the High Director of the Panterian Guard, who were the True government of the world, and were the True orchestrators of the world's economy and security, gestured toward the main doors. "Send in General Eric van Anderson."

"Yes, Your Excellence," First Level Guards acknowledged, and light streamed into the hall.

A tall, lean man in blue military dress followed the light into the room and the General noted that there wasn't a hair on Eric's head that was out of place.

Jeff's anger flared and he felt an old scar begin to itch under his short-trimmed beard.

"Fucking playboy," McDonald said under his breath, commenting on the new arrival. Anderson certainly enjoyed throwing his credit around and also loved hosting lavish parties. Now days, Jeff wasn't invited to such shindigs unless his rank necessitated it. However, when it was all said and done, Eric's tastes were quite epicurean—more like piggish—and McDonald mainly kept the guy at an arm's length.

Granted, the other general was ambitious and used to be good at his job. Because of it, Jeff had given him command of the Army of Mutants decades ago, and things were good for a time. They had even been friends once.

McDonald shook his head in disgust, knowing that rift would never be mended. A year ago, Eric had circumvented channels and authorized a series of experiments that Jeff had vehemently forbidden. To make matters worse, the accursed things had gotten loose and twelve scientists had gotten killed. Then, piling onto bad decisions, Eric had tried to cover all of it up which resulted in a disciplinary action and nearly a court martial.

Henderson was another matter, Jeff thought. Although Eric couldn't be completely held responsible for the massacre, McDonald was already looking at potential replacements.

Eric's footsteps were quick, his stride in perfect parade march. The man did pause when he saw McDonald, but quickly composed himself and moved forward until beside him.

Maybe they are going to kick him out? Jeff deluded himself.

"Reporting as ordered, Your Highness," the other said, quickly bowed to one knee and then rose back to his feet. Anderson was well over average height, and he often used his muscular frame to intimidate those who feared such things. Little good that did him here now.

"Thank you for your attendance, General," the high level priest said and, imperceptibly Jeff noticed, played with his gavel a bit. "We got your last report. How is the FEMET project going?"

"Very well, Your Excellency. The last stages will be completed before deadline." Eric grinned, making it apparent that Jeff had not been kept in the loop.

"How are the Nagis recovering?" the Priest asked.

"Slowly but ahead of schedule: Reinstatement of many members of the old Human Nagephon Force has been ongoing since Henderson." There was a pause and crack in Anderson's voice since both Jeff and Eric had lost many friends that day. "However, it's expected that only a quarter of the remaining troops will return to the AOM."

"Only a quarter?" Jeff asked. "There are over a thousand sur-vivors—"

"I'm still speaking, McDonald," Eric said backhandedly. "It seems that the rest of them are seeking to fill various positions under your new R&D Division. Naturally, I am honored that that type of loyalty will still exist in the new FGGO. The one that I will be leading."

"You goddamn weasel!" Jeff turned on Eric. He hadn't torn someone apart in a long time.

"Stand down, General!" the High Priest yelled, shocking McDonald since they seldom did. "First, this outburst is being overlooked because of your record. Second, it was our decision to work with General Anderson directly. The Guard no longer wishes to have your leadership halter the effects of the FGGO and the functions of this government. From this point on, General Anderson will head the Department of Genetic Research."

"The Decoré, really?" Jeff asked dumbly. "You've got to be kidding me? Jesus! He's lost families and even abducted offspring from the alteration experiments."

"Only eight in that total, General, all blasphemy aside," said the Priest. "You, as you well know, have lost hundreds, including the third Kurgon Beast."

"This is an outrage," he blurted. "You know damn well that we were having difficulty controlling the Nagis before the Battle of Henderson. Besides that, what about the fiasco at Henderson itself? Three thousand AOM troops were slaughtered!"

"General McDonald," the councilman said and shook his head, as though showing pity. An attribute McDonald knew was beyond the thing before him. "Take this for what it is, but we know you love Panteria and we do not question your patriotism. However, we have come to the conclusion that your current command has become a distraction to you when compared to your R&D projects. Should I give examples? For instance, should we discuss your expenditures over the last ten years?"

The High Director acted like he was about to continue, but did not.

Incensed, Jeff was about to reply but quickly bit his tongue, when each of the twelve Panterian Priests suddenly stood up and glared at him. They were challenging him.

"You motherfuckers," he cursed quietly to himself and rapidly let go of his rage when he understood where they were going with this. However, would they cancel the projects he'd been working on regardless? Even worse, mention them to Eric?

He couldn't risk it. "No, you need not continue, High Director," the General swore, voice barely distinguishable from the Guardsman's own. And then Jeff snapped to attention, giving them what they wanted for now—an embodiment of the perfect, taciturn soldier. "Your orders are my command."

"Very good," the High Priest said. "Although General Anderson is now technically your superior, we will be removing your division from his direct chain of command. You will have complete autonomy and will report directly to us. The Ceremony of the Decoré will be held two weeks from today, and the command transfer of the FGGO will occur then. You have up until that time to prepare for this transition."

"Understood," Jeff said and nodded, still surprised that they did not want him to disclose all of his current projects to Eric. And with this change in command structure, it also ensured that Eric would never know.

C'est la vie. He shrugged. Having worked with the Panterian Guard for so many years, Brigadier General Jeffery McDonald understood full well why the Panterian Guard, the true rulers of Panteria and the surrounding Sol system, had managed to hold it all together for so long.

He therefore simply turned, slowly looked down into Eric's eyes, and smiled. "Congratulations on your new appointment, sir! Good luck to you, sir!" He saluted and walked out, not even bothering to ask his leave.

He needed to get back to work.

"Come on, Kevin! That's bullshit." Logan threw a hard stare at his best friend.

"Logan," Kevin said, his eyes met level with his own since they were both about six-foot-two. "You've been here six years and you've never complained before. What in the hell has gotten into you lately?"

"I don't know. It's like I got up one morning, and suddenly my life seemed to take on a different …" he trailed off, seeing Kevin's derisive grin.

Logan McMillian grimaced at the cliché. He rubbed a hand through his black hair, uttering a groan. "Well, I can't really explain it. After what I've done on the past few missions, the recent data we've collected, and the people—I just have to question what we're really doing. Think what you'd like, but it really did just click."

"O-k-a-y," Kevin said, nodding in response, but his gray globes still seemed to hold back questions. "Just be careful about being too preachy around here. There are some real assholes here, and you know that Craig may have to report it eventually."

"Right …" Logan paused and looked down a painted-white corridor, one of hundreds in the CIA HQ. He had joined when he was eighteen, after completing an accelerated college program. Kevin Torleson, a college mentor and friend, had recruited

Logan prior to graduation. Back then, McMillian had wished to make good use of his talents in explosives, weaponry and bio-engineering. The Company had provided him with the equivalents of graduate-level courses, along with the opportunity to bring justice to those who hid from it.

For so many years he thought he was making a difference, but there were too many questions now. Logan's loyalty had finally been shaken lately …

And not stirred. Logan thought of a spy series that was certainly showing its age some thousand years since its inception. It was the realization that that series was over a thousand years old that had sparked Logan's interest in ancient television and cinema. Now he was a glutton for punishment when it came to uncovering such ancient entertainment—good or bad. He'd just watched a terrible flick about some guy that had been turned into a mosquito. A mansquit—

"I guess I'll see ya in Craig's quarters?" Logan asked to end the conversation with Kevin … and, his own tangential thoughts. He realized he had been only trying to start a fight so he could delay the inevitable.

They stopped in front of Kevin's apartment. "Sure, you know how Miles and Craig get when we start that game of theirs. Jeez, it's like playing with a bunch of kids. What? Meet in about an hour?"

"Sounds great," he smirked and stuck around long enough to make sure that Torleson wasn't coming back out. Then, instead of walking back home, Logan walked back to his lab.

Once there, he quickly sat down at his workstation. He opened up a series of files that he still needed to memorize, using the high-capacity neural net in his brain.

"That's it," he eventually grunted, melted the hard drives of the lab's computers, and then got up and entered the main lab.

He didn't bother turning on the lights, since his eyes had been augmented with special implants.

Logan squeezed by, but then decided to move some tables that would be in his way later. Finally, he walked over to the X-1A super powersuit.

He chuckled to himself about that, especially since it wasn't really a "suit" or "powersuit" anymore—more like a walking tank —even though he referred to it as such most of the time. He had added the "super" to the definition during the Product Idea Phase. There had been powersuits roaming the battlefields for centuries; however, this one was the first to house its own linear accelerator, antimatter collector and a host of other advancements. While Logan took pride in the fact that it was under budget, it had cost the Company a fortune and there were rumors that *they* would be demanding the prototype and designs for the production model soon.

"Be prepared for disappointment." McMillian thought of a quote from an ancient movie, when he wondered who was actually coming to take the armor. He just couldn't let it happen. Not with his recent doubts, *Shit!*, it was the first time he'd ever heard of *them*—a mysterious group that was the actual evil entity in those Bond flicks nowadays.

It's not like I don't have super-duper high level clearance or anything, he chuckled, nervously at that. His actions, what he was doing, was finally starting to sink in and he had to get his ass in gear before he chickened out. If they were real, he intended to expose them to the world, and he was forsaking everything to do it!

He quickly kicked off his clothes and slid into the X-1A's biosuit. The material was made from woven carbon nanotubes and very flexible and durable. It also had an elaborate array of microprocessors running the length of his spine, which would come online if the nodes in the drive helmet were ever cut off from the rest of the armor.

"Won't do me any good without my head," some jackass had said during a demo to upper management a few months ago.

Bob Syfried was a total sycophant to the Director of R&D, and often tried to belittle projects that weren't his own. However, since Logan was well liked at the Company, Bob quickly became the butt of the joke, so to speak, when Logan asked him why anyone would assume that Bob's brain was in his head. Hell, that fuck hadn't even noticed the design of the suit prevented decapitation anyway.

The purpose of the electrical nodes of the biosuit was only for backup. They allowed the X-1A to still work, albeit in a safe mode, if the drive helmet, which processed brain signals from the neural net in his head, ever malfunctioned. A necessary feature, since the suit weighed about a thousand pounds, and the "driver" was essentially stuck inside it.

In standby mode, the suit was over nine and a half feet tall, nearly four across its shoulders. It had a four-foot diameter ball of three-inch thick diterium-B1 as a cockpit. The rest of it was covered by various modules, robotic limbs with thick synthetic muscle, pylons for different arsenals, and forcefield projectors. To be fair, this suit was only a working prototype that had been dissembled and reassembled hundreds of times. It was never intended for active duty. Logan wasn't sure if the damned thing was working well enough now, especially since he had just finished rebuilding it a few days ago.

He knew that if he was going to survive long term, he was going to have to make some serious modifications to it once he arrived at his first safe house. He just needed to get out of the CIA in one piece.

Thankfully, since time was of the essence, the suit was relatively easy to get into. It was accessed through a hatch from the back, and he only had to slide into it.

"Yeah, right," Logan grunted as he forced himself into the tight cavity that he was supposed to fit. "At least the tuna's dead before they cram it into the can."

Unlike current powersuits and those of comics, the operator sat entirely in the suit, ensuring arms and legs were safely contained in an armored egg. His future designs looked into the possibility of a more traditional suit, but until then he wasn't going to have his arm or leg blown off because of poorly protected armor.

The status light blinked on and let him know that the suit was ready. Once the suit was activated, its neural link would prevent feelings of claustrophobia by making him feel as though he was actually standing like the suit was now. He made a final check on all the suit's seals and activated the X-1A's QUICK START button.

The Heads-Up Display kicked on and projected vital information on a 360 degree field of view. He quickly turned on the link between the onboard computer and neural net in his head, which pulled the HUD and suit's cameras into his actual vision. And it immediately killed the cramp that was beginning to form in his right hip.

The suit rose up another two feet as it stood ready for action. He smiled as he stretched his new muscles and awareness. His reaction times were now a thousand times quicker than normal; he could now lift over a hundred tons; and he was now almost invulnerable, even without the forcefields activated.

"Yeah, keep it in check, Super Dude. You still have some work to do." He carefully moved to the appropriate cabinets and pulled as many incendiary grenades as possible and put them in strategic locations, but not enough to cause too much destruction.

He worked fast. If he didn't hurry, his friends, his corrupters might—

"I don't want that," he said to himself, feeling the guilt return. McMillian might not have trusted them anymore but he didn't want them to be caught in the resulting fire.

He also worried that someone might bust in at any moment, try to prevent his escape and then get killed.

Logan had been kicking himself for weeks. He knew that he should have kept his damned mouth shut over the last few months, even though he'd only reached out to his friends to help him with his current crisis of faith. But sadly, their patriotic counsel and rhetoric only reinforced his misgivings.

He shook his head. At the very least, he was simply glad that they had never reported him. He also counted himself lucky that due to the sensitive nature of what he worked with, his lab's computers couldn't be accessed from the outside, so his sabotage would be thankfully localized.

After cutting a single wire—a single wire?—and then closing the door of the lab behind him, he couldn't believe that he had put any faith in those fire-suppression systems during the last six years—

Stupid jokes, he chided himself, even though such was his nature and he'd be telling a few more before the day ended.

He was still contemplating that as he reached the guard station at the East Gate.

"So how's it going today, sir?" Johnny, a red-headed kid from Toldeclevchikee, smiled and quickly saluted him, even though Logan didn't technically have a rank. Richard, the other guard, just nodded and went back to watching the monitors.

"Good. Good," Logan managed to cough out something comprehendible, despite being pretty nervous. "Just going to stretch out this bitch's legs."

Both guards laughed at that and quickly waved him through.

Then Logan waved goodbye like he always did.

For the last time, he thought, realizing that this was the last time he'd ever get to joke with these guys, and the last time he'd ever see Kevin, Craig, Miles and Brent again.

Damn. Damn. Damn. He couldn't help but feel a little sick, couldn't help but feel guilty.

But I can't stay, Logan reminded himself, and he needed to put some distance between the CIA and himself pronto.

By the time he reached the nearby forest, he was already running at 128 mph and still gaining speed. The suit was also fully cloaked, essentially invisible to sight and scanners, and was generating a forcefield that was pretty much impregnable.

"It better be," he told himself. "I think that there's going to be some resistance to me trying to figure out who or what the Panterian Guard is. And why it has contracted us to kill so many innocent people."

He ran faster, heart racing because of an uncertain future. His speed hit three hundred, but he kept it there since the forest floor was uneven and somewhat slippery, even for the suit.

He winced when he almost tripped out of distraction. Because of his neural net and already semi-photographic memory, the images of all the people he had killed flashed continuously through his mind. He knew that most of them weren't saints, but he also knew that one innocent person was one too many.

"Someone is going to give me answers. And whoever tries to stop me"—he smiled, anger behind it—"they'll find out what they paid for."

Digit five has been lost. A biotechnician jotted down some notes, while sitting in a dark observation room. She ignored other feelings that were trying to surface, and tried to focus on work.

Hmm, I wonder what Bill would have thought of this, Tracie Myers smirked, thinking of her old coworker, and took a moment to curl a lock of her long, raven-black hair around one of her fingers. Somewhat distracted, her dark blue-green eyes refocused on the biological specimen sleeping on the examination table in an adjoining room.

She looked it over carefully. The creature was a large, demon-like monstrosity. Long, black-green wings stretched out and brushed the floor. A tail, which ended in a frying-pan-sized, spade-like tip, swayed in an unusual rhythm as the beast slept. And four arms and two legs twitched while it slept.

Truly remarkable, she thought, bit her lip and freed her finger from the strands of hair to type her notes. However, she quickly paused and scrolled through what she'd written so far, making sure that she was being descriptively thorough—but also "succinct" enough. The military was full of hypocrisy.

Suddenly, she felt a tear roll down her right cheek.

Shit—she quickly wiped it away and took some calming breaths—*keep it fucking together. I know you can't ignore* IT, *but don't puss out,* she thought, hypocrisies be damned.

Still, this was the anniversary of her parents' deaths—violent, unnecessary deaths—

Come on, Tracie, you can't let it get to you. Not today—especially NOT *today.* She, however, had never gotten nor would ever get over her parents' deaths. Instead, as always, she tried to bury it. But she knew her limitations and was unable to compartmentalize as well as the other members of FEMET.

To be fair, not many of them had their parents killed. She bit her tongue this time and tried not to think about it anymore. On the other hand, to make matters worse, it had been exactly a month since she'd been transferred to this lab, run by a group comprised entirely of former AOM soldiers.

Myers smirked—thinking about the assholes she worked with was actually helping her think of something other than her parents. Originally, she'd been eager to move here, a base just north of Tamorami. She'd been looking forward to hearing the stories of ancient battles and how these heroes had helped curb some of the worst rebel uprisings in history. To her own regret, she'd been ostracized the moment she'd gotten off the transport.

Well, at least it's warmer here. Bill would have hated it, she always joked when she was uncomfortable. She didn't need a psychoanalyst to tell her that it was a defense mechanism.

She shrugged. In spite of everything, she had to admit that she was amazed and impressed by what she had seen at this lab. Her schooling had never prepared her for actually seeing how wild and dangerous Panteria had become in the last three hundred years.

Tracie typed some information about the creature's gender. Then, noticing that it didn't have any claws, she wondered if it would be a real threat in the wild. However, even with her brief stay here, she had already cataloged about fifty monsters that she wouldn't want to startle while on a nature hike.

Like I'd ever go out and go hiking. She noted something about the creature's blond hair and remembered an old movie about an unlucky group of people camping in the woods, and who were attacked by some weird mutant woodchuck. The last time she checked, the number of Red Zones had doubled and the numbers of attacks were increasing, and Extermination Officers certainly had their hands full.

The makers of that pre-FOW movie would've loved to see what we have today, she thought. She eyed the creature on the table in the examination room, and continued taking notes, even though this current task grossly underused her talents.

She assumed that her superiors had determined that a biotech, which was a multipurpose word for a person's summation of skills, a certain class of person or a simple derogative, should be doing something useful. Therefore she, a biotech, was sitting in this room, cataloging the seemingly endless numbers of creatures that were brought in from the wilds by the soldiers of the AOM.

The Biotech swore quietly to herself. She envied the soldiers that were trying to secure the land that had been taken over by the Growth Zones or GZ's for short. Those soldiers—HEROES—were searching the GZ's to eradicate and stop the STIGS!

She suddenly grew angry, a genetically pre-programmed response to the enemy, about how well the rebels managed to hide. No rebel group to date had actually been found in such sanctuaries. Over the years, a few had been lured out by traps, but there were plenty of those bastards out there.

Concentrate on the task at hand. Tracie focused her attention on the creature. Her clearance wasn't high enough to tell her what GZ it was from. Some of them had trees over six hundred feet high.

Bill had the nicest smile, she sighed. That thought reminded her of Captain Bill Cogney, who worked at her old base near GZ-IV, which had the tallest trees and most dreadful of Nagis.

Bill had told her that trying to find stigs was frustrating, so to curb boredom and boost morale, the soldiers were often rotated to alternative tasks, such as collecting specimens for the labs. And there were plenty—

Shit, I'm taking too much time on this. She had eight other subjects she needed to log after this one. One had actually been captured in a city park, proving that even the Megacities were yielding to the pressures of the implacable nature of the Growth Zones.

Thereby offering not only Nagis but also the stigs with convenient access points! Myers thought but buried the anger, which was useless to her here. She looked at her monitor then at the black-green, humanlike form resting on the table in the adjacent room. She wondered if she had missed anything in the visual scan, but eventually thought about her transfer again, with one poignant conversation happening only a few hours ago.

"No, your skills are required here. I understand that you had excellent marks during your time at Kansas Station, and I understand the vital roll you think that you played. However, your request to return there has been denied. Dismissed." She hated her new supervisor. He was a pompous prick, a lieutenant colonel who could no longer keep up in the AOM and who had been passed over for promotion twice already. Also, because she was pretty, he mistook his patronizing way with her as genuinely complimentary.

Who are they trying to kid? She knew the obvious. She was *Biotech*. Even though the FGGO had consolidated a number of different agencies a few years ago and renamed itself Infiltration, the Agency still used inorganic chips in its computers. Unfortunately, Tracie's primary talent from FEMET involved the development and design of organic computers and other systems, which were computers that Infiltration just didn't have. And although she was bright enough to do almost any other task, she had always been overlooked and outright denied transfers to other departments.

Pursing her soft lips, teeth clenched tightly behind them, she eventually stopped typing and rapped her fingers along the desk, realizing she was at the bottom of the ladder.

Whatever. She forced herself to change topics and began the deep tissue scans of the specimen. He, a "male" she determined for obvious reasons and a "healthy 'big' one," had been brought in about an hour ago. He seemed like a dragon squeezed into human form; however, despite a slightly elongated jaw and nasal cavity, he almost looked like a friend she knew back in high school. Still, she labeled him a *Drago-Humanoid*, well, just because.

Maybe I should get a better look and measurement of his—

Hmm? Oh. She blushed, remembering that she wasn't alone. She smelled the stench of tobacco. Its source was behind her, but the smoke now filled the room with its awful odor. Tracie kept herself from turning around and tried not to let the anniversary of her parents' deaths get the best of her.

Compounding her luck, the commander of this base had decided to come by this very day. Myers curled her lip. Apparently, he was also not aware that this was a nonsmoking facility. Something, of course, she did not call him out on.

God, he didn't even introduce himself, she cursed without voicing it. It hit her again—being a FEMET here wasn't easy. Surprisingly, though, she was already getting used to the sneers and comical jabs when she was around. She knew that she could kick about half of these old farts' asses anyway. She hadn't been formally trained as a solider, but Bill had helped.

She smiled, blinked, concentrated and then turned a bit, allowing her self-taught, night-vision skills to see the giant man behind her. He didn't make a sound and his eyes were locked on the drago-humanoid. He might as well have been an apparition, since she could barely hear him breathe. However, she didn't say a word, even as he came up right beside her. She gawked briefly at his height and size, and she then looked back at the other specimen.

"He's awake," she yelped and was quietly silenced by a tap on the shoulder, even though such caution wasn't necessary since the rooms were soundproof. She shrugged and looked on.

The creature had stirred. A black-green arm covered his eyes. She instantly wondered if he was nocturnal for a moment, but smiled by the assumption, since the dragon was in a sterile white room, being blasted by calimar lighting.

Then her smile vanished. The beast seemed perplexed, his ears twitching and his eyes searching as though he had heard her. She instantly scanned the console and cursed when she noticed that someone using the room before her had left the interrogation speaker on. She looked up at her commander. He wasn't pleased. She shook her ahead, turned off the microphone and silently simmered.

Fucking biotech, she thought of the guy that had used the room before her.

Confused and bewildered, her subject rose up and slipped off the table. A wing wrapped around his frame and his tail slid off the flat surface and swayed a few feet above the ground. Standing like a normal—albeit seven-foot-six—human male, he looked around the room, letting its features enter his gaze. Soon, he approached the wall nearest her position and began to feel around.

Impossible, she told herself, her heart pounding as she looked into his frighteningly beautiful sky-blue eyes. *What's it looking for?*

Then he opened his—

"Wot dothe thee de'sire?" His calm tenor-base echoed in the emptiness, knocking the Biotech back in her chair. "Wey hathe ye lock'd mi in dis rom? Spek nowt, ye art en de presence et'nobil. Wher'rt mi cloth, myne plates, et my sword? Und wey dothe thee treat mi en suct ill?"

A sword? But she said nothing in response to the odd English he seemed to speak. It was somewhat like the Middle-English in books she'd read at the University. It even sounded a lot like Neo-Classic, which had been a concocted dialect Panterian Guards and members of the FGGO had used to speak when posing as hired mercenaries during the Apocalypse. However, this was about as much analysis as she could give. Fuck it! she was not a philologist.

They wanted me to be a biologist slash zoologist here, so that's what I am. They can get an English teacher for the other stuff, she laughed to herself and continued her observations.

"I knowith som'un resides near de spak adjoin en dis un. I heardth thee, e'yt dothe I hear thy breath."

Was he bluffing? She held her breath just in case.

Bluff seem called, he scowled and then began pounding his fists ferociously on the wall. He howled too and began kicking the wall as well. Neither would do him any good, since the room had forcefields and there wasn't much that would get through it.

That tidbit of knowledge didn't seem all that helpful, especially when Tracie realized that her hands were trembling and she consciously had to stop them.

A tap on her shoulder made her jump. She quickly collected herself and noticed that her boss's finger pointed at the DOOR OPEN/CLOSE button on the panel. She hesitated but figured he knew best and pressed it down. To her surprise, three soldiers filed into the room. Since having armed guards available was not the norm, she hadn't known they'd been there.

"All right, calm down now. Nobody's going to hurt you." The leader of the entering squad waved his hand in a sign of peace, apparently hoping the creature understood.

"Not good," the Biotech whispered, noticing the tranquilizer rifles in their hands and noted that the Nagi—Naturally Augmented Genetic Individual—saw them too. She heard his growl and saw him step toward them.

A soldier aimed and the Dragon spun, his tail slicing without any hesitation. Blood splattered and the soldiers collapsed before her eyes.

Tracie almost vomited. She covered her mouth just in—

She watched the monster's eyes. He noticed something else and jumped.

No you don't! She hit the OPEN/CLOSE button again, and the door zipped shut a second before the giant reached it. His body slammed into it hard and even buckled it out some. He continued the assault; however, the obstacle, now re-enforced by an internal forcefield, seemed only to mock him now.

The woman watched the creature take some calming breaths and then step away from his quick thought of escape. He paused and stood next to the people he just killed—his face almost sullen as if understanding compunction. Then Tracie watched him shake his head and then inspect the soldiers' bodies, their instruments and even their personal effects. At one point he picked up one of the tranquilizer guns. He looked it over and then pointed it in the right direction and squeezed the trigger.

"Ta-shet," he swore when a thin needle and cylinder sunk lightly into one of the corpses. He bent down, pulled out the needle and held it up in her direction. "Ye cood've teld mi dat this woold ne hathe killayde mi."

She didn't answer. If she needed to say anything she knew her commander would have had her key the mic. Besides, Tracie was in complete awe of the thing before her. She had never seen a Nagi like this. Had some of the creatures in the Red Zones finally become sentient?

Since when can these fuckers talk? She shook her head in disbelief, truly confounded by these events. Then she found herself tapping data into her workstation almost subconsciously. *Possibly, work's a good defensive mechanism as well?* She shrugged.

The beast moved to another soldier, one of his four hands keeping the tranquilizer gun. He fuddled with some electronics, but tossed them aside when they seemed too complicated for him or he deemed them of no use. Eventually, he found a little pocket knife to cut out a small piece of clothing. He made a rudimentary kilt attached to one of the soldier's belts.

Mesmerized by his actions, Tracie almost didn't notice her boss's hand resting on the console in front of her. It pointed to another switch.

Well, that's the end of this party, she sighed and tapped the TRANQUILIZE SPECIMEN button. She knew the soldiers would probably still be alive if they hadn't carried in—

She couldn't help but wonder if they had carried in weapons because they knew a biotech had been watching. Trying not to disrespect the dead, she cursed anyway and watched a nose twitch. In reaction, the Nagi's face squished in fear, then hate. Finally, his blue eyes scanned the room frantically.

Shaken and frustrated, he dropped to his knees and began to groan, while his wings tightened and his tail straightened and his muscles strained. She watched him look at the door again. It was outlined in blood. The creature shook.

"BAAAAASTIIIIK!" he screamed and cursed, and his fifteen-foot-wide wings snapped open. An intense light and an explosion followed.

The woman jerked and looked at her boss. His own eyes were as wide as saucers, and he didn't offer any suggestions. She looked back at her instruments and saw the room's temperature spike past the point of all known plasma. Reflexively, Tracie adjusted the controls and tried to compensate for the blinding light, which soon faded and revealed a hole.

Plasma generation? She felt another tap on her shoulder, but there wasn't anything she could do. With the alarms blaring and fire suppression systems spraying everything with foam, it didn't make it any easier. Regardless, a hole—well, a tunnel—had been blasted through the outside wall of the base, through fourteen rooms and two adjoining hallways. And the Nagi had literally disappeared!

Her mouth dropped wide open, and Tracie Brenda Myers looked over whatever notes she'd been able to finish. There was no way to hide the disappointment. The loss of such a creature was unforgivable, regardless of anything she could have done.

Shamefully, she looked up at her superior. Fortunately or unfortunately, because of the flash earlier, most of his form was now concealed in shadows. His anger, though, was definitely heard in his breathing.

"Damn." A deep base, one much lower than her subject's had been, finally reverberated throughout the room as the giant man walked out the door.

Adding insult to injury, she noticed that he had squished out his tarpik—that nasty, awful cigar—on one of the control panels by the door.

Ugh. Fuck me, she cursed. Tracie wished he had said more than that.

"OK ... uh ... Ecie?" a man asked in a dark, holographic-projection chamber. He looked around the large room for any buttons or switches that he needed to push. He found none. "I'm ready."

"Will do," a quiet childlike voice replied. "I'm looking in the Executioners' Files, personal logs in SET ONE. It's under a subset of 'Extermination Officers: Reports in the Field' and cross referenced with 'Historical Crystal Mountain Events.' For future reference, the file is numbered 5.4739E10M."

Not getting a response, the young computer continued, "This is a personal log slash report that was never filed. Originally listed as 'E.O. file number 534,' it was quickly renamed 'The Pitfalls of a False Alarm in a Red Zone' and was written by Extermination Officer Walter Zimmerman, Badge 890542, on 9/13/3001.

"I'm preparing the necessary parameters of the program. The Holographic projectors have been activated." There was a quick flicker and then a figure materialized. The hologram represented a personification of the original writer of the report. The holographic man or H-man was five-foot-ten and one hundred seventy-five pounds by Panterian measurement. A blond, military haircut rested over relatively normal features that showed no distinctive marks. The H-man was in the uniform of an Extermination Officer, which was mostly gray and olive dress, with no bright colors or shiny insignia to draw the attention of the beasts in a Red Zone.

"Do you wish this to be interactive?" the computer asked.

"No," the man in the room grunted.

"How about with a background? Or better yet a cinematic replay of the event?"

"No, thank you," the man said a bit more taciturn than he'd intended.

"Have it your way," the computer sighed, as Jim had warned him, and prepared to leave him be. "Program engaged."

With that, the holographic *Walter* or H-Walter or H-Zimmerman smirked and came to life.

"This is Walter Zimmerman, Execution Officer, 890542," H-Walter said. "I was called at 0958 hours on September 13, 3001, by a large mob that had alerted me to a possible threat in Medley, a town just east of California's boarder.

"'Help us, help us,' one woman, a Julie Bryant, had cried out, pulling my arm frantically.

"I asked them what the problem was, and all I got was something about 'a monster here for their souls, a medieval demon.'

"I simply nodded," H-Walter chuckled lightly and made a circling motion with his finger near his right temple. Apparently, the computer's holographic program extrapolated quite a bit from the file being shown.

"I was, though, intrigued by the presence of a real-life dragon. So I grabbed my gear and led the disheveled crowd back to the location of the disturbance. However, with someone's importuning, I reluctantly went back for my antimatter rifle.

"As a side note, I prefer my pistol, but I *aim* to please my citizens." H-Walter winked.

"Anyway, as we approached the small establishment, Andur's Café, a mid-sized hover-van nearly ran us down ..." the H-man paused. He made a ducking motion and then continued, "I tried to turn in time to get the ID codes, but it was already gone.

"'Never mind that'—already up, Julie tugged on my coat —'it's right over here.'

"Shaking my head, I simply got up, brushed off my pants and followed her.

"To my own dismay, the place was a mess. I looked around, kicked tables aside and pulled tablecloths off suspicious lumps. Nothing.

"Then of course"—the hologram's cheeks really blushed in embarrassment—"for a moment, my paranoia got the best of me, and I wondered if that hover-van had taken the beast away.

"But, ah-ha!" H-Walter shook his head and appeared to even make his voice sound different. "I remembered that the HV had taken off with such force, the tables and chairs could have been blown around by that alone. Besides, my dear Watson ..." the hologram then paused for dramatic effect.

However, the living person in the room could only shrug his shoulders and ask the obvious question: *Who the hell is Watson?*

"Besides, my DNA scanner didn't pick up anything unusual. And later, I discovered that the cook's medicinal stash had been mixed in with the seasonings. Yah, go figure, he was getting back at his girlfriend, who owned the restaurant," H-Walter smirked. "Therefore, I'm going to consider this event as some type of group hallucination thing set off by a mutated hawk or something.

"I know." The H-man seemed to grow somber. "I have to admit that these people aren't the easiest to live with, but everyone's a bit jumpy out here. Shit, this hasn't been the first time someone has called me in to look for Bigfoot, the Loch Ness Monster, the Boogeyman and countless other pixies.

"But, you know, I can't really blame 'em. I have seen enough mutated shit out here that makes me sleep with a gun under my pillow, and a rocket launcher beside my bed. Thankfully, though, I haven't seen anything like that flying sumbitch they described.

"Still, there's always something new out here, and just because I'm dismissing it for now doesn't mean that I'm not going to keep a better eye out for what's above me.

"Ah, the trials of being an extermination officer." H-Walter then placed an open hand on his chest, and stood tall. "I protect to serve. I carry out this oath and swear that I will do whatever it is in my power to protect my fellow man. Never shall I neglect a plea for help, nor ever turn away from a victim in distress."

H-Walter bowed and soon faded away. It was obvious that the real Walter had taken those words to heart.

Then the room again echoed with the computer's voice: "This file was found, copied and taken back to the Mountain by Lt. Henry Tabloson, Executioners Survey Division, early this morning, September 23, 3001. It refers to the rescue of Arthor Jones on September 13, 3001.

"Would you like to access another file?"

"No, thank you … ah … Ecie," the man groaned and gritted his teeth—not because of the computer but because of his own fate. "I'm leaving. I need to talk with Jim. Thanks again."

"No problem, Arthor" the computer said. "Please let me know if I can be of further help."

"Sure."

"Storalie, keep your chatter down." On top of a nearby building, Brigadier General Eric "Viper" van Anderson commanded and watched the squad move in while barking orders through the comlink. "Turn left at the second tree down the driveway. Remember to keep your head down or she'll blow it off."

"Aye, sir," the captain on the other end acknowledged and turned left with his men. Their natural abilities and armor blended them in with their surroundings. But Eric's binoculars—tied into their bios—showed them as blips as they moved. The house they moved against was double-storied and was surrounded by trees and heavy brush. A stiff, warm wind blew from the east, but large banyans stood strong against it.

All six men were fully armored and holding heavy-slinger rifles. The needle-throwing weapons were anything but clean, especially in a nice neighborhood like this one. But Anderson wasn't going to take any chances.

He bit his lip and thought about the person sitting in that house. She was the daughter of the man who had been conducting extensive research on the real government, the Puppeteer

Government, with Anderson being a focal point.

The General grimaced, wondering how it had come to this. Eric had never met Jon Clayton Alexander and had never wished malice toward him. However, the guy had brought on his own bane, especially when Alexander had prevented a crucial assassination attempt.

That had resulted in a visit from the Panterian Council, who gave Eric a very thorough ass-chewing. In rage, Eric had immediately signed the kill order for Alexander, which, eventually, resulted in the girl's desertion. That was followed by another ass-chewing from someone he once called a friend.

"I don't care what McDonald thinks," Eric whispered. He wasn't going to deal with the talk of "lost honor, the thoughts of betrayal" from the likes of her. Therefore his orders were specific and the Alexander family was no longer going to give him anymore grief.

Her escape was embarrassing enough, but with her history— Jon must have hidden a second copy of his work somewhere.

No, don't worry about that, he reminded himself. *It's only the testimony of a bunch of goddamn stigs.* He knew the information her father collected lacked legitimate proof, even though it probably held true confessions of at least a thousand mercenaries, rebels and whoever had had the guts to speak.

No one had believed it when her father had tried to convince some members of Congress. No one would ever believe it while the Puppet Government—fabricated by the Guard long ago— continued to deal with civil matters like it always had. Such stories were rampant during the last century and no one ever believed them, except people who believed in such conspiracies.

Hell, wasn't there a movie last year about the Guard and the FGGO that starred that chick with the big tits? he smirked bitterly. He thought of the Alexander girl, her escape, and the immediate, not-technically-insubordinate ass-chewing he had received privately from McDonald.

Anderson was still pissed off from that. No defectors from Infiltration lived, especially after post-abduction and the Oath. Unlike his predecessor, his record to date was spotless.

No exceptions. There would be too much time and too much of the Agency's resources pissed away if they captured her and then tried to reprogram her. It was better this way.

Once again, he thought of possible protests, but other orders from the Guard would keep the girl's death a secret long enough. By the time it was discovered, it would be too late.

Then let him object. Anderson smiled and rubbed the butt of his antimatter pistol. Its safety was never on. But, of course, even Eric knew such thoughts were of a fantastic bravado that he would never carry out.

Eric thought of the last few years. Even though they had had a fallen out, Eric still considered Jeff a friend, since the man had saved his life once. Pride or something like it prevented either from really talking. Eric would probably never be able to tell Jeff that he had not been responsible for what happened. And what he was up to now would assuredly eliminate any chance.

But we will live for a long time, who knows? he sighed and watched Infiltration's group enter the house.

Although he had chosen assassins who could naturally cloak their armor, he could have easily disguised them as a police SWAT team and the neighbors would suspected the obvious: Panteria wasn't a perfect world.

Well—he scratched his beard—*in a matter of speaking.*

"General?" His comlink sparked to life again.

"Yes, Captain, is it over?"

There was a pause and then a clearing of the throat. "No, sir, she was gone before we entered, and the patrols behind and beside the home saw nothing."

He shook his head in silence, knowing that McDonald would somehow find out about this. And, naturally, Eric was already preparing himself for the subsequent jokes.

Ah, screw it, he finally suggested. *She's FEMET Spawn. She can be replaced, despite what McDonald thinks. Besides, she probably won't live past Tuesday.*

No truer words could have been spoken. It had been proven several times that FEMET adults who had sworn allegiance to Infiltration simply couldn't live without the Agency. Eric had built that little bit of obedience directly into their DNA. Therefore, it was impossible for them to live without some type of *Ideal* or sense of *Family* to be a part of. He seriously doubted that she'd found such faith in her father's work.

Yes, we can survive without her. She can't do the same. Her death won't be missed by most of us anyway. Eric took a deep breath from the warm air surrounding him. He looked into the sky again and found no clouds above.

Eric absently checked his watch. Since it was March, the Storm Season rarely ran so late. He, however, never took the weather for granted, not since he was a kid.

He shuddered, shaking out a memory that was nearly two lifetimes ago. Then he looked around him, for a moment forgetting that five armored hover vehicles and some twenty soldiers were quietly waiting for him to tell them what to do.

Eric stretched his neck side to side and just let the search teams communicate amongst themselves for a while. Then he looked skyward again, fearing that clouds would form just to mock him and remind him how bad Mortis Tiempos could get.

He bit his lip, triggering a thought about the Meteorological classes he'd taken. Back then, he had tried to understand the reasons why the storms had gotten so bad over the centuries, tried to understand what he could have done to change the unchangeable.

Dammit, anyway. He tensed and then triggered his comlink. "All right, people, there's no use for the entire group to wait here any longer.

"Teams Two and Four, start here and try to track her the best you can. Everyone else, let's clear out. This one's over," he said, giving the order to return to the Eagle's Nest.

Three hovertanks—Light Heavy Assault Vehicles or LHAV's —powered up their repulsars and prepared to return to base. Their cloaking shields were already up. His own transport started and sat waiting for him, while the fifth transport engaged its cloaking shields and waited quietly for the remaining search teams.

Eric knew that the girl had natural cloaking abilities, and obviously she had relied on those to escape.

She was lost.

Lost. Pausing a moment, hearing the ocean roaring and rumbling violently in the distance, he looked at its expanse through his binoculars, before he could bear it no longer.

"Everyone loses a loved one, McDonald," Eric said quietly while stepping into his transport. "But we move on the best we can. We have too."

The saga begins …

BOOK I:
FALLEN

CHAPTER ONE

The road to forgiveness is longer than many think.

(About the Neo-Holocaust)
—Maralie Lopaez, KPX-190
News (2227 A.D.)

"A sea was calm after a terrible winter. The storms had been awful as always, but they had taken fewer lives than before. Spring had come and traveled on. The wind now blew with Summer's dry hand. A new moon kept the night aglow. And gusts brought whispers to be heard amongst waves crashing against the walls of a coastal fortress." Martin Brown smiled after he finished reciting those words to himself. He wasn't much of a poet, but this was one way he liked to occupy his time.

He never said "bored" out loud, even though this assignment wasn't hopping like in a GZ. Because of a mandatory, bi-annual psychological exam, he'd taken an assignment here for a one-month stint, mainly because the two week battery of tests required him to be close to home. A quiet job like guard duty at the General's private fortress filled an Infiltrator's overwhelming desire to work, without causing any stress before and during the tests.

Truthfully, Martin didn't mind getting out of the forests or oceans for a while anyway. The GZ's could be pretty brutal. He hadn't lost anybody under his command yet, but he had heard some pretty horrible stories.

Besides, he thought, *it gives me time to think of my next little project*. Oddly enough, he had initially taken up creative writing because Beth—

Shit!

A piercing pain hammered through his chest. He fell to his knees. He couldn't breathe. Tears blurred his eyes and covered his face. His lungs burned. Stupidly, he looked down.

Oh God, he screamed silently. A small arrowhead protruded through his armored chest. An arrow that was sharp, hard, and surreal.

Warn the base! Surprise quickly yielded to anger, and his hands moved around the arrow in a violent frenzy. Somehow he tried to move it away, move it so he could do something other than weep. His hands repeatedly slapped upon his chest. But nothing, nothing happened! His ultimate reward—alarms in the base— never blasted, never sparked to life.

The only sound was his mouth opening and closing like a fish out of water, and Martin clamped his mouth shut. He realized quickly that the large plate on his chest, an alert for the base, had been ripped to shreds and had been deactivated by an incredibly hard arrow.

Come on, people. Dammit. Come on. Come on! Knowing only a few seconds had passed, knowing he still had some time before he collapsed, he found himself actually back on his feet and staggering around on the balcony. The deck he guarded was out of sight from all the others, but he would try to signal someone, somehow. All he had to do was make it to the door.

Sliiiiiit! Thump.

Something else hit him in the back, another piercing arrow slamming through his right shoulder. His forward momentum immediately stopped. Actually, he was now being pulled back to the far railing.

How convenient. He smiled sickly, somehow still able to stand. But was he dead already?

He managed to turn so that he could see the line securing his shoulder. He then tried laughing, mocking death like so many legendary heroes. But his eyes simply filled with more tears when he discovered that empty lungs prevented even that.

Goodbye, Beth. Goodbye, goodbye, my sweet, sweet —

Another tug pulled on his shoulder. His thighs hit the rails, and he lost his balance.

Following a quiet THUMP that was covered by a series of crashing waves, a black figure jumped on the now empty balcony.

It quickly checked the weapon in its right hand. Made of a flexible composite four times stronger than normal steel, the crossbow and its special alloy bolts could punch through just about anything—including some forcefields.

Tonight it ends, the dark figure thought. Face covered by a skintight mask, the killer lowered the crossbow, briefly seeing the stars glistening on the weapon's surface.

Looking skyward, it took in the sight and remembered something, a different time, a time full of memories—

"Enough. Have to concentrate," the demon said quietly, then

collapsed the bow and holstered the crossbow on its back, and immediately blended into the darkness.

It moved under an overhang and a door to the building. It looked over the PID plate on the right side of the doorknob and then placed an object near the identity scanner. The Hunter took a deep breath, a couple of them before the door slid open.

Let's see. Good, it smirked, waving an invisible arm at nearby sensors before entering the base.

Confident that it hadn't been detected, it moved down the hallway toward its objective, never pausing, never slowing. For whatever purpose it intended … it was committed now.

Like I would stop anyway, it thought to itself. *It ends tonight.*

General Eric van Anderson sat behind his desk. He drummed his fingers with his right ear pressed against the phone-shaped comlink. He was annoyed and tired. The last thing he wanted to do was have this conversation again.

"Yes, I know. I know. OK. What? Yes, I know how much she means to you." He rolled his eyes. "Yes, yes, that's already been taken care of. Come on, Jeff, have I ever disappointed you before?"

Jeff's response wasn't repeatable.

"Yah? Well, you can kiss my ass." Eric actually meant it. "But, really, she'll be found. Don't worry. You have my word on it.

"Yes, I understand. I know," *blah, blah, blah, blah*, he added silently.

Then, finally: "Good." He hung up the comlink and stretched his arms behind him. He thought of mental disorders and diseases, and then he thought of age.

How old is he anyway? He shook his head, turned down the

lights from his desk and got up from his chair. The couch at the other end of his office had been distracting him the entire night. He finally surrendered and fell onto its cushions. Its softness immediately eased his senses, prompting a puerile yawn.

"Simple comforts," saying that and grinning, Eric stretched out and rubbed his eyes. Whimsically, he felt the presence of Hypnos in his room. And although he believed he read too much Greek poetry, sleep came to him anyway.

Outside a thick metal door of an important office, beside two dead guardsmen and in an otherwise vacant hallway, another code was broken. And although calimar light, which like everywhere else, flooded the area, the Hunter had managed to stay out of the sensors and out of the cameras, using its own personal attributes to foil the sensory equipment. Many would have thought this impossible, but only those who couldn't do it, and were jealous.

The Archer stepped over the dead men who had been killed out of reflex, simply because they had been there. It paused, though, taking one last look at a youth who had been telling a joke only a second before.

There was no blood, only a broken neck and an instant death. There had been no convulsions, no squawk of last breath, and no sound from these two boys. The killer had simply snapped their spines and lowered them quietly to the ground. They had never seen—

Enough, it told itself, knowing it was thinking too much of an earlier conversation, a conversation that had not condoned these actions. A fucking speech!

He doesn't know. He doesn't understand. He never will. That was not true but the demon told itself whatever it could to justify these actions.

The Hunter pushed at the door in front of it, opening it without a squeak. Once in, the intruder sneaked into the room and looked around. There was an expensive antique mahogany desk in the front corner. The intruder walked near it and examined it with a steady gaze. Data cards were stacked in a hap-hazard mess, along with a couple of e-pens, Personal Data Links and a stack of other, probably, unassigned PDLs.

The administrative assistant who worked here was either overworked or extremely lazy. Either way, the secretary's workload was going to get a lot easier.

If the bastard survives, the figure only smirked and ran its hand along the inside and outside of the desk.

After a thorough search, however, the Infiltrator found nothing. Cursing softly, seeing that there was no hidden button, it eyed the door it wanted to access.

He'd trust a simple doorknob? Shrugging, it pulled out a palm-sized instrument and scanned the knob. The Hunter turned its head a little sideways, as if it could see something differently from another angle.

The device was put away.

Can something smile with no lips? it asked, feeling its cold heart and praising its chill now more than ever.

Of course, it can. The Assassin grinned beneath its mask, then grasped hold of and turned the knob.

"Hey, take it easy, will ya?" Eric cursed when one of the women jammed her fingernail hard into his right leg. "None of the rough stuff, OK?"

"What are you talking about, honey?"

He was, he well knew, in the middle of a dream, and a good one he seldom had. Two women were astride him. Each were—

"Damn." He cringed. She didn't let up and continued to press her thumbnail into his thigh. He immediately grabbed the red-head by the hair, pulling her away from him. What was she doing?

"Hey, what the hell?" The woman got up, surprised and angry.

But the pain didn't let up, actually it was getting worse. He soon realized it must be an actual cramp and he immediately chided the timing of it. Half asleep, he reached down—

Shit! Snapping awake, adrenaline suddenly pumped through him. He looked down at—

"Oh shit!" he yelled when he saw something actually sticking in his right thigh, just inches below his crotch.

"You know. I did miss on purpose," someone said. Eric jerked his head toward the back of the room, and his eyes suddenly rested on a demon, a monstrosity around six feet tall … more or less. "Be thankful," it laughed.

"Who a-are y-y-you?" he screamed at the monster in rage, his voice only slightly hampered by the pain.

"Hmm, does it matter?" the creature asked. Despite it trying to mask it, its voice seemed familiar, but he couldn't place it.

Then Eric's eyes drifted to the crossbow in the demon's hands. Due to electromagnetic re-enforcement and a draw string of Telson polymer—so called Elastic Steel—it could very well have a four-thousand-pound draw, and could punch a specialized bolt through just about anything. Yet, most likely for sadistic results, he knew that the adjustable bow was now set at one of the lowest settings.

"What do you think?" he finally asked, barely remembering

the demon's question. At the same time, his right hand tested the depth of the bolt in his leg.

"Fuck!" He let go suddenly, accidentally moving the dart again. His stomach reacted and several dry heaves followed.

"How pretty." An emotionless tone—no, a heartless voice entered his ears. He forced his head up and wiped his chin out of pride.

He now knew embarrassment and anger; however, the crossbow's laser sight suddenly blinded him, and he cursed when even the slightest movement made his leg throb.

He kept his hand away from the bolt this time and avoided staring into the laser. In doing so, he saw how bare the room was, how lifeless. There were also no alarms going off, no blasts of intercom chatter. There were no voices of support, no help, and no one was coming to save his ass.

Fear rattled through him for the first time in years. He was screwed. That both terrified him and exhilarated him. He would use both.

"Please." He sat on the couch, motionless. He held his hands out, pleading.

"I don't understand. Why are you doing this?" He still scanned the room for anything he could use as a weapon. However, certainly anticipating Eric's creativity, the dark warrior had taken all of his weapons and potential weapons and put them in the corner. Behind the black crossbow with its terrible sting.

He has to be from Infiltration, but how? Anderson asked himself. *That crossbow's military issue, but who is it?*

"How can this help you?" he asked, killing time, hoping that monster would get sloppy. "Don't you know who I am?"

The assassin said nothing.

"Silly, very silly, why would you come back, what will you gain here?" Eric also fished for more answers. He racked his brain, trying to recall if anyone had escaped in the last week or so. It had been months since the last desertion, too long for FEMET Spawn.

The demon took a step forward. It shook its head, as though mocking pity, and then further reduced the tension on the bow. Its trigger finger began to squeeze.

"For God's sakes," Anderson screamed and stopped the demon from taking another shot. "Think of what you're doing. You'll never be able to sneak past the guards a second time."

Still the intruder said nothing. No emotion came from it except the darkness and sense of hate, a burning that seemed to actually brighten up its ebony mask. There were no eyes to look into, no lips to speak of mercy and no ears to hear his voice. Only a basic form of a head showed, and Eric actually shuddered again by the emptiness it took. Unmistakably, its stance told him the demon was human, but its calm resembled nothing God had created.

Ironically, he had always told the Council that his Infiltrators were the best of all cold-hearted assassins.

"Please, please," he managed to say, and wiped tears of pain from his face. "Is there nothing that I can say to stop this? Anything?"

The dark figure responded with a simple pull of a finger.

"DAMN YOU!" His lungs forced out another scream when the other bolt tore into him. He gurgled, vomited blood, felt the vessel within—its jagged teeth cutting organs and seeming to leave nothing intact.

Now sweat and blood dripped from his face and mouth. Before realizing it, he took in short, testing breaths.

He could breathe! He was still alive! If he could just get his hands on the sonofabitch! He just needed some time to heal.

"Oh God, pity me, a wretched soul." Despite the unbelievable pain, he threw himself off the couch and down onto his knees. The two bolts made it impossible for him to beg properly. But how many people would have guessed that he actually believed in God?

"Please," he said, wheezing because of the spike in his guts. "Please, don't do this. Let me live, and you will gain everything. Don't be a fool."

The Infiltrator stood there. Its head tilted to the side a moment, then straightened back upright. Then it laughed—pain behind it.

"I had it all." A woman's voice broke the carefully masked monotone, one he'd heard enough to recognize. "You took it away from me when you made me remember who I was."

Coughing out more blood, Eric looked down, seeing a red mess. It covered the floor, the couch, himself. And seeing this, he slumped, grew quiet as he thought. He thought of Annie, his sister of all people. His sister, who had died long ago.

He closed his eyes, remembering when he had been a stupid kid. He remembered when his family had stayed at a cottage by the ocean, remembered a freak storm that caught him and his sister by surprise.

But then he remembered something he hadn't noticed before. Did he finally see Annie's face of forgiveness, of peace? Did he finally see that she had not blamed him for losing his grip, losing her?

She had been so brave, so, so terribly brave. His hands fell to his sides, and he just left the bolts where they were. They still hurt, but there was nothing left for him to do.

No more mocked pleads for mercy, no more chances. He had been a man of violence and he would finally join his brethren who had met their ends long ago.

"Fine, Rebecca. Do as you must. I understand. He was a good

man," he said, despite not really knowing her father. He couldn't believe she had survived so long. Hate had proven to be a powerful motivator.

The woman, hidden behind the mask, froze and stared at him. Had she lost her will to end him? But he knew she couldn't let him live now. She just needed that little push.

"Fuck you." He lunged forward, coughed up a mouth full of blood and spat at the demon's face.

"Sol raced to her chariot before the hound awoke," Martin said, reading from his PDL. "She kicked her horses into a gallop and guided them across the heavens. She managed to take several glances over her shoulder, gazing back and wishing he was not there. But he was.

"She knew he would one day catch her, devourer her and start the beginning of the end. But she did not cry. Even though Ragnarok was inevitable, she would never stop driving her ill-fated car."

Rebecca remembered an epic poem of a friend. He had been writing something to impress his wife. Sometimes you forgot that people had lives and dreams other than for war and murder.

"That was another time," she told herself, even though only a week had passed since she'd seen the latest draft. But that was an eternity for an Infiltrator without a home.

"I'll live long enough," Becca said, wiped tears away from her eyes and got back to work. Her fingers typed at a personal computer that was free of the scanners and taps the Guard used to gather private information from its citizens.

The woman worked in a hurry, trying to figure out the reason behind her father's death. The evidence was all here.

But why was he killed for this? There's nothing here nothing, nothing. More tears filled her eyes.

Jonathon Alexander's lifetime work, the millions of recordings and other files of evidence, was on eight separate filaments —kept in separate locations just in case one was lost. But she knew they were ultimately worthless, and the Guard would never have considered him a threat. Her father should have been left alone, laughed at by the higher officials of the Puppeteer Government, but he had not—

Something whispered at her. She spun around and looked behind her. She saw nothing, but the feeling was there. It was the intuition, the disturbance in the smell of the air, and the unusual rhythm in the walls and floor. Something had snapped in the near distance.

The woman quickly pulled out the third memory stick from the computer and placed it in its case, and then into her sidepack with the others. She grabbed her second inheritance, along with its magazine of bolts, and holstered it along her left side. She threw on her long bulky coat then looked around.

Her heart quickened. Looking at her father's den for the last time quickly hit her harder than she's expected. Buried memories of another life, a happy one suddenly rushed to the surface. She'd missed his funeral, hadn't even known he had died until a month after it had happened.

"Just-just give it time," she told herself silently, hate filling the ache, the longing to return home regardless of what that meant. *I just have to be patient, perhaps another week, month, longer?*

No matter, I've found my reason to live for now, and it will be enough, she swore by an oath. *Viper will be killed, and then I can die. Then I won't care.*

She stopped just before getting to a window, took another deep breath and then watched her right hand disappear, followed by the rest of her. She didn't remember exactly when this ability came about, but it was after her Abduction.

Rebecca held back a curse, knowing someone might hear her. If she was perfectly surreptitious, none of the scanners being used outside would work.

I wonder if they should even try. Trying not to be cocky, she straddled the window seal and took a quick scan of the neighborhood, noticing a few lights on in the surrounding houses.

Where are you? Rebecca couldn't see where Anderson was. She had dreamt of what she was going to do to him every night for the last three days. She knew he wouldn't have a chance, since she had been one of his best assassins.

That's pretty humble, right? She smiled, jumped from the window and slipped past a nearby patrol unit, whom she could hear and smell even though they were completely cloaked. They picked the lock of the house's rear door and entered like ghosts.

Sorry, Eric. You won't get off that easily, she smirked and sprinted away, concealing the crossbow the best she could. *You should've left my father alone. We both would have been much happier.*

An alarm began to blare. She looked around—

Rebecca Anita Alexander woke up to the alarm by her bed. "What? Oh—"

"Uuggggh!" She hit the SNOOZE button and was rewarded some by renewed silence. *One sheep. Two sheep. Three—*

"Beep, beep, beep, beep,"—just as she drifted off, Ecie actually chimed in this time—"Becca, it's time to wake up. It's time to wake up."

She had told him how important it was that she got up early this morning. If she didn't—

Shit. Shit. Shit! Her eyes popped wide open and her heart began to race. She wasn't looking forward to today at all. Besides, she had slept enough and the dream hadn't been a good one. The same dream every day for the last five months wasn't helping her constitution even though it had kept her alive. "OK, OK, already. I'm up. I'm up. Give me a break, will you?" she blurted, quickly cutting Ecie off.

"Are you sure?" the computer eventually asked, when she didn't move right away.

"Stop pestering me," she groaned but smiled at how well the Executioner Computer Console took on the brotherly role for nearly everyone. Even though he didn't technically breathe, Ecie was a mesh of organic and inorganic components and was indeed alive. At least, more so than Anderson.

Rebecca smiled but quickly frowned. This day was going to suck. Besides that, she wondered if she'd even be able to move.

"Only one way to find out," she said through clenched teeth. She gently, deliberately, stretched her back on the bed. It was a little stiff but working. The pops from her spine were also good ones.

So much the better. She needed to get back to work and she needed get her lazy ass out of bed. Regardless, she rubbed her eyes and tried self-pity, by telling herself that she didn't get much of a vacation. That not working, she slowly sat up and began stretching her arms and her legs.

"So far, so good." She rolled off the bed and landed pushup-style onto the carpeted floor, her platinum-blonde hair cascading practically everywhere.

Waiting for pain, she held her breath. When none came, she completed a few dozen slow pushups to make sure her elbow and shoulder joints still worked. Then she did a wonderful job of quasi-yoga, by quickly seating Indian Style—without her bottom, legs or feet touching the floor until they were supposed to.

"Hmm," she thought out loud. "I wonder if Jim knows that I used to be a gymnast." That wicked thought made her blush, since she wasn't wearing a stitch of clothing. What would he do, by chance, if he saw her naked?

Stop it, she chided herself. Her body still ached, and her grin vanished, yielding to another frown. He probably wasn't going to be at all pleased to see her this morning.

Reality sinking in and sobering her thoughts, she looked herself over, trying to see anything her healing powers hadn't patched. But only a dull pain and a lot of dried blood remained, despite what had happened only thirty-one hours before.

The kill. The jump. The explosion. She had no burns or anything actually reminding her of past events. Nothing really, except for some scabs that she picked off and threw into the trash nearby. Otherwise, she had been pretty lucky.

Yah, didn't you say you used to be a gymnast? She grinned despite herself, and despite an extremely full bladder and a gnawing hunger.

She pursed her lips, rubbing the last of the scabs from her body, before getting up and pulling the blood-stained sheets from the bed. Eying them briefly, somewhat shocked by the amount of blood, she soon wadded them up and threw them into the washer. She checked the mattress, making sure it was indeed "stainless," and then walked into the bathroom—thankful, again, that FEMET Spawn had such elastic bladders and kidneys.

After flushing the toilet and stepping into the shower, Rebecca zoned out. Mouth agape, soap everywhere, she soaked up the heavenly spray as it washed away every remaining trace of a 210-foot fall into branches, rocks and an unforgiving ocean. However, she began to worry about the upcoming day. Reluctantly, she finally got out and dried off.

"Maybe I should call in sick," she wished. But if she did that, she might actually be visited by worried parties, and that was the last thing she wanted.

"No," she said to herself, not speaking loud enough for Ecie to hear. "I need to get to work. It's been long enough. I don't know what he'll say, but I'll be prepared for it." In fact, she would stop by the holographic imaging center before going into the office and check up on some files, thereby fueling her justification. Then, hopefully, she would be able to get there before … before she would have to face him.

She stretched a bit more and then dried the rest of her body with careful hands. She was still cautious, just in case all her wounds had not healed.

Some more than others. Rebecca cringed. She had hoped that she would have slept better once she had killed Anderson, but the dreams had been as awful as ever. What else could she do?

Enough, she told herself. *Maybe it won't be so bad. Maybe he won't say anything.* In a moment of wishful thinking, Rebecca left the bathroom, throwing her towel onto the bed. She shook out as much water as she could from her long hair and tied it into a ponytail. She then moved to the closet and asked the computer to turn on the news.

"Wot source shall I splick, m'lady?" A mixture of Standard English and Verengoshian came from a voice of a teenage boy. For kicks, the ever-growing computer sometimes liked to talk in the blend of the two languages.

"Scan the local networks. Try to find anything that mentions Anderson's private getaway near Long Island. It fronted as a pharmaceutical company." She looked in the direction of the microphones. They were in the walls, since people generally neglected their comlinks in their private quarters.

"Sure thing," the computer said then quickly snapped off, not really saying anything else. Rebecca still wasn't dressed, and she suddenly wondered if she needed to blush. Ecie's eyes were here too, which was part of a neural net that spread throughout the base. He, literally, could see everything, and Arthor had once mentioned that the sentient computer was now in his "teenage" years. Could he be embarrassed?

"Sorry, Ecie, I'll get dressed." She wrapped the towel around herself again. She knew that she'd have to get used to organic frames and their quirks—if being sentient and virtuous were quirks? Of course, the last three months had given her plenty of time to adjust, and communicating with Ecie was losing its initial awkwardness.

"I'm not a Peeping Tom," the computer protested. "I only look into residences in emergencies and try to blur the images of the cameras when I have to look into people's rooms. I only thought that you might have felt uncomfortable if I talked while you dressed. Some of the Crystalians have mentioned such embarrassment and have asked me for privacy."

"How considerate of you," she said, some of her earlier uneasiness of how this day would turn out beginning to subside. "Thank you."

"No problem"—Ecie probably would be smiling if he had lips—"it will take a moment for the channel. There's a bit of a problem with the station's live stream today, so I'm buffering the info on this side. Call me if you need anything else."

"OK." Rebecca yawned and put on her underwear, slid into the walk-in closet and ignored the bodysuits she usually wore during covert missions. Instead, she selected black cargo pants, a white T-shirt and a dark blue, turtle-neck sweater.

"In Sector Thirty-eight East, a ..." She listened carefully to the news. She hadn't been able to hear what had happened since the reactor breech and the explosion. She was—

"Dammit. An innocent, upstart pharmaceutical company? Figures." She let out a curse.

Ecie, however, didn't respond. He didn't have to, despite Becca wishing that he had. Possibly, she was looking for a fight, but she would save that for later.

"Splicing McNeil," she cursed again and put on some boots. "Ecie, I made sure the explosion would open up the armory. But they were able to keep it quiet, and no one will really know."

"I know," the computer replied, obviously sounding upset as well. "However, it may be for the best. They might have slanted it against us anyway. The latest polls from the Media aren't good. They're starting to compare us to terrorists more and more every day. Being branded as 'vigilantes' was bad enough, but if they start throwing us into the same category as groups like Tek-nah and Vig-Aliac—"

"I know. I know," Becca cut him off, already knowing the truth. The general public knew nothing about what the true government hid from it, which included things like secret dealings in genetic manipulation, the truth about the Resistance, and the battles of Kilogy-Tristis, Garland and Henderson. After nearly two centuries of constant deception, the Guard and its minions could do whatever they wished when it came to protecting Panteria's security.

Like eliminating any possible threat ... She immediately thought about her father and her heart suddenly ached. Despite killing the man responsible for his murder, she began to feel the rage, sadness and frustration all over again. And she thought of what she had done to Anderson, and then of the person who wasn't going to like what she did.

"Aw, screw it anyway," she said, regardless of what Ecie might think. "It's over. Anderson's dead. Good riddance. That's all that matters. If he wants me to leave, then I'll go and it won't matter anymore." Stifling a sudden surge of emotions and any potential tears, she closed the closet door and clipped on her Executioner insignia and rank, Lt. Colonel, to the raised neckline of her sweater. It was a high rank for her, considering she was in her twenties and she'd only been here for a few months, but she had significantly more real-life experience compared to the rest of the Executioners, and would probably be a full general by the end of the year.

The computer didn't say anything else. Either he also realized the possible outcome, or he just didn't know what to say to console her. Even so, the computer knew if someone was talking to him or not.

"It's over," she said. She walked out of her bedroom and out through the living room of her apartment. "If he wants me to leave," she repeated nervously. She noticed a number of ancient weapons and tribal war masks on various walls and shelving. They had been picked up during the last three months, while she was out-and-about with new friends, friends she had made here.

"If he wants me to leave, then I'll go," she sighed. Artwork rested above the artificial fireplace and on the surrounding walls. Many of the pieces were bought elsewhere, but she had made many of the others during some recent art classes at one of Crystal Mountain's many colleges. It was odd that she had forgotten how to draw and paint until she had come here. She had a green thumb too, like her father.

"But then I'll go and it won't matter anymore," saying those words and shaking her head, she thought of the years she had been under Infiltration's guidance. Being a part of Infiltration, Rebecca had gained respect, but it had cost her her father, her life and her freedom.

Such things had meant nothing to the Agency. Before her

father died, she, a child of the FEMET, had believed in the same philosophy. Because of a genetic coping mechanism, she had forgotten many things, important things of her past that had been replaced by the drills of military intelligence and the art of killing and government-sanctioned murder.

Chewing her lower lip, Rebecca walked past and ignored the kitchen. Despite her extreme hunger, she just didn't have the stomach for breakfast.

"I'll get something later. Maybe." She opened the door of her apartment, her new home, in an underground city belonging to the Crystalians. Rebecca now worked for Crystal Mountain's military force, the Executioners.

"Hi, Julie. Hi, Amy. Good morning, Eric." Despite the timetable she was trying to keep, Rebecca Anita Alexander just stood in the doorway for a moment and watched other early birds pass by. She smiled and waved at them regardless of her mood.

About eight thousand Crystalians lived in this area of Cavern Glenn, a residential area that was about an eighth of a mile north of the military base, Delta Six. The rest of the eighty-five-thousand-plus people living beneath Crystal Mountain resided in thirteen other Tunnel Plexes. Quite a few, like Cavern Glenn, were quite expansive, some places with open areas vast enough to project a simulated sky.

She eyed a faux sun and whistled quietly to herself. Long ago, fusion disintegrators had gobbled up millions of tons of unwanted dirt and smelters had processed the resultant ore for girders, tunnel tubes, rails and the like.

"Quite a sharp contrast from the past," she said. In the beginning, many of these areas had been narrow supply and exit corridors. A will to live had resulted in a tremendous achievement.

Rebecca took a breath of cool fresh air, felt the warmth of

the faux sun starting to rise, and touched the leaves of a Japanese maple which grew in a pot with several other plants on her front porch. It seemed all but impossible. But over eight hundred years ago, and just when the Neo-Holocaust first started, a large underground military fortress had been buried by terrible explosions. The people within the base were thought dead and the land was no longer useable by the government at the time. And ultimately, the base was lost and forgotten during the chaos of the Apocalypse.

The people, however, had lived through the explosions. Concurrently, they thought the upper world had died out and that they could never return to the surface. And believing they were the last of Humanity, they'd learned to live rather peacefully.

Over time, the community lost its necessity for a rigid command structure, and much of the military facilities and equipment had been used for other purposes. Nevertheless, about four years ago, when the people here decided to form the Executioners, Jim brought the old military base up to thirty-first century standards.

The new base was named *Delta Six*, in tribute to a division of tunnel-expansion workers that had died five hundred years ago. Since Jim's arrival, however, the rest of this underground metropolis had been called something else.

"Crystal Mountain ..." The words escaped her lips as she thought of Jim and the Crystalians. She grinned, remembering how Arthor Jones, Lt. Governor of Crystal Mountain and also Executive Officer of the Executioners, had once said that someone coined the name during the last stages of the upgrades.

"He's making the place virtually indestructible," he had said. "Like the crystal blades carried in his arms. Hmm, Crystal Mountain?"

That was a cute story, but Rebecca knew the truth and hadn't let Arthor bullshit her that way. Besides, it was referred to in many ways these days, like *The Mountain*, *The Executioners' Lair*, *The Base*, simply *The Lair*, and *Home*.

"Home, despite what I had thought, thought before, before …" Rebecca's smile faded, knowing Jim, the Governor of Crystal Mountain, got pretty paranoid when it came to the safety of his people.

Her stomach tightened when she thought of the conflict she would undoubtedly face in about an hour or so. Becca already anticipated a good deal of what he would probably say—anticipated all the warnings, the concerns, his fears and his disappointment.

But looking around even now, she had seen and inspected the electromagnetic field generators that re-enforced the shell of the rock around them; had seen the defensive modifications, consisting of missile batteries, self-tracking rail-guns, machineguns and electromagnetic pulse cannons; and had participated in the regular drills for Code Blues, Code Reds and Battle Alerts.

"Ecie"—she finally closed the door of the apartment behind her—"can you prep a Holosuite in Pine Place for me? I'll be there in a few minutes."

"Sure thing, Beccs," the computer responded without any delay, even though he was probably talking to thousands of people at the same time. "Do you want any particular file?"

"One of my personal logs," she said apprehensively, but she needed to be prepared. "It's a personal log in Set One, Number 8.967534P. It's also listed as 'Sorry, Dad.' It was written on April 7th, 3004."

"Would you like it interactive?"

"No."

"A simulated back—"

"No, Ecie," she stopped him before he went any further.

"Just play it as a narrative, first person, a simulation of myself standing in a dark, empty room, with a single stage light."

"OK. Will do." If Ecie seemed to actually sense her uneasiness, he didn't show it. "The program will be ready to play when you enter the suite. Standard privacy protocols will be in effect. I won't hear anything."

"Thanks, bud, I'll see you in a bit."

"OK."

Rebecca let out a breath and moved into the large corridor in front of her apartment. In this section, about forty apartments were clustered together in a little community, complete with a park, pool, corner store, and bomb shelter.

She took a right on Henry Street and then into a smaller bypass tube, which would lead to Pine Place without having to take a transport.

A timid grin crossed her lips when she looked at the black inner surface of the walkway. Most of these bypass/safety tubes were covered by a paint that was insulating, could absorb most em-bands and covered the metal behind it like a skin. Beneath the paint, the walls around her were made out of three inches of diterium-D polymer and reinforced with F4 Barium-carbonate ribs. Also, in combination with the special paint, these tubes could be pumped with nitrogen to stop any fires, along with oxygen masks if anyone got trapped inside.

"Just another safety precaution," Jim had said modestly.

"Very impressive, very impressive, my dear friend." She again thought of the man who had coordinated most of this new construction for new safety zones. She would see him today, and she both loathed and looked forward to it at the same time.

Snapping her fingers nervously, she walked out of the tube and made her way to the Pine Place Holographic Imaging and Entertainment Center. She nodded and smiled at one of the attendants, before he scanned her thumb and directed her to the appropriate suite.

The lights dimmed and turned off as she entered and sat down. Then a holo-projection of herself appeared. H-Rebecca —she quickly named—sparked to life under a single spotlight.

"This is an Executioner File. Set One. Number Eight," H-Rebecca named off the file. "A personal Log of Rebecca Anita Alexander.

"These are my personal logs, which are descriptions of important events and scenarios that will remind me of who I was, and who I am now." She had recorded this and many files a few weeks after of arriving here. They had helped her cope and get her thoughts straight. They would help today too.

"'What?'" The simulated H-Rebecca soon got into character and began a monologue. "I sat behind the breakfast table. My frown tugging my cheeks." H-Rebecca took on the image of how Becca had looked when she had recorded this message. Her cheeks and eyes were red and her long, platinum-blonde hair a little in disarray.

"My father tried to make me understand: 'It's true, Becca. You have to believe what I'm saying. We don't have much more time together. Our lives continue to grow farther apart.'

"'How, are you trying to say that those MUTANTs are coming after me?' I giggled by the assumption. Was he serious?

"'Dammit, will you listen to me?' My father, Jon Clayton Alexander, slammed his fist on the tabletop. 'You have to believe this. MUTANTs is just their university. The FGGO will come for you.'

"'What?' I leered and cursed the accusations he was throwing at me. 'That I'm a superhero? Created by a lab no less?' Not believing such Fantastic Fiction and wondering if my dad was hiding some comic books somewhere, I actually started laughing.

I didn't want to, because I really did respect him, but this was too much.

"'Come on, Dad,' I continued before he could say anything. 'Things like that can't happen. That's only an Urban Legend from the Apocalypse, you know, like Bicdové and his soldiers. Besides, wouldn't the Civil Bureau of Human and Animal Rights prevent that?'

"My father cradled his face in his hands for a moment," H-Rebecca drifted off, as though remembering a thought. And the real woman in the room had to admit that she was still very impressed with the holographic program that Ecie had developed. Infiltration had nothing so lifelike, and they had holographic projectors just about everywhere.

"Don't get me wrong," the H-woman continued. "He was a good father, was never abusive and did the best he could as a single parent.

"'I realize'—my father raised his head slowly from his hands —'that you're still young. But you're coming into your sixteenth year, and you had to be told the truth.'

"It couldn't be possible, could it?" H-Rebecca shook her head in disbelief, even though both women already knew the answer.

"'All right,' I gave in for now, growing tired of his signs of irritation. 'What if I am a product of this Fetal Manipulation Experiment, this FEMET? Why me?'

"'Because of us,' he replied, pointing at the pictures on the inner walls of the breakfast nook. The room's outfacing wall was all glass, and its location in the house was perfect for the right amount of light to stream in. And it wasn't wasted. My father had a green thumb and he liked to flaunt it. However, I looked past the tealeaf plants, the hanging vines and the dozens of flowers, and focused on several of the pictures my father motioned to.

"The images of a happy nine year old girl playing joyfully with her parents almost suffocated me. Six years ago, we used to live on Crete. I had been born on the island. I had played on ancient temples. I swam in protected waters so blue that, as a child, I couldn't really appreciate. And I had been rocked asleep practically every night in my mother's arms.

"'It was because of your mother and me,' he repeated, locking his gray/blue eyes with my own and snapping me back to the present. 'They, FGGO scientists posing as researchers for the regular army, said it had something to do with our genetic makeup. After running the tests, out of two thousand pairings, we were one of only three couples that hadn't been sorted by computer.'

"'But what's so important about genetic compatibility?'

"'At that time, I wasn't sure, and they really didn't give us any answers. But your mother and I had been young, brash and very patriotic, especially since it could have meant an end to whatever terrorist groups were out there.'

"My father drifted off for a moment, possibly at the lies he had been told, shook his head, and then continued: 'Several years later, I discovered that this genetic compatibility was necessary to ensure the mental stability of our children. I've heard that the first generation of them, enlisted in an Army of Mutants, went insane because they couldn't cope with their mutations. The FGGO actually had almost the whole lot of them killed before they caused serious trouble.'

"'What was the reason?' He intrigued me. I didn't know exactly how he got this information about the government, even though it did worry me that it was from countless numbers of mercenaries, rebels and other fringe groups.

"However"—H-Rebecca sneered just perceptibly—"I began to get a little pissed when I started to wonder why he had waited so long to tell me about *me*.

"My father shrugged his shoulders, oblivious to my sudden internal conflict. 'Madness is actually pretty common in Nagephon spawn. Scientists believe the mental disorder proliferates pretty quickly if not diagnosed around the time the first powers emerge. In humans, the ages between twelve and eighteen show the most growth, but it can be sooner or later than that. If recognized early, psychoanalysts can help these subjects adjust.

"'Naturally, I'm still trying to figure out how all these fantastic natural mutations in the environment came about. New evidence from the past centuries is always flowing my way, and I think my next inforun might shed some light.

"'Anyway,' my father said, shaking his head. He had been staring at a picture. I couldn't be sure which one, but my father was soon looking at me again. 'Human Nagis, Naturally Augmented Genetic Individuals, or humans that have been deformed by the Naturally Augmenting Genetic Phenomenon, Nagephon, seem to need guidance in controlling their abilities. They are definitely the most powerful beings on Panteria, and without psychological help, they are quickly destroyed by the Extermination Officers.

"'Well, apparently that's true,' he said, derisively. 'But have you ever seen an E.O. kill someone besides a bloodthirsty monster?'

"'So you're saying that the FGGO sought out younger recruits this time?' I quickly asked.

"'Ah, you are listening,' he teased playfully. 'The Puppeteer government that I have told you about did just that, successfully recruiting another two Generations of them.

"'I'm sorry that I don't have any more information about the recruiting process,' my father said. 'I do know that it was a rather costly endeavor. Subsequently, the FGGO decided to develop some Nagephon spawn of its own. Unfortunately, you are the outcome from the union, the surgery.'

"I shuddered." H-Rebecca did, as did Rebecca. "I tried not to, but I did.

"'There is more,' my father spoke, before I could say anything as a rebuttal. But he didn't continue, just simply stared at me.

"'What is it? I can't think of anything else that could hurt me more than what you've said already.'

"'Becca'—my father closed his eyes, pushed back his graying red hair—'I didn't say these things to hurt you. You need to know. I wouldn't have been able to keep the truth much longer.' He took a breath, also rubbing his beard as he did so.

"'All right,' he said, taking a deep breath, and his eyes showed fear, hate and sorrow. 'Someday, they'll come for you, snatch you away fr-from me. You'll never see this place again.'

"Then I saw the tears. Shocked, I reached across the table to wipe them away, but he took my hands into his and began to cry."

H-Rebecca's eyes were filled with tears. "I then watched my father break down, something I hadn't seen since mom died.

"I'm digressing. That was years ago but after her funeral I'm not sure how long he kept his distance. He simply left the house droids to cook and clean, while he sat alone in his den.

"Eventually, after hearing my cries, my pleads, my apologies to him, he soon asked for my forgiveness and promised that he'd never hurt me again. But how many days after that did we move to a suburb of Tamorami in North America?

"I couldn't help but think about my grandparents then. They hadn't been happy. My mother's parents, and my only living grandparents, rarely liked to travel. I seldom saw them, maybe twice a year, less. I missed them.

"And I am ashamed now." H-Rebecca jumped briefly to the time of the recording. "Since I've escaped from Infiltration, I haven't even checked to see if they're still alive."

Rebecca groaned herself. She still hadn't checked up on them. She was afraid to.

"Anyway." H-Becca fell back into the monologue. "The weakness in my father's hand made me shudder. I looked at the pictures in the breakfast room and thought of Mom's death and the days ever since. Her murder had never been solved. But did my father know? I didn't ask him even though I should have."

H-Rebecca rubbed her nose, and wiped away the tears the best she could. "The next few months slowly passed. The day of my sixteenth birthday came and went. I still went to school like any other teenager. You know, I played sports, received so-so grades, the usual.

"And then, I suddenly began to remember lectures verbatim." The H-woman smiled and brushed her left hand through her hair. "I overlooked the truth. But soon it was impossible to ignore, especially when I secretly began to exercise with even heavier weights than the boys, and the coaches.

"Eventually my friends, coaches and teachers became quite obsequious, asking me to run for upcoming student elections, organize special events, help out and teach fellow students and athletes. However, I had found this strange and overwhelming.

"To be honest, I just didn't want to stand out, and all I wanted to do was make it through the year without drawing too much attention to myself." Rebecca looked at the holographic image of her and smiled meekly. She remembered those times all too well. How could she have been so foolish?

"Meanwhile," H-Rebecca said, took a quick breath and crossed her arms. "During this time of my growing self-awareness, my father worked diligently on his logs.

"Ironically, the FGGO had provided generous financial backing so that I'd be raised without any hardships. Of course, I doubt they had anticipated that he would use the excess to fund his research against them.

"Needless to say, when he had almost been killed on one of those damn inforuns, I began to seriously worry about him, and eventually everything else didn't matter. By the end of the school year, I decided that I was not going to participate in any summer athletic clubs, was not going to run for any student offices and was not planning to keep any ties with friends during the summer months.

"Surprisingly enough, I was given my privacy, even though every busybody told me that if I needed … You can guess that I never took up any of the offers. And I wasn't about to admit anything about myself.

Until the accident that is.

"It had been on a dark and stormy night, a night when I was hit by a hovercar," H-Rebecca smirked and then seemed to apologize for that horrid introduction. "I woke up in a ditch a few hours later, merely hurting, even though I'd been knocked nearly sixty-seven feet into the nearby forest.

"I moved my arms, tested the strength in my legs and shook the terrible ache from my head. Rain came down—drenching me, washing away whatever blood should have been there. I looked around. It was late, and no one was around.

"Getting back to the road, I soon saw the gouges in the concrete and the nearby mud, and saw what was left of the retaining wall and the trees that the car must have crashed into. Then I saw the flares and water-resistant paint marks.

"'There is justice,' I mumbled, regardless of my own wretched fate. Even to this day, I remember the smell of his intoxicated blood on the ground, which I still think was in my head. I was either totally hallucinating or there had been a lot of blood. When my father investigated the incident later, he found that the driver was a deputy who often partook in one too many during his patrols. He often disabled the safety systems so that the OBC wouldn't detect his drinking. His resultant hacks also inactivated much of the anti-collision software.

"'I'm home. I'm a bit late,' I later babbled. I barely remembered walking the ten miles back home, barely remembered ringing the doorbell, and barely remembered falling asleep the moment my dad caught me.

"The dreams," H-Rebecca smirked, and Rebecca nodded knowingly. "At first, I knew I was sleeping. But that didn't comfort me with the nightmares. I later found out that they were part of the FEMET Initial Combat Conditioning, the Reprox Coma. They were dreams of actual combat that were buried into my memory and triggered by a maturation hormone all women have. Because of it, I had to endure the terrors, the murders and the wars with every stig in history.

"In time, I woke up." The H-woman rubbed her temples with her hands. "Yeah, nearly three weeks had passed in a 'special' wing of a VA hospital. My father had been worried. He quickly told me the length of my sleep, and then got me something to eat and drink.

"I then told him of the dreams, the nightmares and asked if he could interpret them for me. He didn't or wouldn't.

"Regardless, I immediately told him that I wanted training, military training, anything that he remembered, could show me and could teach me. I couldn't explain it, and he hadn't seemed surprised that I had asked.

"In a nutshell, I was genetically programmed for it. The hunger for combat actually, well, umm, excited me." H-Rebecca blushed, as did the real woman in the room. Although, that particular psychological motivation had been removed once the FEMET children had been brought to Infiltration, the FGGO had known how to encourage their pre-soldiers to learn some aspects of combat before the Abduction.

"Anyway," the H-woman continued. "He began to train me in every tactic he had ever learned. Later, I sought other teachers for fighting, self-defense, education, and military tactics. My endurance, strength and skills increased significantly.

"'Maybe,' I told myself, 'maybe I can somehow untangle my fate.' And believing this, throughout the next two years, I took my life back. I began to participate in extracurricular activities at school, began organizing dances and other events, ran for Vice President of my senior class, and I even participated in gymnastics again.

"But, most importantly, it was like my father began to believe it as well. He stayed home and only traveled for vacations, began writing short stories for some local magazines and began throwing neighborhood dinner parties. Something he and Mom used to do.

"Two years ..." H-Rebecca trailed off and actually looked directly into the eyes of the woman sitting in the chamber. "Two years proved too short a time for adequate training. And, honestly, we were fools.

"A few weeks after my high school graduation and after a rather intense Aikido session in the morning, I was sitting in the backyard. I can't give you a reason, but I was just sitting there, resting and feeling safe. Then I looked up, possibly to see what shape the clouds were that day, and wondered what college would be like.

"However, something caught my attention. Just a second before, it had appeared as only a speck, a bird, a hovercar?

"'Dad,' I screamed when an armored hovervan slammed into and bounced off the ground. 'Dad, help,' I screamed again.

"Splicing McNeil, I wasn't stupid. I knew what was going to

happen, knew what was going on. I tried to run.

"Behind me, the pressurized cabin hissed when the door of the van popped open and a squad of four soldiers rushed my way.

"I fought back. God, I swear I fought back," H-Rebecca shouted and fought with her hands, startling Rebecca some. "But despite what my father and other instructors had taught me, my struggles were useless. These soldiers had been trained for this assignment, and I was only a novice and a routine pickup. Desperate, I even tried to plead with them, begged them to release me.

"'Shut up,' the lead soldier said, hiding behind a thick visor. I gained no sympathy, even though my eyes were tearing up and my hands reached out to them for mercy. They were relentless and cold of heart. My arms were tied behind me, and my mouth was clamped shut by a large hand.

"I bit the hand hard, broke free, and screamed again, 'Daddy. Daddy.' But I was already in the van. And its bare, internal walls reminded me of a box—sealed and ready for shipment.

"Nevertheless, I struggled again with frantic, wild kicks. I didn't know where I was going, but I felt that anywhere outside would be better. Ironically, Rebecca Anita Alexander, a gymnast that had simply declined to participate in the Olympics because she knew she'd get homesick, clumsily stumbled, tripped and screwed her own escape.

"Only as a last ditch effort, I pressed my face to the van's rear window, hoping to see my savior."

There was another long, uncomfortable pause.

"Nothing," the holographic woman said and fell to her knees, tears beginning to fall from her face. "The tears that suddenly came smeared the window, making it impossible to see out any longer. I closed my eyes, shuddered, wailed and fell to my knees.

"Taking advantage of my reaction, the kidnappers got another hold and dragged me back to a seat. I wanted to fight, but I was too shocked and devastated by what I saw.

"'Nothing, not a damned thing,' I mumbled, having seen my house one last time, having watched my house zoom away from me. And in that glimpse I saw a person who witnessed my entire abduction and saw where he had stood and what he had done.

"Absolutely nothing! Tears streamed down my face. Shaking terribly and totally enervated, I simply allowed myself to be strapped into one of the passenger seats with my abductors.

"'Oh, Daddy, Daddy,' I pleaded to him still, even though I had seen him standing in the back doorway, looking up at me and at the van. It was as though his heart had been broken, but he didn't do a goddamned thing.

"My own heart broke," the H-woman sighed and traced holographic tears along the floor with her fingers. Seeing this, Rebecca actually wanted to go over and comfort her, but she wasn't watching this for solace.

The H-woman continued to cry, "My heart broke. How else can I say it?

"Like he had promised, I never saw him again, and, for that one moment, I didn't wish to." H-Rebecca, her monologue finished, got back up to her feet and nodded. "This log was entered into Ecie by me, Rebecca Anita Alexander, on April 7, 3004, in remembrance of my former life. Maybe these memories will help me expiate my sins."

The holographic woman faded into the darkness and the door of the holosuite popped open.

"That should do it." Rebecca held back the tears that tried to form, and channeled that energy for an upcoming confrontation. Regardless of the outcome, she knew what she needed to say.

"She'll be here soon," Ecie chimed in, while Jim St. John sat in his office. Most communication during business hours, whether to computer or person, was directed through comlinks on shirt collars. The Executioners' insignia—in the shape of an executioner's hood with a curved battle axe just to its left side—did double duty. "She healed pretty well."

"I bet." Jim grimaced and thumbed on his Personal Data Link, then rested it on his desk. Preparing for an inspection in Hangar Bay Two later in the morning, he downloaded a file from Ecie and then pushed it aside. "What's the latest on Anderson?"

"Let me pull up the feed on the main screen." The computer obviously wasn't about to get pulled into this fight.

"All right." Jim yawned and looked around. More square than oval and about half the size of an Old Age football field, the Executioner Command Center was quiet and fairly dark during the simulated night. To his right, Arthor's office was beside his, and the large Texic-glass door connecting the rooms was hardly ever shut. His friend's desk was empty too, the Verengoshian currently on a perimeter watch. The other office to Jim's left was also vacant, but wouldn't be for much longer.

Great way to start a Monday, Jim thought and stretched his neck side to side. He looked out his office then, through T-glass that acted as walls, windows and armor.

Other Executioners, working the night shift, sat at various stations below. A skeleton crew manned the complex at night and high-ranking officers took their turns at a swing shift. It had been Jim's turn the night before, and he had volunteered again this night. He was thankful nothing happened.

Well, almost nothing. He eyed the giant view screen Ecie mentioned. The large monitor took up a quarter of the far wall, and ten smaller screens also lined the forward section of the Command Center.

Obtained from the Media, cloaked satellites, hidden cameras, reconnaissance patrols, and other various sources, Ecie's monitoring programs fed the screens with hundreds of pictures within pictures. With only a scan, Jim could take in the actions of the government, the rebels, the crooks, the civilians, and just about anyone else. For a moment, he tried to see everything he could, but it was a lot of information. Really, too much.

Then a face entered his vision, a man he had come to know over the years, especially in the last thirty hours.

"Why did she do it?" he asked the simple question.

"It's obvious why she did it," Ecie quickly responded. "But you're wondering why *she* did it?"

"Why do you ask, when you already know?" Jim thought of the other night, of the alarms running in silence. Despite her authorization and clearance, Ecie had been worried about her and had told Jim when she had gotten back home. *But couldn't she have come to me afterwards, instead of sneaking into her apartment and enduring her injuries alone?*

"I'm just repeating what you've said every five minutes for the last two days."

"Thirty-one hours," Jim said tersely.

"Do you want the exact time?" The sarcasm was thick, like a teenage son talking to his father.

"No," he conceded, rubbing his hands together, and looked at the man on the main viewer. Although the General had developed vehement allegiance amongst many at the AOM, Jim had tried to avoid contact with Viper during his service, since there had been too much scuttlebutt about the man's extravagance. Always somewhat humble despite his abilities, Jim had done his best at simply limiting contact to Agency functions only.

Later, about six months after Jim had escaped the Agency, some type of power play had given Eric control of the FGGO. Back then, Jim and other members of the AOM hadn't even known that they were simply a subgroup of the FGGO. Instead, until everything was rebranded as Infiltration, they had thought that the FGGO was just the research arm of the AOM.

Assuming that there had been one, the former FGGO leader must have considered research more important than the day-to-day tasks and hadn't even known about the subversion until it was too late. To this day, Jim hadn't been able to find out who the former leader was, since Viper—and/or the Guard—had erased the person's history completely.

C'est La Vie, Jim thought. The former leader of the FGGO had never even bothered to make a visit to the AOM by the time the Third Generation of AOM soldiers had received their commissions. There might have been records that still existed somewhere, but the FGGO had been a mystery even by the time Jim had been with the AOM. And if the other Generation of Nagis soldiers had known anything, they hadn't talked.

"Ecie, what's the score of the game on Screen Seven?" he asked. That screen was showing a Little League Baseball game. He watched the kids play, watched them laugh and cheer. He'd been barely older than them when he'd been recruited by the FGGO.

"The Ravens, the blue team, is up four to one," Ecie said quietly. "You said that you played at one time?"

"Yeah, a pitcher," Jim chuckled. "I was awful."

"Apparently, the AOM and the Panterian Guard knew your true potential. When did they recruit you?" The computer was digging, usually asking Jim questions about the past during these shifts.

"Sixteen. I have to admit that I was impressed when I saw the inside of their palace for the first time. I know its somewhere in Phijeyoton, but the transport they used didn't have any windows. And all of the other meetings I had with the Guard were in the field, through operatives."

"Do you remember anything about the Governing Council?"

"There were twelve of them, sitting in seats like a panel of judges. That group referred to themselves as the High Priests. I only remember being nervous as hell. Lauren, the AOM recruiter, told me to keep my mouth shut and listen. That was easy to do."

"You being a kid or not, I still can't imagine you falling for what they told you, saying that they needed to keep themselves a secret from the rest of us."

"Thanks for the vote of confidence," Jim groaned. "But by then, it wouldn't have mattered. They were already giving me the hormones to control me."

But, thank God—he grinned, frowned—*thank God, Lisa didn't know about the hormones. At least, she hadn't kept that a secret.*

"I really don't know if it was the drug that drove me, or my own desire to perform for them," Jim said.

"There had to be something," Ecie smirked. "They fed you the steroids and growth hormones to help unlock your physical potential, but you still managed to gain several graduate degrees at their university. I couldn't imagine such a schedule for most people."

"Yeah, I know." Jim waved his hand in dismissal. "I trained like a scathing lunatic, a freaking monster with nothing else to do except study, workout and train."

The Crystalian Governor stroked his chin in self-disgust. At that moment, he wondered if, during his training, he'd ever thought about his family, the loved ones he'd left to join the AOM. His sister, just a toddler when he'd been recruited, had never known a brother.

Like they would've recognized me. He pursed his lips and fiddled with the corner of his desk. He knew that even if he had returned his parents wouldn't have known him. Too much had changed by then.

So I stayed away. Jim closed his eyes in shame. In reality, he had thought of them but only in passing. He figured that the AOM had created letters, emails, holographic greetings for him so that his parents didn't worry. However, empowered by the knowledge of his future, he had foolishly believed that there were things simply more important than family.

"By the time I turned eighteen," Jim started again. "I was stronger than anyone else in the AOM. They didn't stop me either and kept pushing. There was even a petty bet when I pressed a Bratilina cruiser above my shoulders."

"That's about a thousand tons." The computer was impressed.

"Yah, stupid show," Jim cursed, knowing he was a lot stronger now. Being so pumped up with adrenaline and stimulants, he vaguely remembered the actual moment. His instructors and future commanding officers had seemed to always bring up that story for the new recruits, as if they hadn't believed it themselves.

Idiots, wasn't I your prize, your find of a century? The Crystalian Governor stretched his neck and eyed the main view screen a moment before tracing his right index finger along the edge of the PDL on his desk.

"Ecie, can you give me a moment?" Jim asked the computer when he remembered a choice, a choice he had thought was voluntary until Lisa had freed him.

"Sure, Jim." Ecie, although sounding a bit worried, clicked off and gave him some privacy.

I was such a fool. He looked down, seeing his forearms in the light. Instantly, they seemed to burn from the memories he replayed in his mind. It was as if the adamant within his arms had its own desire and would never let him forget it.

"You would feed. I know," he mocked the weapons hidden from his eyes, which were three indestructible Kurgon Blades resting between the wrist and the elbow joints of each arm. It had been a horrible operation, during which the bones of his upper and lower arms had been replaced by adamant sheaths, posts and cords. Naturally, they kept the muscles strong and made sure that they'd never tear off the artificial bone. And they reinforced the bones of his hands too so that they'd never be crushed.

He eyed his right hand for a moment, picturing the curved, long razors hidden there. "I know you'd kill me too"—he smiled sardonically—"just so you could feed again, wouldn't you?"

Jim held his right arm out and slowly flexed special muscles, triggers that had been added with the crystal blades. He waited for pain, but of course it never came. Nor did he ever bleed, even though only flesh provided a barrier between them and the outside world—

Shlisst-hymmmmmn, a start of a hymn, a prayer—what it had once been compared to anyway—whispered in his ears. Although he could control the speed and number and extension, he allowed all three, fifteen-inch-long and transparent, weapons to fully spring out into the open. Each blade rested between a knuckle of his hand, positioned in front of an artery and modified muscles, as though feeding on his life rather than using the blood and tissue as a hydraulic release.

"How long ago did they make you?" The crystal glistened in his eyes, and he clenched his fist. "How long had you been waiting for me?"

But a Kurgon Beast must be made whole. He shuddered from his stupidity, when he thought about the Reformation, which had transformed him into an inhuman killer. He winced, seemingly always able to perceive the alloy throughout his frame. Truthfully, his very bones—

Cheap bastards. He sneered, making his skull ring like a bell when he flicked a finger hard upon it. The supply of ore for making adamant had been growing thin for decades. The Panterian Organic Computer Matrix—or Panocomptrix, the Panterian Guard's super computer—had perfected a way of making the remaining ore last much longer than what the Devil ever intended. By using Silica, the only other element capable of forming a stable matrix with adamant, the FGGO had been able to stretch the supply the Guard had provided for Jim's Reformation, thereby covering the rest of his bones with a sheath of indestructible fiberglass.

"They read way too many comics," Jim sighed and made another bell sound with his head and finger. Less than a sixteenth of an inch thick and nearly as tough as the pure crystal, the fiberglass guaranteed the AOM that his bones would never break, even though Jim had never been stopped because of a few broken bones.

Suddenly, without warning, he wished to scream out, but he calmed himself before the outburst, knowing such was pointless. He knew it was the Beast anyway, knew that it often tried to take advantage of his anger.

"Look at me." He tapped his fingers on the desk and drew M's along its top. He no longer had conversations with the Beast —getting off of the mind-controlling hormones had ended that. However, he knew who the Beast was, knew that it wanted to hear its name once more, and knew that it had tasted too many battles. And, despite what he tried, it would see many more.

"A fool, always a fool," he whispered and slumped down in his chair, thinking of a past that never seemed to be such. His armament, his augmentation, the training, and the knowledge of the true government were his admonitions of pain and foolishness. And the death of his love.

"But Henderson was so long ago," he said to himself as if time should make a difference. Over five years had passed since then, but he remembered it all too well. And he thought of when Lisa had called to him and when he had seen her plight, her suffering.

Henderson Prairie was a large swatch of land in Northern Tundra of North America. The AOM had thought that *they* had lured the Night Rangers there with false information. And unexpectedly falling into an ambush, the Army of Mutants nearly had been destroyed on the Autumnal Equinox.

"Lisa, why did Medical move closer in?" He would never, could never forget what happened. She'd called to him, had broken the control of the drug herself, and had told him about all the lies. Then she—

His hands still shook, and he had thought about her death nearly every day for the last five and a half years. Years later, he now wondered if he had accidentally killed her. "That last explosion had been so close, but it never should have had enough strength to force my hand."

In nightmares, he dreamed the Beast had done it and laughed at his foolishness. In other dreams, Lisa mocked his efforts in trying to save her and pulled his blades into her herself. Then in others, she screamed and shouted and cried, questioning his betrayal, wondering why he never stopped the slaughter.

No. He hadn't killed anyone, but the Executioners had. And he had trained them.

"Too long ago, too long ago," he whispered, clenched both

his fists and retracted his blades. He did not want to experience the pain again. Having a near photographic memory didn't help matters much, but he had learned to bury it, despite what he was doing and what he had promised.

"But isn't it different now? We no longer kill the just, the good. After five years, shouldn't that count for something? How can anyone say that I like to butcher?" He shook his head, knowing his former worth to the Guard, the AOM. He remembered how they had searched the globe for him, trying to regain their Beast, their Rouge Killer. They had had ample opportunity, especially before he had managed to find all of the tracers that they'd hid inside him.

Although not much could pierce his skin, adamant was different. Like the spots between his knuckles, his body had quite a few scars from where he'd used his blades to extract those cursed devices. Still, it was one of the few times he'd praised his ingenuity, since the Agency had never been able to retrieve him. And apparently, they had grown tired of the hunt themselves.

"But how had they expected to kill me? By Kepler bomb? Antimatter? Nazer rocket?" he mocked, knowing he'd reached a level of invulnerability that few ever had. Comic-book levels even.

"Fools, I was your prize," he said with a teasing laugh. Then he whispered, "Ecie?"

"Yes?" ignoring the comlink on the collar of his neck, the computer answered him through the speakers of the office. "Jim, is everything OK?"

He tapped his fingers on the control panel, and pressed a button to hold the image of Viper on the screen. "Sure. Have you heard anything from Captain Tirson?"

"Nothing except for yesterday's report. They're going to meet in Toldeclevchikee as planned."

"Fine, keep me informed. Let me know immediately if there are any problems."

"They'll be fine," Ecie reassured him.

"I know. I know that I'm being overprotective, but we're starting to become too visible. I've been letting them take on too much. I need to reel them in a bit," he cautioned. Jim remembered how he had come to Crystal Mountain—a refugee fleeing the AOM's one last attempt at capturing or killing him. These people took him in, fed him and told him stories of their past. In return, he had helped renovate the Mountain—a civilization buried for over eight centuries, and living in virtual harmony. A society that had set aside aggression and hate and violence because it simply thought it had to in order to protect the last sliver of Humanity.

Then, of course, Jim came.

"Ecie, why did I stay?" he asked the computer a question he asked himself practically every morning.

"To help them."

"Right." Jim had tried to convince himself with the same answer so many times. How many people had died from cave-ins before he had decided to help them? How much fear and shock were present when he had told them about Panteria? But hadn't he kept his promise to Lisa by helping people instead of killing them?

"But why did I let them form this righteous wretch, the Executioners?" He clenched his jaw, imagining that he heard the adamant blades calling for a true battle again.

"They're a righteous people. You couldn't have stopped them once their minds were made up. They would have gotten into far more trouble if you hadn't helped them."

"Ecie, a lot of problems have been caused by righteousness and a sense of justice. We might bite off more than we can chew." He suddenly had to suppress the Beast when he realized that it knew what he did. Thankfully, he knew that he'd have to lose total control for it to resurface now days.

Still, every-so-often, Jim dreamed that he was leading an attack against Infiltration or the Guard itself, and the Executioners would either win or lose. No matter what the outcome, however, he was always alive at the end. Left alive, to count the number of dead and to say a prayer for everyone who died for the cause of enlightenment.

"The Truth. They've sworn to expose the Guard to the world," he laughed but could not mock it, knowing he was bound by that same oath.

"It'll happen," the computer said, repeating what countless numbers of Executioners said too.

Jim looked around, not thinking, not saying anything else. He thought of Lisa now, about her dark red hair, sparkling eyes— her death.

He bit his lower lip, remembered Henderson, remembering every twig, rock, ditch, every cry for help and sudden silence. He remembered Lisa's wounds, her blood, and her last good bye. And he remembered her blood, her pale lips, and her burial. In a deep, incredibly deep grave, but a location he would never forget.

So long ago, so long ago. Indeed, over half a decade had passed since he'd buried Lisa, his lover, his wife.

No, he reminded himself, *we were never married. We couldn't be. The FGGO never would have allowed it. But what we had was good enough.*

Enough. He thought about her blue eyes and her gentle voice when she preached to him about goodness and salvation. He rarely called himself a man of faith anymore, even though the duty of Governor necessitated such piety on occasion. The Crystalians were a very religious people and still a very tolerant people. He didn't judge them for such naiveté. Well fuck, they *had* survived an apocalypse.

"You know, it might have all been over if I had done things differently, so very differently."

The computer didn't comment. It knew the possibilities of a world in which Jim never found the people here.

Immediately, Jim wanted to take those words back; however, the Beast, possibly even the man, regretted not trying to destroy his former organization minutes after Lisa's death.

Maybe then Crystal Mountain never would have surrounded me, and maybe my death would have been quick. But where would my soul have gone? he smirked.

Could he even die and did it even matter? He had taken religion for granted with his own family—just a place to hang with friends and smooch with Becky Marumoto. But Lisa's teachings had meant more to him at the Agency—love had a way of opening one's heart to things other than self. Now, though, he questioned everything.

Jim took his eyes from the monitor, thinking about the direction of the Executioners' goals. His group had already brought many to justice—and not all through indiscriminate murder. But he had to admit that he sensed a bit of satisfaction from the pain and death he was responsible for. But would he dare call it pleasure?

Could Lisa have been too late? Jim rubbed his eyes, not able to give an answer but never seeming to tire of the constant puzzles. How much of his promise to her was he actually keeping?

Maybe so, but I'm just a Kurgon Beast. That's all I'll ever be. He ignored the sensation from his adamant blades and sensed a familiar figure about to enter the Command Center.

"Ecie, Rebecca's coming." Jim sat up a bit straighter, trying to look professional. "You know, I'm sorry about my comment earlier. I was just in a mood. I couldn't imagine a world without you with us."

"Thanks, Jim." Ecie perked up a bit. "I know."

Rebecca placed her hand on the faceplate near the right side of the Command Center's door, and said, "Rebecca Anita Alexander, identification number, 77897, military council and recon."

"Welcome, Rebecca. I beat you here," Ecie laughed. Rebecca didn't have Logan's spunk yet to say the computer's jokes often needed work.

Give me time, she thought, as she watched the thick door made of diterium-D, a stronger form of diterium polymer, swing open.

"Fine," she conceded, although she did her best to produce a scowl for his benefit. "Thanks."

She walked through the doorway into a dark control room. Technically, it was still night in Crystal Mountain, so her night vision compensated easily—

The screen. Her knees almost buckled beneath her when she saw the eyes, the strong cheeks and rectangular face. It was the mask of Viper. The General. The Genetic Overmaster. The Infiltration Decoré. The man she had killed.

"Becca." She jerked her head around, wishing she had brought her crossbow, something—

She smiled, but that did not last.

Damn, he's already here, she cursed, her heart starting to pound. "Jim, good morning."

"And you. Do you mind coming into my office?" he asked, saying nothing else. The T-glass of his office was already darkening.

Stand firm, she told herself, even though her legs felt like spaghetti. "Sure."

Jim watched the woman enter the office. He could tell that she was anxious; however, her movements were as graceful as any dancer or gymnast. She closed the door behind her. He'd already closed her and Arthor's connecting office doors, and he'd asked Ecie for privacy too. He didn't want anyone else to hear this.

"Becca, welcome back. I hope you enjoyed your vacation," he poked, despite himself.

"It was fine." She didn't look him in the eyes. "Thank you for asking."

He bit back a grimace in response to her nonchalance. He wasn't looking forward to this. "Right. OK. Look. You know that I know—"

"Now look here," the woman shouted before Jim could finish, as if she was prepared for this. Apparently she was. "You know damn well why I joined the Executioners. You know I believed that we were going to bring justice to the likes, the likes of him." She jammed a thumb at the image of Viper that was blocked by the darkened T-glass behind her and then crossed her arms. "Splicing McNeil, Jim, Eric was responsible for the deaths of my dad and over a hundred other innocent people. He was guilty and I collected on that debt.

"Shit, isn't that what we swore to do? You told me that you trusted me, the reason why you asked me to stay. What? Are you saying that you don't trust me now?"

"Damn it, Becca," Jim cursed. Her accusations and hostility

had tested his patience. He didn't see himself in the wrong here. "I know what he was. He was a terrible bastard, but why did you lie to me? Why did you do it, when Logan—"

"Logan?" The ex-Infiltrator shook her head, waved her right hand in protest. "The Panzer didn't have anything against Viper. He didn't need to be caught up in this mess."

"Is that why an Infiltration Forensics team found Eric fucking pinned to his sofa? Sure you blew up his fortress, but you didn't make it a clean hit. You let your emotions get the best of you, and you got sloppy at a critical moment.

"Becca, Infiltration already thinks we did it!" He was breathing hard, trying to make her understand. *Doesn't she know how worried I am about everyone here? They're still training and aren't experienced. Does she even know what the Guard can do?*

He was on his feet now too. He looked into her ocean globes and knew they appeared like ice when she was angry. But they now took on the characteristics of the sky, freedom and openness.

Her lips parted softly, a lot of the initial anger and defensiveness had already drained from her. The fingers of her left hand played nervously along her thigh. "Jim, I know I did that in haste. I know it's impossible to apologize for what I might have done to the base, to the people of Crystal Mountain, but I just couldn't stand it any longer.

"For the last two weeks, I watched him parade around the news as the president of that new pharmaceutical company. He was mocking us all with that fake shit—launching a new drug that treated depression. A drug based on the hormones that the Agency had used to control our kind!

"Face it, Anderson had to be taken down. I did it and won't apologize for that.

"But"—she shook her head quickly before he could comment

— "I'm sorry that I disappointed the Crystalians and disappointed you."

She paused and took a deep breath.

"Jim, if you want me too, I'll leave," she said, sincerely, despite what that would mean. "I'll turn myself in, and tell Infiltration that I acted alone. I know you think that I acted in haste. I know that I did. But if Logan had done it, you could not have had that deniability. I wanted to give you that at least."

He saw her lifeforce flicker, noticed how shame, embarrassment and betrayal were taking more of a toll than what she really showed. He studied her face, imagining the terrible pain she tried to conceal, as if she dreamed about her father's death every night.

"Becca, that isn't an option. This is your home," he said, and immediately saw her relief. How could she think that he'd ever ask *that* of her? "I know that I asked you to be patient and let Logan take care of Viper. However, I now realize that I was inconsiderate and belittled your convictions."

He looked into her eyes, then away at the dark T-glass wall. He knew how she felt. He knew how much she hated Viper, and he knew that his request had only looked good on paper.

"Rebecca, you know …" At a loss for words, Jim looked at an interior monitor in his office. He noticed that the President of Panteria, the puppet office, was making a speech, talking about something, the anniversary of the Civil Code of 2878?

Shit! He frowned. *Our freedom is a mockery, and no one knows any better. And we are branded the terrorists for trying to show them the truth?*

"Rebecca, you're right," he said, his anger coming to the surface. "The Guard continues to do anything it wishes to its people —use them for experiments, employ them in wars, assassinations. Whatever it considers necessary for the sake of global security.

"And like you said, like the Executioners have stated countless times, we can't let them continue doing it. It must be stopped. It will be stopped."

He'd been letting his anger simmer even more so during the last couple of days, since he knew that deep down he envied what Rebecca had done. Deep down he wished that he'd let the Beast feed one final time at Henderson.

"But I swear that if they come for us, if they somehow make it into these tunnels, they will see Hell for the first time. They will understand fear. They will understand pain. They will understand fury. They will understand me."

Rebecca listened to Jim and her heart pounded in fear. It wasn't often she saw the anger he held in his heart, but she admired him at the same instant, realizing his strength and his ability to keep that rage in check.

Long ago, she remembered a lecture he'd presented at MUTANTs, Military University for A-Natural Terrestrials, of the FGGO. He'd discussed the role of Berserks in modern warfare and she still remembered the vibrancy of his speech and articulation.

Many of her classmates, she included, had expected a blathering idiot: somebody green, big and taciturn. And, afterward, she remembered shaking his hand and commenting how she would like to work with him one day. He simply smiled and gave her an AOM souvenir pin.

Sometime after that, Jim St. John had seen his lover die in battle, causing him to desert the AOM. He had been chased all over the world until the FGGO had thought that they had killed him with modified nazer rockets. Subsequently, he had found the people buried here in Crystal Mountain. And they, together, had rebuilt their home into a fortress. In time, he and the rest of the Crystalians had asked Arthor, Logan, John, and Rebecca herself to stay and find a home here in Crystal Mountain.

She stared at him, her heart still thumping hard in her chest. He had left the FGGO long before Rebecca had joined the Army of Mutants. He had left long before the FGGO had been renamed Infiltration. However, almost six years later, he was still pissed off.

Jim didn't say anything else, neither did Rebecca. She simply nodded, went back to her office and started working.

"Doctor Murphey?" With little pause, another student raised his hand in Cassie's history class. Dr. Anna Murphey had been prepared to provide a historic retelling of the Discovery of Crystal Mountain, a guide to the Executioners' base and a list of the Mountain's defenses only if no one actively participated. To her mild surprise and immediate relief, the questions had started the moment her friend Cassie had introduced Anna to the class. "Why was the Ter-rex created?"

"Good question, Josh." Eyeing the seating chart, Anna smiled at the ninth-grader. She drew a figure on the demonstration board at the front of the room with her PDL, which was linked to the board's control. "The Ter-rex, or T9A6 amoeba-bactivirus, was bioengineered to breakdown weapons of mass destruction. The ancient U.S. military created it as a last resort to target missile silos and hidden caches of nuclear and biological weapons of both foreign and domestic aggressors."

Anna paused, waiting for another question. Practically all the children raised their hands. She pointed to a girl, Teri, with blonde ponytails, who asked, "But with the Neo-Holocaust going on, how could anyone still be thinking about war?"

"One thing you must never forget is that military strategists always seek out weaknesses in their opponents," Anna warned quickly. "The Neo-Holocaust was a volatile time. True, many nations had actually collapsed from the violence caused by its own citizens, but invasions from neighboring countries were also common. In this case, however, the United States was worried that the Death Cults were going to escalate the death toll by more extreme and horrifying methods. Many of those groups weren't exactly sane or understood science."

"I remember reading about the Ter-rex when I was in sixth grade," a boy named Brant said, pursing his lips in thought. "I still don't understand exactly what it was."

"It was indeed a hodgepodge of life, pseudo-life and nano-machinery," Anna smirked and continued drawing her little diagram. "The first biolab began with cellular slime molds. They modified them with bio- and nano-reactors so that they could manufacture several corrosive enzymes, and then adapted them to survive in extremely radioactive conditions."

"Like making them capable of eating through nuclear warheads?" Brant asked. He was following along fine, while the other students in the class were nodding their heads too.

"Correct." The Director of Medicine smiled and began adding little ovals and crystal-like figures to the diagram. They weren't to scale but would serve the purpose here. "They also grew them in a radioactive medium, using newly created Iridietum-317m. Essentially, Iridietum, originally developed for the 'botched' experiments in nuclear isomer explosives, was to spread the Ter-rex over the blast area."

"You mean they intentionally created a 'dirty bomb,'" Brant interjected, shock easily visible on his face.

Anna grimaced. She could tell that some of the students were trying to grasp the concept of such a warhead, which spread radioactive particles throughout an area to make it uninhabitable. Others seemed to understand it completely, and she wasn't sure if either group comforted her.

"That's right. Iridietum explodes with less velocity and radiation, but creates an extensive shockwave," she continued regardless. "The Ter-rex warhead could spread the organism, as blast-resistant cysts or spores, a significant distance. One warhead, for example, would easily have covered the Mountain."

"Umm, sorry to go off topic, but I heard that Crystal Mountain had been abandoned at one time," a girl named Julie commented politely and timidly.

"No problem and very good," Anna said. "That's not common knowledge. The original base here had been shut down. It had been a military museum for nearly fifty years before it was hollowed out and retrofitted during the Neo-Holocaust. Can anyone tell me what this base was called before it was renamed?"

Julie was the only one with her hand raised. She answered, "I heard it was called Cheyenne Mountain, a former Center of Operations of the old North American Air Defense Command, or NORAD for short."

"Right, NORAD updated it, expanded it significantly, and then began tracking the worldwide violence associated with the Death Cults. Ultimately, we were pretty blessed, considering that General Martin Lee Wallace had requested tunneling equipment, arboreta and manufacturing and food-processing facilities to be built within the new base. Our ancestors wouldn't have survived long if these hadn't been available to create a complete, self-contained biosphere."

"I still don't understand how the Ter-rex was released over the Mountain in the first place." A boy named Chuck shook his head. "And why didn't they try and punch them into the ground to actually hit the base?"

"It certainly would have made a difference if the latter had been the case," Anna added. "Can anyone tell me why that didn't happen?"

Teri hesitantly raised her hand. "The complementary 'bunker-buster' project was never completed?"

"Right," Anna agreed. Usually only upper-level students or even college-level classes seemed to hit on such detail. Cassie definitely had a talented group here. "However, before I answer that completely, Chuck asked me how it all happened.

"Sadly, inforuns suggest that one of the Death Cults managed to locate, recruit and corrupt several soldiers at bases with Ter-rex mobile launch systems. I guess you can't blame those who had been recruited, since people were dying by the tens of millions and the recruiters must have promised some type of salvation. They ended up firing off 20 Ter-rex missiles, a total of 255 warheads, at Cheyenne Mountain and the surrounding area.

"But can any of you surmise why the Death Cults wanted to knock Cheyenne Mountain out of the picture?"

Anna gestured to Brant. He nodded and cleared his throat. "If NORAD updated Cheyenne Mountain to monitor and direct operations against the Neo-Holocaust, eliminating the Mountain would have crippled the government's efforts."

"Right, the new base had already identified and killed several death-cult groups, which had been sponsored by high-profile leaders of various countries and corporations. We speculate that several well-founded death cults got together to take out the threat." Murphey pointed at the diagram of the T9A6 on the demo-board. "And they succeeded, while also wiping out a megacity called Denver-Springs and much of an old state called Colorado, from which the current Coloradan forest gets its name.

"Even more tragically, these warheads were never intended to be used. Weeks before the incident, the U.S. government—under pressure from its allies—decided to scrap the entire lot.

"As a side note, Ter-rex missiles weren't housed in silos or protected like nuclear weapons, even though they were no less terrifying," Anna said. "Instead, under new security protocols, they were placed on mobile platforms so that they could be moved at regular intervals, regardless of how dangerous they were.

"Think about it. Just one missile carried fifteen individual warheads in its nose cone. And just a single warhead could spread radiation and Ter-rex over about 120 square miles—well, without wind of course."

Anna paused a moment to let that sink in, especially when twenty missiles had been shot at Cheyenne Mountain. "You can see why the U.S. government was planning to dismantle the missiles and send the warheads to a disposal center in West Point, Pennsylvania. Horribly, red tape delayed that action and eighty million people were eaten alive.

"OK," Anna said and shuddered, not really comprehending so many deaths—let alone the seven billion people who died during the eighty years of the Neo-Holocaust. "OK, guys, looking at the diagram of a single amoeba of the T9A6, what can you tell me about it, specifically how might it multiply?"

There was hesitation, many of the students looked at each other. Josh finally raised his hand, and said, "If it was part of a cellular slime mold, it could reproduce asexually by means of sporangium, releasing spores or reproduce sexually." He then bit his lip, certainly unsure of what he was about to say. "However, the diagram seems odd."

"How so?" She was hoping her sketch would show this. To

her credit, it would have been difficult finding the clues by looking at an actual picture of one.

"Well, hmm," the boy started, but then seemed uncertain. "It looks like bacterial, viral and biomechanical components have been added to its inner make up."

"Are you sure that I didn't just add them to show phagocytosis?"

The boy shook his head. "No, they aren't closed off in vacuoles. It doesn't look like the T9A6 is eating them."

"Good, Josh, that's right. Biolabs added bacterial and viral bodies and self-replicating nanobots to help in its proliferation, allowing it to spread in three ways: as slime mold colonization, as a viral infestation and as a bacterium.

"The latter, of course, was the most destructive, since its enzymes were capable of breaking down anything. And all three T9A6 forms could spread from it as well."

There were gasps and then a bit of silence, before Teri raised her hand. "So after the Ter-rex was released, the U.S. government pretty much wrote off the Mountain?"

"You can say that," Anna acknowledged grimly. "The Ter-rex missiles detonated over southern Denver-Springs on April 24, 2177. It spread over 36,000 square miles—about the size of Indiana—and it wiped out the surrounding populations. In fact, the Iridietum-317m radiation is still around today."

"36,000?" Brant's right eyebrow rose. "Isn't that the area …?"

Anna nodded. "Yep, Ecie developed a protective field to simulate and amplify much of the Iridietum's effects. The area called the *Wasteland* that surrounds Crystal Mountain is still pretty much the original blast zone."

"Then is it harmful?" Josh asked.

"No, surprisingly enough, there were never any biological problems associated with Iridietum. Ultimately a failed nuclear-isomer explosive, it was originally created for EMP warheads to kill enemy electronics and create long-lasting electronic disruptions. The targeted populations were meant to be spared."

"I still don't understand why our ancestors didn't try and dig around it." Chuck shook his head. "We did have the tunneling equipment."

"Good point," Anna conceded. "However, Wallace had no way of knowing how far the T9A6 had spread. Despite the buildup of a small stockpile, a Ter-rex warhead was never detonated in the open. Regardless of the protests from its allies, the U.S. had decided to eliminate the Ter-rex anyway, since computer simulations suggested that even a small detonation would spread across the planet.

"Thus to answer Chuck's earlier question, they never got around to developing a bunker-busting bomb, since the weapon was scrapped."

"Soooooo since several hundred warheads hit the Mountain our ancestors figured that there was no world left to rejoin?" Chuck asked.

Anna smiled timidly. "In a sense, they had no contact with the outside. The Ter-rex had eaten everything. It tore through transmission lines, satellite links, radio transmitters, the surrounding forest, an entire megacity and almost twenty feet down into the ground. Even if they had tried tunneling out, it would have taken a decade to make it past the initial blast zone, and no one had known how far the T9A6 had expanded beyond that."

"But we found out that it didn't go any farther beyond that," Julie smirked, significantly less than what Anna had done when she'd discovered the odd fate of their ancestors.

"Yep, once Jim came crashing through that sealed ventilation shaft …" Anna remembered the day Jim had found her. He was immense. Surely Crystal Mountain had tall people. But, compounded with his mirror-like bodysuit and round mirrored helmet, he had looked like a demon.

"I remember when you brought him to us in the Spring of '99," Brant chuckled. "Many of the Elders hadn't believed that anyone could survive the T9A6. I remember hearing that many people feared him."

"Yeah, since the radiation was still present after all this time, we thought the Ter-rex was still up there. As you know, we used to take regular readings to see if it was making any more movement downward. Needless to say, when Jim fell through the ceiling, I didn't know what to do. In shock, I thought about running home, regardless of breaking possible quarantine. But he caught me before I had a chance to move."

"Weren't you scared?" Teri asked mouth agape.

"Are you kidding? I almost peed my pants." The class roared and Anna laughed too, knowing this was a ninth-grade class. Still, in the back, Cassie seemed to bite down a smile. "But he immediately pulled off the helmet, showing me his big, brown eyes. He showed me that he was still alive—that I was still alive! And amazingly, I sat with him for most of the day, and we talked, just talked and answered each other's questions."

There was awe in many of the faces of the kids. Anna had seen it before. Many people hadn't believed that she had been so brave. Thinking about Jim now, even though she knew they had drifted apart, Anna knew bravery had had nothing to do with it.

"So what were the questions he asked?" Josh's question quickly brought Anna back to the present.

"Well, he asked things like how long we had been here, how we could have survived down here this long, how many there were of us, how big the complex was and things like that. I told him what I could, but I also asked him about the upper world."

"It must have been quite a shock," Chuck smirked sympathetically.

"I can assure you it was," the doctor confirmed. "My God, the Fall of the World, the War, the Apocalypse, the FGGO, and Panteria. After hearing Jim's words, I pulled him into an elevator and took him as far away from the surface as I could.

"And you should have seen the look on his face," Anna noted. "He really hadn't believed that we'd been buried here for over eight hundred years. Naturally, upon seeing the lower levels, he immediately asked more questions about our survival.

"I couldn't answer many of them," she added, thumbing the edge of her PDL for a moment. "The Mountain, if you remember, wasn't in the best shape back then. Many of the manufacturing facilities were deteriorating, the botanical gardens were growing out of control, and many of the older living areas were collapsing, thereby costing many, many lives."

Anna shook out a thought, and then said, "I saw the look in his eyes when I told him these things, and I knew what he was thinking."

"But didn't he refuse to help us at first?" Teri protested.

"He did," the doctor admitted. "However, that was an entirely different request, and I'll get to that in a bit." Right now, she didn't want to change the subject, not wanting to think about Jim's reaction to those pleads just yet. "Anyway, I brought him before the Elders, and our world changed forever."

That was a cliché, Anna knew full well; however, it struck home and everyone in the room nodded. "He started by pulling our antiquated aircraft out of storage, getting them back up and running, and flying them out for new supplies.

"Some of them he sold to discreet collectors for funding. And, even though this predated both Ecie and credit modifier chips, this still gained us huge sums, allowing us to purchase the necessary materials to update our manufacturing and medical facilities. And quickly enough, these same complexes began to churn out 31st Century products: our own hover vehicles, modern medicines, computers, schools, shops, auditoriums, subways, turbo lifts, etc."

"Uh, so did Ecie come online before or after the Executioners were founded?" Brant raised his hand in brief interruption.

"He was born before that, since Jim had been very impressed by the Panocomptrix, the Panterian Organic Computer Matrix, during his first visit to the Panterian Council. He simply wanted our own home to prosper with such a caretaker. However, by the time Ecie achieved consciousness, many of the initial upgrades of the Delta Six military base had already been completed."

"Wasn't Ecie the one who reconstructed the inforun file, the one that had told us the history behind the name *Crystal Mountain*?" Julie commented.

"He was," Anna confirmed with a grin. "Can you elaborate?"

"I know a little." The girl hesitated.

"It's alright," Cassie added, warmly. From what Anna gathered, Julie was usually pretty shy. "We'll all help fill in the gaps if necessary."

Julie beamed. "OK, I heard that the T9A6 was spread out by the initial blast waves, but the organism thrived only in the irradiated areas. I just don't understand why."

"A bit of a design flaw," Brant explained. "Several of the nanobots and organelles, which made the more potent enzymes in the T9A6, were kept in check only by that radiation. Without it, special proteins didn't form and they disintegrated."

"Ah, thanks." The two students smiled at each other, and then Julie said, "Being restricted to the blast zone, the Ter-rex amoebae and bacteria ate whatever food was available, ran out of it and died out fourteen days after detonation."

"Fourteen days," Anna repeated. She had cried herself to sleep when she had read that the first time, thinking that thirty generations had been buried for no reason. But then she had read another report that vindicated Wallace's efforts, which she would explain later. "So how did the name come about from this?"

"Right the name," Julie laughed, soon conscious of her digression. "Well, the Ter-rex had managed to eat as far down as the radiation had penetrated, so the remaining cysts and viruses had bound to most of the underlying rock as a hard, organic crystal. Three decades later, the U.S. government dedicated the site 'Crystal Mountain' as a memorial to the people who died there. Later on, the Reforestation Projects claimed it as an ultimate proving ground for Growth Zone Four."

"And that was that," the Director of Medicine sighed. "But remember that even though most of the T9A6 cells had died after only fourteen days, research teams discovered the area was still contaminated after losing several probes. Essentially, even though Growth Zone Four thrived in it, its spores remained dormant and viable for another three hundred years, which prolonged the quarantine."

She noticed that she was getting short on time. Hoping to move things along, she cleared the demo-board and drew a semi-representative picture of Crystal Mountain. "Fifty years after the Ter-rex attack, Growth Zone Four—along with the Pacific and Atlantic Oceanic projects—achieved an optimal amount of growth, and the Reforestation Projects succeeded in ending the Neo-Holocaust in 2227.

"And even though our home has been covered by a vast six-hundred-foot-high forest ever since, Jim and Ecie figured out how to keep the new entrances and hangars free of vegetation, and to hide them with holograms that can work in the *Wasteland*.

"Ecie developed the tight-line communication system, which allows us to punch through the radiation field so that we can synch up with satellites, beacons and other electrical communiqués. To retrieve less accessible information, we've also traveled and explored and built up thousands of outside contacts."

"Have you traveled much?" Teri asked.

"No, I really haven't had time," Anna admitted. "I'm always working on new medical techniques that we've learned after the Discovery, and since I've taken over the Director of Medicine position from Dr. Tevalos Hendes ..." she paused, realizing that she was babbling. "Yah, uh, I think I can count the number of times I've been outside the Mountain on my right hand."

The children laughed and Anna smirked. Truthfully, she didn't care much for travel, and Crystal Mountain had everything she needed.

"Jim traveled a lot though." She remembered how busy they had been. "However, as info- and supply-run groups got more experienced, he accepted the position of Governor and focused his attention here at home."

"But I still remember the Governor turning down our requests to lead us," Teri persisted.

Anna recalled that moment almost four years ago. It was not associated with the events of the Discovery, but she digressed, since it did concern the current defensive capabilities of the Mountain. "You're right. He did refuse, but you were all too young to understand. He turned us down when we wanted to form the Executioners."

Josh shook his head. "Why? From my understanding, he's one of the greatest soldiers that have ever lived."

The Chief Doctor shrugged. "I don't know. He's never told me why, and I've never asked him." *We were close, but not that close.* Anna took a breath and didn't say anything else right away. They seldom spoke to each other anymore, and she had stopped trying to understand.

"I remember that meeting in the Great Hall." John, a boy in the back of the class, brightened with recollection. "Weren't you the one? Didn't you change his mind?"

She nodded, wondering now if Jim secretly hated her for that. "Yes, soon after the Discovery, we ultimately saw the problems associated with the Puppeteer Government, which, as you know, is comprised of the Panterian Guard and its minions. Although democratic governments in our history books weren't at all perfect, we couldn't believe the lengths at which the Panterian Guard was taking to maintain global security. It puts all of those silly ancient secret-society-world-domination movies to shame.

"So a few weeks after he became our Governor, we all gathered around him again in the Great Hall. And then we—all eighty thousand—asked him to teach us, show us, and provide us with the means to fight this wrong.

"Taken aback and despite our pleading, he shook his head and started to walk away. Shouting to be heard, I stopped him and told him the things we had heard and had seen.

"I spoke for everyone, and I asked him what else we could do, asked him if we should just go out and become a part of the senseless, the mindless and the misled.

"He had no answer but he still resisted.

"But I was relentless. I reminded him of how he had told us the truth and how we couldn't let the Panterian Guard continue on with this injustice. Right or wrong, we had to try and bring about a different world.

"Immediately he countered by asking us how we could bring our own peace to an end.

"I told him that that was irrelevant. We had lived in a society where truth and peace were parts of life, and we could not live idly in this one.

"'We are creatures of God,' I had said, standing proudly. 'How can we let our brothers and sisters live in such deception, even if they are distant?'

"He had smirked, possibly at our innocence and ultimate sacrifice. But he then submitted to our request," *even though*, Anna thought quietly, *he had asked God's forgiveness.* "Therefore on November 23, 3000, the Executioners were born."

"Was that when we updated the old military complex?" Josh asked immediately, giving Anna little time to think about events nearly four years distant.

"Yes, the shock-absorbing springs beneath the initial command modules were re-enforced with electromagnetic shielding and struts. A geothermal-powered force-field soon began to beat fifty feet beneath the surface, thereby protecting us from the outside world and remaining invisible beneath the cloak of the Terrex explosions. Hangars One and Two were then constructed and fitted with heavier blast doors.

"Literally, the armor and defenses around our civilization are greater than practically any other force on this planet." Anna stopped, smiled at Cassie and then cleared the demo-board.

"Do ... do you think we'll ever need to use them?" Teri squeaked silently.

Anna Murphey, Chief Medical Officer of the Executioners and Director of Medicine of Crystal Mountain, suddenly got a lump in her throat. She thought about Arthor, Jim, Logan, John, Rebecca, Cassie, and these students. She thought of Dr. Tevalos Hendes and when she had succeeded his position after he had retired.

She remembered walking through one of the arboreta this morning before coming here, remembered going to a new holo-suite facility to brush up on her history, and remembered getting a cup of coffee from a new pastry shop.

While sipping her cup of Joe and thinking about her upcoming presentation, she had not at all been bothered by a little baby in a high chair, who had been making considerable noise and had been beaming happily in her direction.

Anna remembered the day the Executioners was formed. She also remembered that she was one of the key people who had petitioned its formation. Naturally, Doctor Anna Murphey was older now, and it certainly made a difference.

CHAPTER TWO

There is a violence that liberates, and a violence that enslaves; there is a violence that is moral, and a violence that is immoral.

(Speech, Udine)
—Benito Mussolini, Fascist Dictator of Italy (1922 A.D.)

The morning sun flared into the lobby of the courthouse. Steven Henry smirked and put on his sunglasses. It was going to be a bright sunny day.

"This way, sir," his bodyguards grunted and used their massive strength—by real and/or synthetic means—to hold back the reporters and protestors that rushed him once he got outside.

"What an ass hat," someone cursed nearby.

Steven smiled at the police escorts who were assisting his hired goons. He didn't know which one of the officers had said it, but it didn't matter as long as they did their job.

"Suck it up, boys," he told them as he started walking down the steps toward his limousine. "You can get back to your donuts soon enough."

Another wave of reporters surged up the steps of the courthouse. Police shouted at them to stay back, so the reporters screamed, trying to have their questions heard. It was all noise, and he ignored it. He'd wasted enough time here over the last couple of weeks. It was obvious that there hadn't been enough evidence for a trial.

"What a beautiful day," he said and looked up. The police were directing hovercars—HCs—away from the area for his added safety. Apparently, the drivers weren't all that happy about the detour. Hundreds of them were stuck between and around elevated walkways, supply lines, transport tubes, sculptures, banners, billboards, and other designated routes to get them around the mile-high buildings of Toldeclevchikee, which was a massive, ancient city surrounding much of the Great Lakes.

Henry looked up at all the glistening panels of the hovercars set aglow by the morning sun. He reveled in the warmth too. He was amazed that its rays hit him, despite being surrounded by hundreds of fifteen-hundred-foot-tall pyramids, which were intersected with even higher towers, steeples and megascrapers.

The people—protestors, reporters, whoever—still shoved to get closer to him, but his bodyguards and police still kept them back. Steven simply shook his head, having been asked question after question. His own attorney, Martin Slivers, repeated the NO COMMENT sign and helped Steven toward the hover-limousine.

The lawyer had said nothing to him, not a word since the case had been dropped.

"Right, whatever," he whispered to himself. Henry ignored the cold shoulder of his attorney and walked down the steps, vaguely feeling the undulating movements of the reporters as they moved with his entourage. He likened them to hungry wolves, piranha, sharks, and rabid dogs. How long had they been following his life? How many slanderous accusations had been made? How many times had he been on the news? He wondered when these assholes would let him be and allow him to do his business in peace.

You know what? He smiled. *I'll give you something to suck on.* He stopped just before he was about to enter the black limousine, a large antigrav hovercraft able to seat twelve. Feeling generous today and a bit giddy, Steve Henry decided to give them a spontaneous Q&A session anyway.

"Mr. Henry?" A young, beautiful interrogator quickly broke in with an inquiry, practically stealing his heart. He pointed in her direction, giving her the opportunity.

Blonde hair swirled, green eyes perked, and a lovely smile curved the woman's lips before she spoke. "Now that the court has found you untouchable for these crimes, what will you do in your efforts to … to redeem your soul?"

His cheeks twitched a bit, and his own green globes squinted by something other than the sun. "What?"

Slivers immediately jabbed him in the side, but Henry hardly felt the cue. And the blonde remained where she was. The smile had not left her face, even though Steven's had been lost the moment she began to laugh. "I am asking you this for all those people you screwed. My God, you wiped out any records that ever linked those accounts to them. Some people have a conscience. I was wondering if you, well, you … *did*."

Damn, will you stop poking me? He shoved Slivers away and turned back to the blonde. "Now listen here, you little slut. I run a business, not a goddamn nursing home. I bought their company, dissolved it and gave them all generous severance packages. It is unfortunate what happened to their pensions after the company was liquidated, but I'm not responsible for that. I didn't do anything illegal.

"And as for that ridiculous slander about me funneling their money into my personal accounts? Come on. They were trying to pull something out their—out of the air." He'd sworn once on camera already. He wasn't about to let her razz him anymore.

"I see." The woman jotted some notes, and then threw him another mocking look. "What about Jason Tammer?"

"It's terrible that he threw himself off of that damned building. Maybe the guilt of fucking up and ruining your own company and the lives of two hundred people affected him?" The last question was meant to be rhetorical.

"And why should we believe you? This hasn't been the first time that people who could've blocked these deals have disappeared or committed suicide. Any evidence to the contrary always ends up missing."

He held back a curse. "Look, this isn't the first time someone has tried to throw shit on me." His eyes stared at the lovely woman, but could no longer find Venus in her form. "Tell you what, you find something that sticks and I'll wear a target on my head!"

The woman didn't say anything else. What could she say? She, like the idiots who tried to indict him, had Jack and Shit. And Jack left town.

The crowd, which had been quiet during the exchange, again burst into questions while he waited for the limo's door to open.

He only turned his head this time. "No more questions, you damned leeches!"

"But, sir?" someone broke in just before he started to enter the limo. "What about the vigilante groups, like the Night Rangers or the Executioners? Don't you think you may still have to answer to them?"

"Why should I fear a group of outsiders?" he laughed. "The Night Rangers are too clumsy, and the Executioners could never touch—"

His forehead suddenly began to burn. Then he heard a pop.

Logan Brant McMillian, encased in his impregnable armor and cloaked to invisibility, sat on a skyscraper's rooftop, which was a half mile away from a huge crowd of people in front of Toldeclevchikee's Fourth District courthouse. There wasn't any wind today and, thankfully, because of the detours, no hovercar was going to get in his way.

He breathed quietly and aimed his proton/antiproton accelerator at his target. He was listening to the distant conversation through his parabolic mics. That Henry was a pompous ass. Then—

"Yep, can't touch you," Logan smirked, pulled the weapon's trigger and watched Steven's head disappear.

A good deal of the crowd scattered instantly, running from the scene, unsure of who would be next.

Henry's now "unemployed" goons cursed and swore. Police officers activated their handheld shields, pulled their side arms and rifles and looked frantically around.

By contrast, most of the reporters and some of the protestors stepped closer, forcing Logan to wince. He knew morbid curiosity when he saw it, especially when they shoved cameras near the dying corpse.

He'd had enough anyway. He had confirmation of death. He got up and secured the antimatter rifle on the back of his armor.

"That is that," he said to himself, thinking about the rest of the plan. Now, a small section of Henry's company was going to be dissolved, and all of the stolen assets would be returned to the people he had wronged. Needless to say, it would never have happened if Steven Henry had been around to stop it.

"I want to find out who did this on the double. Give me possible vectors. H-Squadron, scan the buildings." Orders blared from fifteen different positions, while Logan listened in on the police channels. He watched their vehicles zip up into the air, watched them scan the area with instruments and modified eyepieces, and then noticed that somebody had called the paramedics instead of the coroner.

"Little good they'll do him." Logan sneered, looked around, gazed at the patrol-hovers, and then back at the corpse.

Near the body, he saw a visibly pale Martin Slivers, formerly Steven Henry's lawyer but still the executor of the man's estate, answer a quick question and walk away. That man's involvement with the Executioners was over, and now his parents and thousands of other people would be fine.

"Thanks for the call, Martin." Despite being invisible, Logan nodded toward the man once and then walked to the other side of the megascraper's roof. He looked down and saw the sidewalk twenty-five-hundred feet below.

He took a calming breath and stepped back. His friends always asked how he could be acrophobic when he had no problems getting into an HC or any other type of aircraft.

Logan knew there wasn't much to contemplate, since he simply hated heights. However, in spite of that, he took three more quick breaths and then jumped over the edge. Just before he hit the pavement, special jets kicked in and slowed him down. A second later, he hit the street, got his bearings and then turned off his suit's cloaking field.

McMillian made a two count and sprinted off. He'd left his vehicle a few blocks away from here, making it necessary for him to transverse the area with plenty of spectators.

"Let's see, Market Street, near 327th Avenue. Bit busy today, I see," he smirked. Ground vehicles were gridlocked and pedestrians flooded the sidewalks. There were quite a few people who didn't look happy.

"And John jokes that I should take a part-time job in the city —funny, real funny." He stopped briefly and eyed the crowded walkways going in every direction.

He noticed the hovercars flying high above. Some of those were gridlocked too; being in Toldeclevchikee's airspace, the cars' navigation computers were restricted to specific aerial routes. He could imagine someone, locked out of manually controlling his/her craft because of city restrictions, pulling his/her hair out and yelling at anyone who gave him/her a questionable glance.

Nothing like a little air rage in the morning, he laughed to himself and then looked into a darkened alleyway, which was an entrance to a network of huge, enclosed areas that always seemed to tempt the foolish or brave. It actually took him a moment to see the bewildered looks of the people around him.

"That's the Panzer!" a little boy shrieked and pointed, his mother quickly pulling him into a little shop for safety.

People reacted instantly, pointing and stopping dead in their tracks. To which, the Panzer waved and then activated his cloaking device again, blurring him out of sight.

"Well, that should do it." He smiled to himself, knowing his presence here would suggest involvement with Steven's murder, but not directly link the Executioners to it. Logan crossed the street then and passed by the hundreds of onlookers that were still trying to find him—

"Geez, sorry buddy." He skidded to a halt, almost stepping on someone who hadn't bothered to take a look. The guy was either in his own little world or, or possibly wasn't a fan.

McMillian watched the man walk into the crowd until he was swallowed up by it. He grimaced again, thinking about recent events. The Executioners weren't being portrayed in the best possible light lately. Some people were trying to regard them as terrorists and their voices were beginning to be heard. Obviously, he figured he knew what group was behind it; however, it still stung a bit. If the general public began to regard them that way —

As fucking terrorists, really?

He admitted that the Executioners sometimes took drastic measures for the sake of justice, especially when they made severe examples of some people like Henry; however, a lot of good had come out of it. How many people had they saved since the Executioners were founded? How many people had he personally helped since he'd joined awhile back? But would people begin to start shrinking away when an Executioner offered help? Would people begin to start fearing them?

We're right in what we're doing. It's the only way. We're not a group of senseless killers, he told himself, despite feeling that he needed no justification.

"All right, fields off," he said into his comlink when he turned into a secluded alcove.

"Affirmative"—voiced a reply—"cloaking field and defensive shields off." A black fighter craft, the *Blade*, suddenly shimmered into existence. About twenty-four feet long and ten feet wide, it hovered quietly above the pavement. He walked over to it, turning off his own cloaking field, and opened a small hatch in the armor so he could stick his arm out.

"How's my baby?" he asked rhetorically. Even though he had included an organic computer into its systems, he had installed growth inhibitors so that it would never reach consciousness. He felt guilty about limiting the computer's potential; however, while he enjoyed the luxury of the processing capabilities of such a computer in his craft, he still wasn't sure how a living entity would feel about being locked in something not much bigger than a hovervan.

He ran his bare hand along the length of the *Blade*. The fighter's indented front made its two oval-looking forward weapons pods protrude like potential claws. Mainly, they housed the latest in scanning equipment, forcefields and communication nodes; however, these pods also carried a heavy 30mm e-cannon on the driver's side, and an antimatter cannon on the passenger's side. Between the pods were a couple of smaller nodules that held a sonic disruptor and an ammunition drum with over eight hundred 30×150mm caseless rounds.

Not to be overlooked, a nazer rocket pack rested in a compartment in the back, located under a storage area that ran behind the cockpit. Outside of those, two larger pods, containing fourth generation repulsar drives, were incorporated into the last half of the fighter.

He walked up and slid his hand onto a panel between the *Blade's* roof and one of the rear repulsar pods. A red glow pulsed beneath the pressure of his palm print—a rather technophobic and weird method of entrance he figured—and the vehicle opened in the morning light. He was going to have to update that with a neural link, just in case he ever found himself in an area that wasn't safe for him to pop open his suit.

But the craft is a prototype, he reminded himself, as the cockpit clam-shelled open and slid forward. The rest of the craft accommodated his armor by collapsing the seats and widening the cockpit area.

"General McMillian?" An indicator light triggered in his helmet's HUD and he saw motion in his 540 degree field of view, which he had modified a few years ago. Pulling his hand back into the armor, he turned and saw a lovely woman—a blonde, green-eyed woman—smiling back at him.

"Thank you for this opportunity, General," she said, quickly saluting.

"No problem, Captain." Even though he hadn't had a rank at the CIA, Logan, per Jim's request, had taken on the role of a general due to substantial leadership and field experience. "Thanks for your help, Tara. Have a safe trip." He returned her salute with a robotic arm and then watched her enter a camouflaged hovervan across the street in another alcove.

A moment later, the HV took off and headed west. Soon its pilot activated its cloaking field and it faded from sight. Eventually, it would enter the forest surrounding the city, and they'd be home soon enough.

"Hello, darling." Logan minimized the armor's arms and legs and jumped into the *Blade*. It was a craft he'd constructed a few months after he'd accepted the post of the Executioners' Chief of Weapons Development. Although it was initially designed to be a testing platform for new combat systems, Logan now used the craft personally to field test new components before final approval.

"A necessity," Jim had suggested and had encouraged.

"Yeah, Jim was right. As usual," Logan smirked, even though it hadn't taken much coercing on St. John's part.

"Nope, not much convincing at all," McMillian laughed and activated the restraints and communication nodes that plugged him into the *Blade's* irresistible panels and gained him mental control of the craft. He engaged the core, the lifters and the repulsars. Then, after the vehicle rose a few feet higher, he throttled up—

BAMM. BAMM. BAMM. Sonic booms echoed in the police radios behind him. Logan immediately checked the rear-view scanners, making sure he hadn't taken out any windows as he rocketed out of Toldeclevchikee. He then hit the supersonic buffers, which instantly smoothed out his flight path and allowed him to continue on without further noise.

"Halt. Unidentified vehicle, you are to slow down immediately and surrender to pursuing craft." Logan listened to the threats, immediately gave them *the* finger and accelerated the *Blade* through a megascraper's dark shadow. A moment later, he activated the cloaking field, and his craft disappeared from scanners, radar and even sight.

"All rise," a powerful voice said in the Infiltration Great Hall. Many of the thousands here jumped to their feet like perfect soldiers, while some tried not to show their hesitation.

"What? Do some think it happened too quickly?" Jeff asked himself quietly, standing on the Hall's central platform, which was three hundred feet above the main floor. To give them credit, it had been only a couple days after Viper's death.

"He certainly wasn't hated here," McDonald whispered. "And it hadn't been much of a surprise that he'd been circumventing me for years, maneuvering his position at just the right time. He conned just about everyone."

The General made a quick glance around him. Giant tapestries, tens of stories tall, flowed from the polished granite ceiling to a floor of marble, which was etched with black and gray patterns. Too heavy to sway in the breeze, each massive drapery held scenes of battle spanning the ages. Terrible wars like the Triblé Faction, the Kilogy Trestis, and the unforgettable Battle of Henderson lined the Great Hall as numerous, multi-story works.

There were also several battles not portrayed, making him realize that many in Infiltration had no idea who he was. However, not succumbing to anger, he simply shrugged and looked across a sixteen-foot-wide, rail-less bridge, which stretched three hundred and thirty feet from the outer upper landing pads to the central platform.

Several dark figures marched toward him. Hoods were drawn over, faces shrouded, weapons hidden. The Eleven Exalted Guards, the High Priests of the Council, had arrived only moments ago. Eying them now, the General listened carefully to their monotone voices, which echoed their prayers and words of ceremony throughout the Great Hall.

He watched them move closer, whispering their sacred vows as they approached. Behind them, High Director Tedrick Vardson walked quietly, but with a considerable presence. Being the Supreme High Priest and ruler of the Guard, the Council and Panteria itself, Vardson was dressed and hooded in blood-raven red, and was holding a crystal-tipped, gold scepter.

The change has begun. McDonald bit down another smile and tried to shed the feeling of excitement trying to creep up. He knew this was all pompousness, and he knew that he should have never had to go through this again. But he also knew that the office had changed considerably in the last six years. Eric, despite his megalomaniac flaws, had provided Jeff a more streamlined organization.

But those were the same things the Guard never allowed me to do, and others that should have never ... Jeff held back a curse and now simply waited for this ceremony to be over.

"By our power ... in the strength of our great nation ... to the honor of our fathers and mothers, brothers and sisters ..." the High Council spoke their oaths while they walked—Jeff hearing bits and pieces. Infiltrators lined the walls and stood at attention, with each man, woman and creature holding his/her/its sword close to his/her/its heart. All their eyes rested on the man they'd soon call Decoré, the leader of Infiltration.

Not moving his head, McDonald eyed them with his peripheral vision. Altogether, there were about six thousand here, and they waited in patience, in perfect silence. Many looked like they were eager to get back to whatever hunt they had been called from to be here.

They wouldn't have to wait too long. "Welcome, prestigious Council and His Supreme Majesty," McDonald said when the members of the High Council stopped a yard from him. As ceremony dictated, he also said it very loudly and in a tone of G flat. He really hated such rituals. But, nonetheless, he quickly knelt down on his right knee and bowed.

"Grand General Jeffery Neilson McDonald has accepted the office of Infiltration Decoré, the Genetic Overmaster," High Director Vardson said. "Upon his oath, all of Infiltration's facilities and associated organizations will be under his direct command." And with that, the High Director stepped closer and lowered the ceremonial scepter.

The General needn't say anything. This was only a show. He simply pressed his lips on the pure adamant head of the scepter, sealing the agreement and pledging his loyalty. A loyalty he had given Panteria over a century ago.

Then he rose and bowed before the High Council again. They nodded, crossed their hearts and left the hall. The door closed.

"Hail the Decoré. Hail the Decoré. Hail the Decoré," the Infiltrators suddenly chanted and cheered. He stepped over to the platform's edge and looked at his compatriots and the hall that surrounded them. There were no windows, no skylights and no calimar lights. Old fashioned torches were placed throughout the Hall, and immense three-dimensional displays showed his image as he waved to them.

"Great Panteria, Great Panteria, our home, our life, our joy," the Infiltration Chorus and Instrumental Band began to sing and play the Panterian National Anthem. The music surged with a growing crescendo and a resounding forte; however, the chorus held their own, and Jeff sang along with them, as did nearly all of the Infiltrators. The song had always struck a soothing cord in McDonald's heart. It, above all other things, had always gained his loyalty, his respect. It was the only reason he needed to serve his country. Well, amongst others.

Eric led us astray, he thought to himself. *The assassinations end now, Special Projects will finally get sufficient funding, and destinies will come to fruition.*

On that last thought, his stomach twitched, a lingering ache he'd felt for a long time. He buried it as quickly as he could. For now, at least, she was lost, but he never believed that *she* had died. Eric should have trusted Jeff on that.

Then the anthem stopped, and a full four seconds passed before he realized everyone was waiting for his next order.

"Thank you for coming today," Jeff chuckled. Allowing himself to be distracted by such thoughts was just silly. "I know you are eager to get back to work. Let me just say that I am very proud of you. Very proud of what you have accomplished.

"All right," he laughed, allowing a smile to also show. "Most of you don't know me from Jack and I apologize. For the last few years, I have been running Special Projects, and as to some of you that know the drill, it can be a bitch."

Several laughs echoed in the chamber. A few "Boo-yahs!" followed to.

"However, despite being buried in research for so long, I am familiar with all of your training and know how much you have all sacrificed. I only hope that I can honor you as you have done me today. You are dismissed."

Infiltration Guardians—mutated humanoid animals—quickly saluted and opened the doors of the Great Hall. There were many corridors that led to this center of their base, and it wouldn't take long to empty out.

"Yes, Decoré," the rest of the Infiltrators shouted and began to exit.

McDonald turned and walked to a temporary throne, which had been placed on the platform for the ceremony. He flung his cape aside and plopped down to think.

"Well, Eric, it's been a long time, eh?" he asked, thinking of the days before his demotion, remembering when the Army of Mutants consisted of more than just being hired killers.

"You were such a conceited prick," he cursed. "When was the last time they've fought as a cohesive force? Henderson? You know what's happened since then? The Night Rangers are starting to show signs of strength again. There are more terrorist groups than ever. And there's a new rebel group.

"But I guess you're aware of that, hmm?" Jeff mocked. "I'm taking back what we've lost, Eric. Rebels and other scum used to cower from the very thought of facing the AOM. They knew us as mercenaries that wouldn't stop until every last one of them was dead or captured.

"We used to be elites, but now?" Jeff cursed, shaking his head. "Now the Guard is relying on groups like the Blood Raiders—the Blood Raiders?—to do the job for us.

"Never," he shouted and got up from the ceremonial peace of crap that Anderson had used upon his inauguration, which would be promptly burned. Then he walked to the lift system, which would take him back to his office.

It would take some time, but he was determined to gain the same prestige for Infiltration that the AOM had appreciated long ago.

"Those days will live again," he promised, no longer trying to think about General Eric van Anderson and the mess that man had managed to accomplish in only six short years.

"But, yes, I was to blame too," Jeff conceded, knowing that he had spent too much time in R&D, rather than actually seeing what had been going on around him. Still, despite these setbacks, he'd never turned his nose at the Norns and had never once spat at his destiny. He'd known that things had their order, had known that all things fall into place over time, and had known this long before Anderson had taken control of the FGGO.

"Yep, Eric, you need patience, need to understand the forces of the chaos around you, and you need to resist temptations you might not be able to control."

Jeffery Neilson McDonald had done so. Infiltration, the Military University of A-Natural Terrestrials, Special Projects, and half of the Panterian Prison Facilities were now under his direct command.

"To be fair," he laughed to himself. "You did decide to wait, expecting her to die on her own. I remember your grin when you told me to 'let the Norns do their thing,' and throwing my advice back in my face. It's funny how things turned out, huh?"

The lift stopped in front of his new office and McDonald walked out with a bounce to his step.

Rebecca closed the doors of her office after Jim left to inspect Hangar Bay Two. After asking Ecie for some privacy, she darkened the T-glass walls and thumbed on her workstation. She opened her personal files and tapped on the one labeled JONATHON CLAYTON ALEXANDER.

A holographic image suddenly appeared, sitting on a chair in front of her desk. The image wasn't nearly as good as a holosuite but it would do. The flickering likeness of her father smiled and rested hands on crossed legs.

Becca pushed back her hair and smiled timidly. "Hi, Dad, it's, umm, done."

"I see." Her father grimaced. This program was the last file the real Jon Alexander had made. He had tried to make it seem sentient so it could answer questions as well as he could have, and essentially help her sort through any of the thousands of files that he had collected over the years. However, with the additional boost of Ecie's personality software used in h-suites, Rebecca often talked with him like, like her father.

"I know." She shook her head. "It doesn't matter. I know what I almost gave up—"

"Do you? Do you really?" her father snapped. "So tell me. Do you feel any better?"

"That's not the point. I'm not going to go over this argument again. Not with you, not with Jim—"

"I'm sure he took it well." Jon smiled sardonically. "If everything you've told me about him ... he must have been pretty disappointed."

"Yeah, maybe he was. It doesn't matter."

"I'm sure it doesn't. It sounds like you haven't told him how —"

"Not now," the ex-Infiltrator sighed, wondering if she should just end the program and get on with her work. What was she doing anyway, seeking his approval, approval from a simulation of her father?

"OK, OK," Jon Alexander sighed too, and just sat there for a moment. "So what? Was that all you wanted to say? That you killed Anderson?"

"Yes, no, I don't know," she said and shook her head. "I just wasn't expecting Jim to allow me to stay after this."

"You didn't think he'd forgive you? You thought he'd let you surrender yourself back to Infiltration? Come on, Rebecca, you're lying to yourself. You need to—"

"I'm not going to tell him," she shouted. This was absurd. It was like she was a kid again and her father was chastising her. This program was the first opened when she'd found the data files he'd left for her. She remembered crying when his image appeared to her on the computer screen for the first time; when the program welcomed her home; when it—he told her how much he loved her; and when he had told her how much he wanted to hold her in his arms again.

"Fine"—the hologram flickered and her father glowered at her—"I understand. Is there anything else then?"

"I guess not," Becca said tersely, but even she knew she didn't mean it. "Sorry, Dad, I'm just hungry and ... I don't know. I just —But, but do you think they'll actually come for us? Do you think they'll find us?"

"It's hard to say." Her dad grimaced—not pleased with the change in subject ... or her. Ecie had told her that the program *had* become sentient; it was pretty much her dad in there... "The FGGO was around a long time before it was changed into Infiltration on November 25, 2998. They have a lot of resources; however, you should know better than me. By the time you left, you told me that Infiltration no longer engaged in all out warfare —focusing, instead, on subterfuge and assassinations."

"There were little skirmishes here and there, but never more than requiring a few squads." Rebecca nodded, pondering a bit about what she really did at Infiltration. Her primary job had been in Military Intelligence, trying to locate and map movements of smaller rebel and terrorist groups in Sector California and in Growth Zones Five and Six.

Very good at what she did, Becca had been responsible for locating and ultimately wiping out seventeen such groups. In some cases, she had actually led a few squads to deal with them personally. Even today, she did not feel guilty about some of those she had eliminated, since they had been very bad people. But naturally, she thought about the others.

"You once told me that the FGGO has been around since 2712." She pursed her lips, and immediately tried to shake out the thoughts of guilt. "If groups like the Blood Raiders are slowly supplanting the AOM, I don't understand the point of having the Army of Mutants around anymore."

"Your guess is as good as mine, Rebecca." Jon shrugged his shoulders. "It might be that Anderson understood that and started to focus on another niche. I don't know why the AOM wouldn't have been recommended for such assaults, even though a wholescale army hasn't been needed for some time. It was always very thorough, and the children of the FEMET obviously replaced any of the numbers that were lost at the Battle of Henderson."

"The Fetal Manipulation Experiments." Rebecca shuddered, remembering the experiments that her mother and father participated in, which gave rise to her incredible abilities and her ultimate fate.

He cringed. "I'm sorry. I didn't mean to be so crass."

"No, it's OK." She waved it off. "So when was the AOM created?"

The program knew she remembered just fine, but he humored her nonetheless. "As you know, the Malix Campaigns brought the world under single Panterian rule on May 9th, 2860. Many of the battles were fought by FGGO soldiers in the guise of mercenaries, which were hired by their own Puppet Government. However, the AOM, a military subgroup of the FGGO, wasn't officially organized until 2964, which was in response to rebel and terrorist threats after the Unification."

"You know," Rebecca smirked. "Infiltration didn't teach me much World History, unless it pertained to military tactics. Come to think of it, Jim once told me the FGGO existed before the Guard. I thought he was pulling my leg, but is that true?"

"He wasn't kidding." Jon Alexander's brow raised a bit, seemingly impressed. "The Foundation of Greater Genetic Organisms, a military subgroup, was organized by the Panterian Congress in the summer of 2712. Once established, the FGGO quickly began to manufacture vaccines, medicines, artificial limbs, et cetera. It ultimately made the Panterian armies quite formable and nearly indefatigable.

"Interestingly enough, it was the FGGO's success that caused it to adopt its secret existence long ago."

"How so?" Rebecca felt like she was only fifteen again—young, naïve and captivated by his stories.

"Well, realizing that Panteria and the FGGO were a threat of the highest magnitude, EuroAmerica, Moranica and Tangia banded together and attacked the FGGO's primary complex in 2732. At the same time, they also planned and assisted a coup d'état in the Panterian government.

"Of course history books don't mention the latter event; however, these city-states did manage to place and maintain a Puppet Government in Panteria for over thirty years. That is, up until the Peoples' Revolution of 2764.

Jon Alexander nodded and said, "Yah, the FGGO had a hand in that upheaval. It survived the attack of 2732. It continued drawing funds from untraceable accounts and continued on as an independent entity." Her father appeared flabbergasted. "You know, one of my informants said that the FGGO was obligated to bring back a sovereign Panterian government. My God, the guy almost seemed like he was proud of what the FGGO had done. It's like complimenting Hitler or Anwalter!

"Anyway," the man sighed and nervously drummed his fingers on his right thigh.

Rebecca didn't say anything, still awestruck by how her father seemed to be sitting in that chair in front of her.

"The Panterian Guard, headed by the Panterian Council, rose up in 2837," he finally continued. "I still don't know the entire history behind it or how the Guard gained so much power. Nevertheless, it and the Panocomptrix secretly took control of almost every aspect of Panterian life a decade later, incorporated the FGGO, and then created and organized the structures of the Puppeteer and Puppet Governments we now have.

"But, Rebecca, you know as well as I do that Panteria's history isn't going to help us," he pointed out the obvious. "I think the question is 'Do you think Infiltration will find Crystal Mountain?'"

"I don't know," Becca conceded. "We weren't even really looking for the Executioners at the time. We had suspicions of where they could have been based, but not to any particular Growth Zone."

She spat out those words with clenched fists. An old frustration that was linked to her old job at Infiltration suddenly flared up, and she let it vent: "Sorry to change the subject, but I don't know what's going to happen in another century. The GZs and Red Zones keep getting worse. The latter keep getting more dangerous, while both keep expanding. The GZs are responsible for the Season of Storms and provide shelter to some of the worst —"

Rebecca cut herself short, not wanting to be hypocritical by saying the word "stigs." As an Executioner, she was in league with, supposedly, the worst of them; however, she still had distaste for some of the bastards out there.

"Dad, what was Jackson McNeil thinking?" she sighed, knowing hunger was making her lose some focus.

"He did take some liberties with the project, eh?" he agreed. "But you have to admit, if he hadn't added other organisms to the genetic templates, the Neo-Holocaust would have continued unabated for some time."

"I guess so." She shrugged, agreeing reluctantly. There were six primary growth zones—numbered Four through Ten—in the Northern Hemisphere. Initially, the first batch of super trees, Plantae Omnibus, had been terribly difficult to grow. Although around in name only and now overgrown by the other seven, earlier sites like Growth Zones One through Three never took root, which had spelled an early disaster for the reforestation programs.

Dr. Jackson McNeil had been responsible for getting the projects refunded and back on track, when he used his own money to plant GZ IV. By chance, he had discovered that Plantae Omnibus, Phase One, thrived only in irradiated areas, notably in those places blasted with Iridietum-317 particles. He rented a crop duster and dumped the remaining seeds of that first batch all over the Mountain. Within weeks, the media suddenly took notice of how well the new GZ was doing, which, along with the reviving oceans, eventually ended the genocides.

Nearly eight hundred years later, everyone still celebrated June 8th, which was the day when Growth Zone Four began its first signs of life. Even Rebecca haphazardly took part in the annual festivities, knowing how much the Growth Zones meant—despite how they, including hundreds of minor GZs, had been spreading unabated since the late 26th Century. Shit! Those next batches of Plantae Omnibus in GZ V–X hadn't needed the Iridi-etum "kick start" at all.

"But I still think the Neo-Holocaust would have ended even-tually," Rebecca countered. "New oceanic vegetation, algae and phytoplankton were much more important for replenishing global oxygen and food stocks. And McNeil's Pacific and Atlantic projects had been flourishing decades before GZ Four succeeded."

"Yah! It's interesting how perception makes such a differ-ence." Her dad shrugged. "Who knows? The world might have been a bit different if people had decided to start planting nor-mal blight-resistant trees again."

No one was sure if that was really true. The blights popped up in the Southern Hemisphere on occasion, and the only way to stop them were controlled burns.

Rebecca said, "Yep, except for some aqua farms on the coasts and some land in the northern tundra, we don't have much room to move around."

Her dad kept quiet. He was well aware of what Rebecca knew. Truth be told, in the Northern Hemisphere, there wasn't much arable land, even though every square inch of it looked green from space. What farms existed were small and well within the limits of the Megacities, or were small, temporary pockets of land that the GZs hadn't spread to yet.

Oddly enough, no one ever really thought about where most of the food came from nowadays. Clearly, there was a dark his-tory she didn't want to go into at the moment. But, sadly, there were only a couple of Megacities in the Southern Hemisphere. There used to be over a hundred before the Neo-Holocaust.

"Well, if the GZs do take over, a lot of people might have to move," her father smirked and tapped his holographic fingers on a knee. "I don't think Jim's going to release the knowledge of how to inhibit their growth. The Guard, Infiltration, the Blood Raiders or anybody else may decide the Growth Zones aren't all that necessary."

Jim and Ecie had come up with a simple but very sophisticated method to both prevent the surrounding growth zone from reclaiming areas cut back for the hangars and other entry points ... and also to power the holograms and the *Wasteland* around them. They had developed special nanobots that continuously ate the trees, which in turn powered their hologram projectors and the enhanced field that scrambled just about all electronics and communication systems. Who knew if the Guard would risk unleashing those little monsters into all of the GZs to flush out hiding rebels ... and risk another holocaust? Even though she wasn't sure such would work. The nanobots could only keep a relatively small area clear, and Jim still had to go out and help clear those areas with his claws every few months.

"Point taken." Rebecca nodded and subtly pulled up a calendar on her PDL, making sure she wasn't missing any appointments. She was losing concentration and was obviously hungry. Jim said he'd take her to lunch when he got back. Despite the argument they'd had earlier, she hadn't declined.

Her dad eyed her curiously. "Well, looks like you better get back to work. Sorry I couldn't help you, but I'm glad you made it back here safe, Daughter."

"Thanks, Dad, me too." Becca closed the program and sat in her office alone. She still missed him, even more now, despite what she had done and what she had tried.

Anderson had him killed six months ago. She hadn't even known until a friend had seen a news report and had told her about it. She had missed the funeral.

Rebecca quickly blinked back the tears that tried to come. She didn't know when she had forgiven him for not trying to save her on the day of her abduction, since she would have just watched him die if he had intervened. She never mentioned forgiveness to the program either, even though she always seemed to see the yearning in his eyes.

"Ecie, clear the T-Glass, and can you get Arthor for me?" She rubbed her eyes and drummed her hands nervously on the desk.

"Sure, Rebecca," the computer chimed in. "Oh, Lt. Tagget got your assessment of the disperal operations in Sector 49 South. He figures that they're pretty small and Logan's team shouldn't have much trouble with them. However, he noticed that you pinpointed a number of cocaine and heroin facilities there too, and he was wondering if you still wanted those left alone."

"Yep," Rebecca said with a sneer. She was not fond of drug use in any shape or form, but she wasn't going to get into another argument with Jim this morning. "Just focus on the synthetic drugs like disperal and Darmbats."

"Sure thing," Ecie said. "Rebecca, is everything OK?"

She smirked, rubbing her eyes again, making sure she didn't have a tear that had managed to get past her defenses. "Everything's OK, Ecie. Thanks."

"Sure. No problem."

"Jim headed to Hangar Bay Two to inspect its hologram. He should be back up here in an hour or so. He's taking me to lunch. Interested in joining us?" Rebecca asked on the other end of the comlink. "We all haven't been to Bailey's Grill lately. Cherie keeps asking about you."

"Sure she does," he laughed. "Who doesn't like my jokes?"

"Well, just don't tell Ann—" Arthor could tell Becca cut her sentence short. He wouldn't have to comment. "Anyway, I figured after your watch, you'd be a bit hungry. Jim wouldn't mind the extra company either."

"That's OK." Arthor stretched a dark wing in the daylight, while a pair of eyes scanned the landscape. He'd give those two their privacy. *God, it's like watching two slugs trying to date, and they need time work this out.* "I was planning on swinging by to see Anna this morning. It's been awhile, and I wanted to see how her presentation went."

"Sure, tell her 'Hello' for me. See you later."

"OK. Oh, and Rebecca?"

"Yah?"

"I'm glad you made it back here in one piece. You honored your father's memory."

"Ah. Thanks. It's just good to be home."

That spoke volumes. "Chetok," Arthor agreed and smiled, ending the conversation, and rubbed his eyes with his upper-right hand. He knew Jim wasn't at all happy with what Rebecca had done, but Arthor had warned Jim of the inevitable.

He should have helped her. He shrugged. It was getting late and he was getting tired. He'd pulled the swing shift and it was about eleven hundred hours. It was about time to call it a day.

He yawned and scanned the landscape one last time. The invisible platform he sat on was amongst the tops of the six-hundred-foot-tall trees covering the land. Being from a world that didn't even have electricity yet, he still couldn't believe their majestic nature, couldn't believe such wonders. Hell, these were trees that could resist sub-arctic temperatures, fire, blight, radiation, and that could even regenerate quickly after physical attack.

Chetok, I was amazed when my mother showed me a lantern when I was a kid, he chuckled to himself.

He sighed and gazed through the telescoping lenses of his

helmet. He didn't see anything suspicious, and he figured he should be happy about that, despite his overall feeling of boredom.

Jim had been pretty paranoid that Infiltration would seek retribution for what Rebecca had done. And, even though the Governor had thought that the Executioners' location was still a secret, Arthor knew this had been a pretty good test.

The Crytonian sat quietly on the platform. The forest remained still, much like when he had first come here about an hour ago, just leaving him alone to his own thoughts.

Thump, thump, thump. His head spun to the side, a response to almost a feeling rather than an actual flapping noise, and he looked down in time to see an owl flying away.

He unfolded his other wing. He welcomed the stretch, extending both tips out to about fifteen feet—wings that his friends would describe as those of a giant prehistoric reptile or a bat.

"More like a zarmbat's," he said derisively and tried not to think about his home as he sat on this small obstower. He didn't mind its simplicity. In fact, he'd always hated leaving this spot. It was here where he always ended his watch.

"But it's time to go," he said to himself, with a stretch of his wings and another. Then he flapped them once as a test—knowing it was just a psychological thing, since his power of flight had nothing to do with his wings, except for some rudimentary movements. Regardless, he flapped them again and then shot into the sky.

He swooped, he soared and he jetted across the heavens. Tucking his arms in and using his tail to help stabilize him against some crosswinds, Arthor smiled at the thrill, but he quickly subdued the joy. It didn't take a lot to remind him that by coming to Panteria he had lost his world, lost his family, his

armor, his sword and his—

He cursed and buried the memory as deeply as he could, then contracted his wings and dived to another obstower.

Harold Taylor and his partner, Joe Tillian, had been working this morning shift periodically for two years. Despite having to start it at zero four hundred, he always loved seeing the sun break over the Rocky Mountains and enjoyed the peace and quiet.

Such as it is, he thought, brushing his thumb over the safety of his high-powered e-rifle, and scanned the horizon. Thirty-five hours ago the Governor had called in and asked them to keep their eyes sharp today. Lieutenant Taylor had sensed some tension in the man's voice. If there was going to be trouble—

In his helmet's visor he noticed a "friendly blip" approaching at high speed. Taylor checked the power rating of his armor and then the cloaking field surrounding the watchtower. He never much thought about the powersuit encasing him, until he had to take it off at the end of his shift. Also, he usually took for granted that this entire platform was completely camouflaged by a powerful hologram, neatly blending them into the forest and sky.

THUMP. Something huge landed hard in the tower, and Harold felt Joe jerk beside him. Their rifles were already aimed— just in case—at where the sound of the thump originated. Where the "friendly blip" was, a large figure materialized out of nowhere.

The figure was in specialized armor, which could oscillate from black to shimmering Quicksilver and every other color. Like the Governor's and Rebecca's suits, the tall figure's armor amplified and extended the field that the man could create to disappear from sight. Thanks to McMillian's Armory, Harold and the rest of the Executioners would hopefully have powered armor that mimicked that affect—an army of invisible soldiers.

"Good morning, Gentlemen," the man said as he took off his helmet. General Arthor Jones quickly nodded to both of them.

"Good morning, General! Area's clear," Harold shouted and simply lowered his rifle. He didn't salute either, even though the hologram concealed them.

"As you were." A quick order followed. The blast and impact shields were up, having allowed the general easy access to the interior of the main obstower, which was one of many spread throughout the *Wasteland*. "Good news. I spoke briefly to Jim on my way here. Looks like we're in the clear and we'll be changing the threat level."

The tension in Harold's shoulders fell away. He grinned in response—his helmet concealing it—but his hand quickly making an appropriate gesture.

"That's great news, General. And good morning," Taylor said. He extended and offered his armored hand to the man. "How was your watch?"

"Dastil es, Lieutenant—It was fine, Harry." Verengoshian— one of the languages of Crytonia, a country of Deliplain, a world quite distant from Panteria—briefly registered in his ears. He watched too, as his armored gauntlet was engulfed by Arthor's armored, upper-right hand. He'd made it a point this time to have Joe snap a helmet cam picture when he stood next to their EXO. "Bet how art thy wife y children?"

Harold wondered when he had ever gotten used to hearing Verengoshian and why it sounded so much like English. "They're doing great. Billy's just starting to get the hang of Weeter Smitz, Angelica is taking her first steps and Margaret's finally getting back to work."

He enjoyed these talks with Arthor Jones, who was the Executive Officer of the Executioners and also the Lieutenant Governor of Crystal Mountain. Naturally, Arthor had a very time-consuming schedule, but the man always made it a custom to stop and talk with anyone when given the opportunity.

"That's great, my friend," Jones spoke softly, focusing on his English, and turned to chat with Joe a bit.

Harold chuckled to himself and took a brief look toward the horizon, then closer at the trees. Jones had told them all about the world of Deliplain, where its sentient creatures, the typhons, lived. To this day the Crytonian man could only guess how he had come to Panteria, and less still about the ungodly powers he was able to wield the day of his arrival.

"Well, Lieutenant, am I relieved?" Harold stretched his neck a bit and saw a huge grin. Soft, blond hair seemed to offset the color of the dark skin, while blue eyes caused another striking contrast.

"By your leave, sir." He nodded and moved with Jones to the entrance of the obstower. "Oh, and if Jack's working in the Command Center, can you pass off a 'Hello' for me, and remind him that he still owes me a bottle of Scotch."

"Sure," the Crytonian laughed, put his helmet back on, and spread his wings, preparing himself for flight. "Have a great day, Lieutenant."

Harold watched the giant step onto a small balcony just outside and look up into the holographic sky. Was he calculating exactly where to go, or was he wondering how much the sky had really changed?

"Oh, I almost forgot." The general turned to him just before he took off. "Taylor, I have scheduled your ninth-level evaluation on Tuesday at fourteen hundred thirty hours. Tillian, your seventh is on Wednesday at fifteen hundred hours. Until then, good hunting."

"Aye, sir. As to you," Harold said and grabbed hold of the railing before him, preparing for the surge of wind to come from Arthor's takeoff. The gust quickly hit his armored frame and he watched Jones zip up into the sky, almost faster than anything he'd ever seen. He, however, quickly remembered the Governor and the *Blade*, and how fast those two could fly.

"Eh, Joe?" He turned to his partner, his best friend since Sixth Grade. Harold was roughly the same age as Tillian, maybe a few years younger, but he knew friendship had erased the gap.

"Yeah?"

"I'm glad that he and the others decided to stay with us."

"Will you get to work, sir?" Joe quickly joked, and also tapped him on the top of his helmet. But then Harold watched his friend look up into the sky, as if trying to locate their now invisible Lieutenant Governor. "But yeah, I know, Harry. They're definitely good people."

"Yeah, the best," Taylor agreed and smiled.

"Ecie, I don't want you to engage the crash netting. I'll be fine," Arthor reassured the computer and snapped off the comlink. He did an aerial somersault and then sped in a different direction. He then accelerated around Crystal Mountain and shot skyward, seeming to stretch the stratosphere thin. He flapped his wings hard to help him occasionally stop and change directions, never tiring of the exhilaration he felt when he tore through the sky this way. He had always wondered how he had gained these abilities but was never disappointed.

"But again, at what price?" He shook his head, never being

able to forget about the sword, his existence. "Aren't these only simple pleasures?"

He folded his wings and dived.

One. Two, eyes closed, he counted. He had to keep training himself, which was his only distraction. But there were only so many times a day he could really think about the name *Omniemnan,* which was the unattainable symbol of his dishonor.

Three. Open. Four. He imagined a small door whisper open. Then his wings nearly pressed against cool metal as he fell down a narrow shaft.

He continued counting with his eyes closed, relying on memory and reflex. His breath quickened. His tail adjusted only minutely, keeping him from slamming into the narrow shaft.

Seven. Clear. Eight. He stretched his arms out and he readied his legs for the shock.

Nine! He opened his wings—

Ka-crack!

His feet hit something hard, and his legs bent to absorb the impact. And his armored, lower knuckles drummed against a painted metal deck. He opened his eyes and scanned the Western Receiving Chamber, where several emergency entrance shafts from the surrounding obstowers fell into. He'd told Ecie to turn off the catch unit, despite really wishing otherwise.

"Yeah, I've been around Logan way too much lately." Arthor tapped the metal beneath him in three sharp rhythms, before he pushed himself up and walked over to the door.

But I guess Jim's not much safer. I wonder what Anna's up too, he chuckled, removed a gauntlet and pressed his hand against the PID plate for entry.

"Ah, Arthor," Ecie popped in. "Nice landing."

The door opened and he walked in. "Thanks. See, nothing to worry about. Has Jim come back from HBII yet?"

"No, he's just about done though. You want me to patch you in by comlink?"

"No, it's OK. I need to check the status on one of the medical facilities anyway."

"Which one, you know I can tell you right now."

"Ah, that's all right. I can do it myself. You know, ask her while I was already there? Besides, I could use the walk."

Ecie paused a moment. Then his voice went a little higher when he asked, "Should I tell Anna you're coming? She's back from her presentation at Wallace High School. She wore something pretty. Meow-rowl."

Arthor felt his tail twitch. "No, will you please do a multi-linear calculation or something?"

"What do you mean? I'm working on nine trillion right now."

Despite it being a joke, Arthor clenched his teeth. "Well do another one then. Anna and I are just friends. That's it. That's all it can ever be. Got it?"

There was a long pause. The corridor was empty. No one had heard his outburst, but why did he bark?

"I'm sorry, Arthor," Ecie apologized. "Not being human or humanoid, I forget about the differences. I shouldn't have joked."

"No, it's not that, Ecie." Arthor lowered his head, realizing he had been reminiscing about Verengosha, his home province of Crytonia, way too much lately. He also noticed that his upper-right hand was absently grasping at open air again.

He needed to think of something else. "Oh, I don't know. Can you tell me a joke?"

"Sure," Ecie accepted the apology and obviously changed his tone again to lighten the mood. "Logan told me this one. Did you hear about the Cathar, the Magician and the Scholar …?"

Arthor tried, tried to give the computer his full attention, but he soon became distracted by the continuous opening and clos-ing of his upper-right hand. A nervous twitch he had developed a year ago, it often occurred during times like these, when he obsessed about his lost home, honor and sword.

Omniemnan. His heart began to pound hard in his chest. It was object that his hand tried to grasp, even though he had no idea where it was.

Like, he thought to himself, *like some damned tic of a woeful hero from one of Logan's awful movies.*

Jim heard an adjoining office door open and a tired sigh echo in the room.

"Arthor, how was your shift?" Jim asked.

"Was slow, Jim, really slow. There was nothing out, very quiet. Looks like you were right."

"Well, there might be something out there soon enough." St. John tried not to grimace, but he wondered if Arthor actually wanted a fight. He, however, suddenly had to clench his own fists, when his own heart began to beat in anticipation.

Arthor Jones walked to the back of his office and up to the hot water dispenser. There was something about his friend this morning. The guy's depression was evidently getting worse, and Jim was running out of any possible remedies.

"Anything else?" the Governor asked anyway.

The Crytonian made himself a cup of tea, gestured if he wanted any. St. John shook his head. He wasn't a big fan of tea, but that didn't stop Arthor from praising its benefits.

"Not really, Jim. I visited the main hospital before I came here. It seems like everything's working fine. There are two trainees trying to get used to the new life-support systems, but

Anna says they'll be ready in a few months."

Jim remembered his early days here. "Anna. How is she? I haven't talked to her much since she accepted Chief of Medical. Well, honestly, even before that—" He cut himself off.

"She's doing great. Work's kept her busy. She's pulling thirteen, sixteen hour days. I haven't seen much of her myself."

"Well, if anything gets past our defenses, we might be seeing a lot of her. Worst case scenario, Ecie might not see them coming." Jim stepped through the doorway, closer to his friend, and whispered, "The investigation has been dropped, but who knows what they have—"

"I don't know, Jim." Another voice joined the conversation, and he turned to see Rebecca walking up behind him. She was close—what had she heard? "When I was working with Infiltration, I never saw anything really capable of stumping the Statcom, and that was only a synthetic frame."

"Possibly," Jim said, rubbing his chin. *Maybe I should have accepted a cup of tea and kept my mouth shut,* he thought, but then said, "But remember, Becca, you didn't see everything there. And quite a few Nagis are still around.

"You've told us a lot of info about the Eagle's Den since I've left, but Viper was an eccentric man. There's no telling what he did after the FEMET experiments. We have to take every precaution as a plausible one."

"Sir? Excuse me, sir?" A knock on his office door and a new timid voice sought Jim's attention.

"Yes? Come in," the Crystalian Governor said and gestured to a young man he hadn't met before. A private, Nathian Bryon, entered quickly and snapped to attention. He held a PDL tightly in his hands. He was one of Jim's new Administrative Assistants.

"Sir"—the boy gulped—"Lans-Delta has just landed. Captain Tirson says the mission went well. She said the Panzer was up to his usual stunts again by waiting for just the right dramatic moment to detonate. And he did his best—I quote this, sir—'in scaring the hell out of everyone.' She, however, liked the assignment, and she wishes to be a part of his team again. I also have her request to transfer to his unit."

Jim remembered meeting Tara Tirson once. She was a very smart woman with the most piercing green eyes and lustrous blonde hair. He figured Logan would agree to the transfer without much problem. Smiling briefly, the grin was soon lost when he thought of something else. "Did she say anything about his destination afterward?"

"General, he was just beginning a new mission when Captain Tirson's group left." Bryon almost seemed out of breath, as if the entire conversation had been on one draught of air.

Jim motioned toward Arthor's office. "Great, Nate, thank you for your report. Have some coffee or tea, won't you?" He smiled again, when he heard the quiet snickers from both Rebecca and Arthor. They knew he hated formalities on shift, as much as the other Crystalians did after work; however, the private still looked at him curiously. "Mr. Bryon, I left that type of military long ago. My name's Jim."

The assistant grinned, politely declined the cup of tea, and returned to his post. St. John soon watched the youth relay the story to his workmates, who only smirked and continued working, obviously having heard something like it before.

"So, Arthor," Jim said, while looking back at the Lt. Governor, thankful of the brief intrusion. He didn't want to talk about what Logan was up to either. "Rebecca and I were about to get some breakfast—Well, I guess lunch now. Interested?"

The Crytonian, holding a PDL of his own, gazed up and laughed. Jim noted that despite Arthor's trials, the man did tend to laugh a lot. Was it all just a careful mask?

"No, Jim," the Crytonian replied. "There are a couple of things here I wanted to take care of before I checked out. After that, I was planning on going to bed."

"Well, have it your way. Rebecca, are you ready?"

"Sure, it's about time. I'm starving." An arm slid around his and he was nudged toward the door. "But I'll have you know, I never put out on the fortieth date." She jabbed him in the side, while he heard Arthor bellow light amusement.

"And I thought my charms were going to work this time," he joked as they walked out of his office. But what if it was more than simple horseplay—

He quickly shook off that thought when he looked into her eyes. Was it the strange face she suddenly made? Was it a face of worry she held? Wondering too if they were just kidding themselves?

Arthor watched the two leave. He wished they'd just tell each other how they felt. Hell, thinking of a human phrase, he'd even "pass the notes between classes" if they were too chicken.

Ah, humans and typhons, the similarities abound, he chuckled and immediately thought of what Aenglan, Arthor's old teacher and father's bodyguard, would have said or would have even thought about this situation.

He dared not answer it himself, of course, and instead immediately started to review upcoming training schedules on his PDL. He tried not to think of the sword again. But, most of all, he dared not think of anyone capable of loving a … *knight* such as Arthor Jones.

CHAPTER THREE

*Cruelty is a tyrant, that is always attended
with Fear.*

(Gnomologia, No. 1213)
**—Thomas Fuller, English
cleric (1732 A.D.)**

John Henry Powers tucked one side of his overcoat into the other. He walked away from Medley Tavern, a humble establishment he had grown used to during his vacation.

He looked around. It was about midnight, so he walked on an empty sidewalk. Few people lived in this town and tended to commute. He'd heard the bartender talking history to a group, and John gathered that the town of Medley was founded after the turn of the last century.

He figured it really didn't matter. The few people who actually lived here would be evacuated someday, since Medley was smack-dab in the middle of a red zone. To boot, it had only one Extermination Officer, and he covered most of the Rocky Mountain Region.

Walter's pretty damned good. He tried to smile. But he knew, like always, that it just didn't come out quite right. So, while he walked, he tried smiling again, knowing nobody was around to judge. To his own "delight"—if he were a different person, he would have laughed at his own joke there—the smile felt better the second time around. Hell yeah, it just took practice.

"Repeat. Rinse. Repeat," Logan had said, but what did Logan know anyway? That guy wasn't entirely wired right himself. Still, even though the guy could be a smartass, he was John's best friend.

Hmm, I guess I need better friends. He tried another joke, but then just mimicked a sigh and quickened his pace down the sidewalk, while listening and scanning the area around him carefully. For now, only shadows crept close to the buildings where the street-lights couldn't reach, couldn't touch.

"A kid was nearly mauled here a few nights ago," he talked to himself, purposefully, to make some noise. "The boy was lucky getting away. Four other people have died so far.

"The boy told the EO that it was big, armored and strong. This should be as good a place as any." Medley was in a red zone, a big one. And despite the number of Nagephon beasts being killed in this sector by the United Eradication Council of Hostile Beasts and Biological Survey, the creatures were frequenting this area more and more often.

Many people in the Megacities protested the slayings, saying that no one should live in these places. John had his own opinions, and he pretty much agreed with the "live and let live" policy. But he also had killed quite a few of those monsters that had been driven crazy because of their mutations. And he knew the world was the better for it.

"I draw the line when something kills for pleasure, crazy or not." He stopped, took a deep breath and held it, trying to listen for heavy steps, something, and anything. He'd done contract work for other EO's in the past, before he'd been asked to join the Executioners. The work had kept him fed, and kept him in a pretty good network for important scuttlebutt. The latter was his main reason to continue these contracts nowadays, but he also did it as a general service.

He yawned but kept up his guard, not letting drowsiness get the best of him. Despite lacking most emotions, he could feel pain. And he wasn't going to be eaten by some giant demon—

Rooooaaar ... He heard something growl. John held his breath again, concentrated and listened. There was no wind, no breeze.

Grrroooaaaarrrrr. Screech. Rrrwoowww! It was louder this time. The voice wasn't human and was about a block away.

Here goes, John thought to himself, ran and climbed to a building's rooftop in a matter of seconds. He moved to the back of the roof and looked down, his special eyes compensating for the darkness.

He saw what he thought was a lioness. Unable to see for sure, he assumed it was female unless it was a young male without a mane. The large cat was being pushed backward by a pair of creatures, which were obviously distorted by the Nagephon.

He eyed them closely, recognizing the bigger, armored one immediately as his bounty. The word "enormous" was an understatement for the first one. The other beast was a bit smaller than a person. Neither of them seemed to have descended from anything human.

The lioness screamed again, a frightful hiss. She took another step back when the others moved closer.

John's intended kill, an armadillonoid, reared up to its full fifteen-foot height. It suddenly lunged forward, trying to grab hold of the cat. But the lioness was too wily. It slapped at the beast and backed away, pulling free from the behemoth's claws.

Kikooooooaaarrr! the monster screamed. The lioness obviously had hit a sensitive spot, and the armadillonoid almost toppled back, nearly crushing the jackalpod behind it. The smaller creature barked in protest but ducked down when the bigger beast raised menacing claws.

Hmm, she should be able to keep them distracted long enough ... John pulled the overcoat from his shoulders, exposing ancient, illegal weapons to a moonless sky. His hand rested on one of the katana sheathed on his back. He felt a light, cool breeze blow through his hair as he looked over the edge and prepared himself for the inevitable.

Powers imagined grinning like Logan would have done in faux self-pity for the beasts, but he simply stepped over the side. Four stories zipped by and he landed with only a slight bend to his knees. Instantly, he wondered if one of his former Masters would have asked if John was part demon or angel.

Well, Jupa never quite understood the FEMET project, John told to himself and waited in the darkness, waiting for the right time to strike.

It didn't take long. The armored monster got a better angle this time and surged forward, grasping its prey in its giant claws. The lioness screamed, but this time couldn't break free from an iron-like grip.

Seeing an opening, the jackal leaped forward and tried to get behind the cat. She caught him with a rear foot, and the jackalpod screamed and covered a huge gash on the right side of its face.

The lioness shrieked. She tried to free herself again and again, but there was no use. Powers could hear her shortened gasps. She moaned pitiful cries, and all her struggles were being wasted. She needed help or she would die.

Now! Like tremendous springs, his legs catapulted John into the sky. He pulled out his swords at the same moment and pointed them down hard into his target.

SHHLIIIIIISSSSSTTTT. The alloy of his weapons sliced eas- ily and deeply, and John guided the two fearsome blades like he was carving a fish. Bones, joints, blood vessels and flesh slid away from the armadillonoid's spine.

The behemoth screamed the best it could without working lungs. Arms and legs, no longer under its control, burst into spasm. The monster crashed to the ground, blood spilling every- where, and its armored tail violently pounded and tore up the asphalt. And John, with another strike, decapitated it and cut off another limb before it slashed his way.

"*Eiak-ka-ka-ka*", howling in terror, the jackalpod tried to escape. John whirled around and threw a razor sharp spike in its direction. Its skull popped from impact and the beast fell for- ward and shook until it finally died.

"*Werrrrrr, ki-kuk, ki-kuk*". John spun back around, wondering if another—but he quickly cursed, as with any one of his friends would have done. He sheathed his other sword and grimaced when he looked at where the armadillonoid had finally collapsed.

Shit! he thought as he walked back to the lioness. She was try- ing to pull free from under the dead monster, which must have crushed her back legs and spine. She wouldn't make it.

The cat moaned again pitifully. However, despite what any normal human might have experienced, he felt no sorrow or pity for the animal he had tried to save. He was unable to … simply born without that or any emotion. Still, John believed he under- stood pain, suffering and mercy. Readying the longer of his swords, he drew closer to her, his eyes staring deeply into hers. He aimed the blade then and prepared for a final strike.

"Woorruupp?" Then there was another moan, like a question. He paused and turned around, looking at a metal dumpster behind him. "Woorruupp?" The moan came again.

The lioness suddenly stirred back to life. She yelped, cried, anything her damaged lungs could muster. She never stopped, never allowed her breath to fade.

A small, furry head popped out from behind the metal box, and the lioness stopped for a moment, eyes watering. It was a younger cat, but John noticed its markings, and immediately questioned its lineage when he saw its face.

A liger? He could only guess, since the cub was a lighter yellow than a deeper orange. It eyed him curiously and cautiously, fear obviously present.

John stepped back.

The lioness cried again, a paw reaching out. Two little, golden eyes jerked from John's direction to those of its mother. The cub moaned again, a gurgled cry, and moved forward. It, a male cub, plopped down next to her, and she immediately began to lick his face and began to puff soothing sounds between staggered breaths.

John watched the little one rest his head on her shoulder. She continued to lick his face. He watched curiously, wondering if these animals actually understood death. Old Age reference books mentioned how wild elephants used to react to the remains of a dead bull or cow.

He wondered how much had been lost from such extinctions. The elephants and many other animals in cloning zoos were oblivious to everything, except a child's handful of peanuts or other treats. And many people nowadays wondered if it would be more humane to simply put all such beasts out of their misery.

Jim once said that it's important that the zoos exist, reminding us all of what natural beauty was lost during the Neo-Holocaust, Powers thought of an old argument. *Logan said that the impact would be more effective if the children could only see it as a hologram or in a book. Rebecca told them that they were being "preachy" and needed to focus on eating their* synthetic *eggs.*

He put off the thought as he watched the scene before him unfold. The lioness continued to stare at him, even while she comforted her son. Most of him didn't understand what came from the contact, but his honor made up for it.

He sheathed his other sword and nodded reassuringly to her. "I will. I promise," he said.

Pitissssss. There was a fizzle, and the night quickly enveloped the group when one of the streetlights that got damaged in the fight went out. The man's eyes instantly adjusted for the difference and saw a final spasm. A cool breeze blew in too, and Death came and went, flowing in and out of the shadows to take His new charge.

John sat down next to the cub and took the animal into his arms. It moaned and tried weakly to rest near its mother. But it finally collapsed on John's lap, where it cried and wailed.

John cuddled the little cub, rubbed it behind the ears and tried to think of some words to comfort it. Even though none came, Powers knew what he had to do. He knew where it would be loved and cared for. He was going to take it to a place where the animal would be readily accepted, to a place where a Crystalian could be anyone. Even an orphaned cat.

<><><><><><><>

In the *Blade's* cockpit, the scanners went dead. Logan had just entered the *Wasteland.* He smiled at the Crystalians' euphemism, considering the area he'd just breached would certainly be a literal hell for anyone looking to cause trouble.

"Well, good thing Ecie isn't trigger happy," Logan mused, knowing that an occasional hovercar would get lost in the area every now and then. For hundreds of years, Panteria's Department of Transportation had been advising wayward travelers to drive straight ahead until their instruments would come back online. Apparently, it was good enough for everyone, since no Executioner to date had had to pose as a rescue worker to help a lost vehicle. And thankfully no outside hovercraft had crashed in the area either.

Logan smirked, tapping his left armored fingers on one of the panels, while his mind spun the *Blade* in almost every direction.

Eyeing Crystal Mountain in the distance, he maintained the erratic course and even periodically changed his altitude. Executioner landing protocol stated that any craft traveling to the Mountain should slow well below 160 mph before it hit the Terrex field. Once within its boarder, the craft was to perform a series of random vector changes—the number and intensity limited to how well the shields and velocity envelopes of the craft prevented any potential atmospheric disturbances. Consequently, the *Blade* zigzagged and spun at well over three times the speed of sound.

Hell, Jim's always been so overprotective, he thought, since the *Blade's* instruments were beyond dead right now, and the radiation was as strong as ever. No foreign monitoring equipment could track the airspace within the *Wasteland*, even though Ecie had perfect vision here.

Now there's an idea, Logan laughed at nothing in particular and then activated the proper link between the *Blade* and the Control Center. With that, the craft's scanning equipment snapped back online after it synched up with Ecie's communications.

The Guard and its minions obviously must have questioned the existence of the *Wasteland*; namely, it being stronger in this area than it had been for over five hundred years. However, because of the ancient importance of Iridietum-317m, there were other areas around the globe similar to this one, and they also fluctuated in intensity due to the planet's magnetosphere.

Ecie was a pretty smart cookie. "But who knew he'd be so spunky?" he asked aloud. Ecie definitely liked to yank Logan's chain. Well, he had to admit, they both couldn't help it. Practical jokes a constant game between them.

Logan put off for now what he'd do to Ecie to get back at him for filling Logan's toothpaste dispenser with bubblegum. He thought about someone else who might be able to see him by now.

"Lifeforce detection and tracking aptitude," McMillian mumbled. The FGGO had given a name to the phenomenon Jim had gained on his nineteenth birthday, which was an ability to literally see living energy. Only a few individuals ever had such a gift, and those few had been enlisted for recon work.

Jim had been an exception, a Kurgon Beast. He had used his gift to search out his enemy wherever it was and simply eliminate the threat. No one had ever been able to hide.

Logan smiled uneasily, even though St. John would never have reason to find him in such a way. Nonetheless he mused himself with Arthor's words: "Chetok, Jim sayde thy soul was black wit'tinee yellow y pink poke-a-dots amongst de edges. A trace peculaer if ye'ouldth ask mi."

"How convenient," he remembered saying. "At least you'll remember to bury me with matching shoes."

His friends had laughed, but he sighed woefully, wondering if they were just joking or would actually honor his request.

"That would be awful, especially if He judges by attire," he said, glancing up.

He rolled his eyes and tried to think of something else, since religion just wasn't his thing. But the Crystalians might have been wearing off on him, since they had enough for him and the rest of Panteria. Well, that wasn't entirely fair. They weren't "judgy or preachy"—

To his relief, a beep echoed in his ears, reminding him how close he was to Crystal Mountain. Nowadays it no longer held the crystalline appearance of its namesake. With six-hundred-foot-tall trees hugging its slopes, it simply looked majestic.

"Beautiful ever so, a garden crafted by God," Logan repeated a Crystalian poem, and then accelerated the *Blade* to circle his home. It looked so peaceful, but his heart quickened when he wondered if this place would ever be found.

"Come on. I'm just letting Jim's paranoia get the best of me," he said, even though the Crystalian Governor had every right to be paranoid in this world.

For a second, Logan wondered if people were actually look-ing for him, people who had every reason to find someone who used to work for the CIA.

"No, they don't know where I am, and they're dead, dead," he said. He was just being ridiculous.

Ultimately, Logan decided to concentrate on his flying. He slowed the craft as it circled the Mountain's southeast slope. As he did so, a green, holographic dot morphed into an arrow, which pointed downward. He increased the output of the hover-drives, slowed to a stop and adjusted his altitude.

The craft promptly sank through the trees, without even a bump. As always to Logan's gratitude, the primary, secondary and backup holograms above the hangar's doors were proven to be working just fine.

Someone would have to be damned lucky to find us, he thought, and then in his best imitation of Arthor Jones: "Bastik! The Pan-zuer believes ne in such whimsy."

But, then, he noticed that his armor's right hand was shaking even though it was locked down. And he knew his suit wasn't malfunctioning.

Jim stood with Rebecca and Arthor in the dark while they waited for Logan to land. As a safety precaution, all the lights in Hangar Bay Two had been turned off so that the holograms wouldn't be compromised when the outer doors were opened.

St. John looked to his right. Rebecca looked his way briefly and smiled. Any hostility from a few days ago was gone. They even had their routine movie fest last night and had watched a terribly plebeian horror picture Logan had recommended.

They'd woken up the next morning snuggled up to each other on the couch—innocently!—enjoying each other's warmth.

He smiled back at her, the light from the holograms making her eyes twinkle. She, in turn, winked his way, and then looked back up at the ceiling.

He avoided reading her bioenergy. Afraid too—

Lisa.

He needed a distraction, so he glanced around the huge hangar, which was about three Old-Age football fields laid out side-by-side. It needed to be rather large, since HBII was where larger transports and hover vehicles took off, and where all vehicles landed. By contrast, HBI, named Agatha's Field in honor of the great General Lee Wallace's wife, was only the launch facility for smaller transports like HCs, HVs and fighter craft. Both new, they had been designed, tunneled out and built after the Executioners had been founded.

The original 850-year-old underground hangar had been decommissioned, and now housed the Crystal Mountain Museum of Science and Industry. Jim was glad he hadn't sold off everything in the old hangar. As nearly priceless relics, the vehicles had been perfect center pieces to start with, and from there other artifacts had been added to expand the museums' exhibits. With no other museums existing before, he'd been surprised by how many potential curators had been living here, since the Crystalian Natural History Museum, Center for Art and Culture, and many others quickly followed.

A light blinked in the corner of Jim's eye and he looked over toward a workstation. "Problem, Ecie?"

"Logan's exceeded the 160 mph protocol and circled the Mountain," Ecie sighed but didn't seem annoyed or worried.

"That's OK," Jim chuckled. "The *Blade* could probably do high Mach with those velocity shield envelops it has, and still do the random vector changes without any problems. Just make sure he doesn't crash."

"I know, but he's the one flying. I'm not promising anything."

Arthor and Rebecca heard that and laughed too. Jim had heard the Panocomptrix make a joke long ago, and he could only assume such behavior was normal.

"Well, do what you can." Jim nodded and looked at those around him. Unlike Jim, Rebecca and Arthor, the other Executioners, wore special eye pieces which allowed them to check their instruments without any trouble. They appeared perfectly content in the darkness.

Jim remembered what Anna once whispered to him during an extended walk long ago: "Living underneath, we got used to the long nights when the power went down. We didn't enjoy the raven's cloak, but we learned to feel some comfort by its presence."

He shook his head silently, thinking of those times. He thought of Anna. They hadn't spoken much—

"Where is he?" Rebecca whispered impatiently, and Jim

smiled, thinking about grabbing dinner with the tall blonde later.

Up above, the doors of the ten entrances were quite large, each 80 by 80 feet. Regardless of being made of state-of-the-art, harder-than-steel diterium-D, each weighed nearly eighty tons apiece.

Jim remembered the day they installed them, about three or so years ago, just before Arthor had arrived.

My luck the antigravs weren't working that day, he mused, thinking he had stopped loaning himself out as a mini-crane long before he had finished his accelerated schooling at MUTANTS. But the doors had not been heavy by his standards—far from it—and he figured it had given the Crystalians an opportunity to boss him around.

He looked up and tried to spy some type of flicker or other problem in the holograms above the doors. The H-grams, the fields, were perfect in fabrication—an appearance of reality and a form of substance to scanners if Ecie's disruptive realm was ever discovered. And they had been running in perfect precision long before the forest had been torn away and forced to grow around the openings with a specialized electromagnetic shield. Still, Jim eyed the simulated picture of dirt and rock above him very cautiously.

But no one will EVER find the Lair, he told himself. It was a promise he intended to keep.

"He's coming through," he said as he watched Logan drop down through the open set of doors.

"Where?" He heard the tone in Rebecca's voice, some envy there for the power that allowed Jim to see the Panzer through the hologram and the *Blade's* cloaking field. He grimaced, since it was a power he had once used to slaughter hundreds during his time with the AOM.

"There." He pointed just as the *Blade* de-cloaked above them.

The charcoal colored fighter craft, which often changed color depending on conditions, floated down, deployed its landing gear and settled quietly on the hard, composite deck. Then, the *Blade's* cockpit opened—allowing the large, weapon-covered ball, which was sitting in the middle, to dislodge and hop out. The ball quickly formed into a tiny walking tank with the power to destroy an entire army.

"Hey, Jim, what's up?" Logan said cheerfully, walked toward them and stopped near a receiving area for his suit.

"Logan, you're late. We were about to start breakfast without you."

"And you know how much we enjoy your stories," both Rebecca and Arthor jested in unison, knowing full well that the man couldn't tell a decent story worth a shit.

"Sorry … *Jim.*" The voice was muffled some when Logan popped the seals on the suit, removed the drive helmet and crawled out, revealing a black-haired man in his mid-twenties, who was older than Jim by a year. "But the last job was a tough one. I never realized that the Night Dragon was going to resemble an actual dragon. Maybe you should have taken care of Kenkaid's security system for me, Arthor?"

Jones gave an uneasy acknowledgment, knowing St. John's reservations about what Logan had done. That, and Arthor *used to be* a knight.

Fuck. Logan could really stick his foot in his mouth.

McMillian continued not even realizing his faux pas, "But everything went fine. The results should show within the next couple of days."

Jim was still uneasy about this whole plan, but it was too late now. He should have never underestimated Logan's resources and tenacity. Nevertheless, the Executioners were dead set on doing this, so Jim did his best to keep the fallout as minimal as possible. "Good, I hope those drug czars weren't too much trouble for you."

"Oh, Heaven's no." Logan pointed a thumb back at himself, while Jim smirked at the man's act of cockiness by trying to take on the perception of the perfect, stereotypical hero.

"Need someone to take out the trash? Who you gonna call?" Logan even did a little dance, as he mashed those two different movie quotes together. He was actually a very humble guy and, despite the bravado, he really didn't take killing lightly.

Jim just played along though, made the "fake phone" motion with one hand and pointed at Logan with the other, while both Arthor and Rebecca said, "Bruce Willis!"

Logan, throwing on some overalls to cover his biosuit, gave Jim the THUMBS UP, blew the other two a raspberry and signed in with the deck officer. All the while, Jim watched as the hangar's doors closed above.

Thankfully, nothing else came in—

"Well, OK then," Jim said, while blowing out the breath he was holding and started moving toward the exit. "If the big hero isn't too full of himself, we were planning on taking you to brunch, hungry?"

"Ecie isn't cooking, is he?"

Jim heard the computer snicker through their comlinks, then a snort. Logan laughed too.

"No, but we'll put the shells in the eggs anyway, since you seem to like them that way," Jim said as they walked out.

"Hey, HEY," came a shout. Jim turned, seeing how Rebecca had ruffled Logan's hair. She was trying, well not *really* trying, to give him a Wet Willy. "Dammit, Jim, now I know why I was brought here, eh? Just so I could be the object of everyone's sick and twisted jokes?"

"That's right," Jim readily agreed, turning back around, and heard the others catch up with him. Rebecca grabbed his right arm with a playful tug, while Arthor walked to his left.

Logan was to the right of the former Infiltrator. "Great, that's just great. What else have you got to say?"

"Well, you haven't been really eating synthetic 'chicken' eggs."

"God dammit! I knew it," Logan cursed. And Ecie's laughter followed them down the hallway.

Step. Slide. Step. Slide. Step. Bigsby Hammerson grimaced from the ache today. The bionics had never quite adjusted. They were always a constant reminder of his foolishness. Some people got to live with heartbreak and some, simply a scar. Not him though. Not him.

But we adapt. Have too. Thinking of that, the man smiled uneasily, while he walked down an immense hallway. It was draped with tapestries, representing figures in the Good Book. It was also lined with related sculptures of supposedly significant people who seemed to eye him as he walked.

He shuddered despite himself. It was always here—just as he passed *Abel*—when he would get a shiver. This part of the hallway always reminded him of betrayal.

His right cheek suddenly twitched too but not quite as much as it used to. In truth, he had adapted just like the old cliché. He had adapted, regardless of dreams and nightmares that seemed to manifest only on the quietest of nights.

But it's not the same, not nearly the same, he reassured himself. He'd been employed here for about six years. Yet the surroundings were similar enough, and they constantly reminded him of past mistakes. Ones he would never allow to repeat.

As long as I'm appreciated, that's enough, he smirked, more confidently this time. He nodded as well, and his right hand gripped the information that was enclosed in a yellow packet.

Thinking of something more immediate, he shook his head while he waddled along. *It feels pretty thick, and I'm sure he's going to say something about this,* he sighed, eying the envelope. *He's told them, what, a hundred times, more?* he then chuckled as he fingered the seal along the packet.

"But they work hard, wanting to please him." He shrugged, knowing that his boss paid everyone very well and was actually well liked. He had to admit that even he liked his boss almost like a friend, all tirades beside.

But I'll never trust anyone that much again, he told himself. He'd managed a strict professionalism for six years now, and didn't have any plans to change it. An Accounting professor once told him that friendship blurred professionalism, and you should never be friends with the boss. Bigsby's mechanical leg reminded him of that advice every day.

He moved past the cathedral-like ceilings capping the hallway. He listened as he went. His walk toward his boss' office caused echoes to bounce here and there and back to him. Again, he looked at the statues, which seemed to grin as he slid by them. Were they laughing at fate, his foolishness and his overconfidence in friendship?

Laugh all you want, he thought and otherwise ignored these villains and heroes of superstition and myth of an old world. He was content with the knowledge that they were immobile and could not move at all. Therefore he continued on in—what he considered at least—his own sardonic and wistful way.

The air from the HVAC system blew his curly brown hair with its subtle touch. It was hot today and his face was covered in sweat, and his cheeks sagged and pushed outward. Adding to his discomfort, his red "power" tie was knotted tightly around the collar of a shirt that was one size too small. By now, his face probably matched the color of his tie.

He laughed to himself and questioned why he seemed in such a mood. But like it or not, this was his style. And, even though he felt his tie digging into his neck and despite his boss frequently telling him not to bother, Bigsby fashioned it anyway.

Bigsby. His past should have forced him to change his name; however, it was the memory of his parents keeping him from changing it completely.

Besides, Marie—He came up to a set of doors at the end of the hallway. They were solid in modest words, a core of steel covered by expensive oak and mahogany from the Southern Hemisphere. It completed its purpose—preventing him from entering without invitation. He shrugged his shoulders and rapped the obstacle in three sharp rhythms.

"Yeah?" a sharp retort. Muffled curses followed.

Bigsby's cheek twitched again. He knew and disliked the tone that had lashed out from behind the barrier. He had witnessed similar confrontations long ago, from another time.

Why do I care? he asked himself. He didn't need this today. He began to turn around.

"Come in." There was a click, and he knew his bum left leg hadn't moved fast enough. With no other option, he just waited for the double doors to open fully.

Sunlight entered his gray globes as he walked into Henry Harvardson's office. He noticed a faux fire pit in the center. Lining the left and far walls, books were collecting dust, waiting for the day when Harvardson would have some free time to read them. Armor and ancient weapons decked the human-size figures standing like guardians for the person that practically lived in this place. The person whose screams now pounded on the stout CFO's ears.

"I don't care what you do as long as it's done. You *got* me, Smithers?" Brown hair, about sixty years-old, shook with the same rhythm Henry Harvardson kept with his baritone curses and bobbing head.

Bigsby made a face. He only knew the age of his boss because the old guy had told him once. Otherwise Harvardson didn't look much older than middle-age. Even his voice sounded youthful.

Harvardson was standing behind a large mahogany desk. He rolled his eyes after each apparent excuse from the VP of Operations on the other end of the line. Hammerson, still in the entryway and yet thinking about age, figured his administrator could easily live to a hundred and twenty.

If, that is—he walked halfway to the desk before stopping again on an Old Russian rug—*if he doesn't get a coronary.* Bigsby, with some satisfaction, didn't let the smile slip.

"OK. OK." Harvardson calmed a little but the irritation still seemed to persist. He sat down into his chair. The big desk in the back of the large room seemed to dwarf the man, but he was still a head taller than Bigsby's five-foot-eight. "All right, just make sure you get those things operating by Sunday. We can't afford to have them down for much longer, not with those bastards out there. Got it?

"All right, good." The receiver was slammed down, and Harvardson let out another curse. For the last few weeks, the new missile defense systems had been creating havoc with the security net, and the old man seemed to have had enough.

Subsequently, the CFO decided to wait it out and not add to the commotion; however, despite his wishes, he had not been overlooked.

"What is it, Bigs?" His employer brought his hands to his temples, as though trying to rub the life back into them. "You know, if you stand there too long, Bertha might start dusting you as well?"

"Sorry, sir, I just didn't want to disturb—"

"Bigsby, how many times do I have to tell you? It's Hen—Ah, never mind, just give me the packet."

"Here you go, Mr. Harvardson. The labs were one hundred percent accurate in their findings. I'm sure you'll agree that their efforts were worth the—"

His boss snatched the packet from him and shook his head, while he searched for the letter opener. "Geez, did they ever get my memo? Don't they know the dangers of paper cuts?"

Bigsby stepped back a bit, preparing himself for another outburst. "Well, I don't really—"

"Relax, Bigs. It's a joke." Henry rolled his eyes and looked down at the book his people had prepared for him. Bigsby thought about the thoroughness the labs and research teams went through, but he knew Harvardson had only wanted a simple synopsis.

"Ah, let's see"—Henry thumbed through the document —"Table of Contents … 23 chapters? One of them is about discrepancies in competitive supply stations, another about overall output in the next four years. Hmm, growth rate for the subspecies Ancacharthus Poliproium? Oh, here we go, on Chapter 17, Competitors' Current Status."

Bigsby had been Harvardson's Chief Financial Officer for six years, but he had never seen a smile as great as the one his chief now presented. For a moment, he wondered if he would have to ask Dr. Stein to come in and fix it, but he decided to put his faith in the elasticity of the human skin for now.

"Do you know what this means, my boy?" Henry shouted. Bigsby, however, noted that it almost sounded musical. "Why, with those deadbeats out of the way, we'll finally be able to ship our exports out in full.

"Get your books in order, son, because in the next few days we're going to make quite an impact. Woo-hoo!" Bigsby actually took a step back. Henry actually hooted. "Tell Smithers, get the computers going, warm up the trucks, check the status on our own supplies, and let's prepare to fill the void."

"Yes, sir," the bookkeeper "whooped" back too. His boss' mood was a bit contagious. The information had instigated a better response than what he had even anticipated. He turned toward the exit. "Anything else?"

"Thanks, Bigs. No." Harvardson shook his head and grabbed for the phone-shaped comlink.

"Very well." He walked out of Henry's office, almost feeling the same excitement the old guy had seemed to unleash. However, hearing something just before the thick doors closed behind him, he soon shook his head and frowned in concern.

"Get me Frugal," he repeated Harvardson's order, and quickly felt the facial tick—a sign of stress that had developed after the shit that was his life.

Bigsby quickened his pace to his office. The statues tried to mock him once more. But, if his fears came to life, they would be the least of his worries.

Jennifer Hendricksen risked a glance out the window. A bonfire roared next door. An occasional explosion echoed in the distance, but the automated bell at the nearby church still rang at noon. Screams and howls came from alcoves she could not see.

She knew Hillmount Estates would never be the same. She shivered, like countless other times in the last few hours—but less than before, considerably less than last night.

She eyed the bars outside the window. A testament to her family's stubbornness, the self-installing barricades had been put in place so that her family could stay until the numerous criminals and nightboys—ruthless cyborgs modified for various illegal professions—could be rounded up. Her family hadn't really thought there would be much trouble this far deep into the town but this simple precaution had already saved them countless times. That is, until they hadn't.

"Still, there are others that it keeps out." She gripped the pistol that was in her hand. The Hi-Ball Eliminator's kick was heavy for its size, less than ten inches in overall length. But she was getting used to the recoil.

Despite her age, her parents had given her the weapon a few years ago. She didn't know why, and had rarely ever shot it until now. None of her friends had had any interest in firearms, and she never mentioned that she'd owned one around any of them. Naturally, it wasn't illegal to own a weapon outside of the megacity or otherwise. Even kids could get special licenses to own one for competition. However, Jen didn't have such a license, and, even though she was quite accurate with it, had no desire to compete as a marksman. Nor had her parents suggested she ever do such a thing.

So what would I have used it for? she asked herself derisively. Now knowing the answer, she laid the weapon back down on her thigh.

A whine entered her ears.

"Sorry, Max," she said and rubbed her little furry friend behind the ears. "I was just checking my gun."

The owner of the long snout, black coat and forest-green eyes looked up at her, as if mocking interest.

"Just go back to sleep then," she said, brushing his brow. In response, the animal that had been by her side for the past hour, yawned and laid his head back down. She stroked his head lovingly.

There was a creak upstairs. Max's ears perked. She listened more intently too. The world squeaked again, and she raised her weapon. She scanned the living room and soon focused on a red dot trekking across the far wall. She tried to find a target within the walls and ceiling, anything she could unload thirty 8.5mm high-velocity rounds of steel slugs into. But she only found vases, plants and paintings stacked against her.

The ceiling groaned again, followed by frantic footsteps. And suddenly having to resist the tears that tried to fill her eyes, Jen chuckled instead, when she realized that there was someone up there trying to cram twenty years of her life into a handful of suitcases.

"Mom, is everything all right?" she asked, having to make sure.

"Yeah," an anguished moan flowed down the stairwell, but Jen somehow knew the difference between this and other. "I'll be down in a few minutes. Any sign of your father?"

"No, not yet." Jen squeezed her pistol's grip, seeing something near a neighbor's garage. "I'm sure I saw a piece of vibranium armor near the Tortelli's garage. I don't know how much time we'll have."

"Don't worry. He'll be here. Just relax and keep a look out." Quiet, then a bump from upstairs, and then another pause, before: "But how … how are you doing?"

"OK." Jennifer trembled, holding her gun a little more tightly, and brought Max even closer to her after she heard her mother's tone and the nurturing in the voice.

Last night a K-5-packing nightboy had made it through the perimeters, broke the code to the electromagnetic lock and had walked into where she'd been sleeping. Until that moment, Jen and her family had told themselves that they'd be safe. The bars would hold and the security system would keep anyone out until the Army National Guard arrived.

She remembered how terrified she was when she woke up to see a large helmet that covered half a face; the massive cannon a biomech-surgeon had molded to the nightboy's arm; and a twisted smile on pale, nearly dead lips.

Jen felt her palm grow numb, as she pressed it hard into the pistol's grip, wishing she had had the weapon then. Even now, she could still imagine the cyborg reaching down to touch her. And she raised her legs up as she did then too, trying to prevent the inevitable and resist the might a NB could wield.

She shook suddenly, when a sharp, "after-a-storm" smell seemed to reenter her nose—ozone released by sparks from his circuitry. She still thought she heard his rapid breath of arousal, and envisioned the color of his pale-white skin, which also hinted of poor biomechanics and questionable bioelectronic surgery.

Death, Oblivion and Eternity plagued her thoughts now too, remembering how she had tried to scream. But he'd clutched a cold, armored and lifeless hand over her jaw.

"I never thought my savior was going to be in the form of a dog," she whispered, snapping out of her dark vision, and petted her companion, lightly as not to wake him up again.

Max had come unseen, had howled and growled. He had risked being shot by a ten-millimeter cannon, thereby alerting her father. Mr. Hendricksen immediately ran into the room and sprayed the monster with a few rounds of a heavy slinger rifle, which had literally painted the NB's body across Jen's wall.

She had tried to sleep in her parents' room the rest of the night. Hadn't dared enter her room, nor would ever do so. Her father, having had enough, was out looking for an armored van to move whatever meager stuff they'd take with them.

Hendricksen looked out the window again, seeing the burning bonfires on the lawns next door. A couple of police cars lay in pieces a block away. She couldn't see them now, but she knew they were there, part of a blockade the escapees from the Rockford Criminal Corrections Center had wiped out.

Understandably, many families had left the city of Hillmount Estates just as hundreds of rioting night boys, prostitutes, drug assassins, racketeers, and whoever had broken out of the prison's southeast wing. Left before that scum had made their way here to this once thriving community.

She, as with her parents and many other inhabitants of the community, had thought the police would have stopped the detainees. To their dismay, the villains had quickly slaughtered the waiting patrols and then had decided to take up residence, spreading themselves throughout the city. Meanwhile, the governor of Toldeclevchikee had declared a state of emergency in regards to the "Hillmount" matter. And, before communication networks died, he promised to send in the National Guard.

Where the hell were they? That had been three days ago. Everyone she'd known was gone. A tear forced itself out and rolled down her cheek anyway when she thought of the overused saying.

"Home is where you hang your hat." She had hung her hat here for seventeen years of her life, which was the total existence of Jennifer Terrisa Hendricksen. And although she was currently emotionally numb, she also knew the sadness would hit harder later.

Thinking about the locked door to a room that she would never open, and thinking about the fires that burned on so many of her neighbors' lawns, she simply wiped the tears off her upper lip and cheek.

"Let it be later then," she whispered.

"Hey!" someone shouted.

She spun her head to look out a window and spied the person who shouted. He was across the street, where an arranged agreement must have gone sour.

An assault nightboy, much like the one she had faced last night, jumped out of a downed hovercar and sent a series of rounds through his unarmored adversary. There had been a shout and a *thump*. Then a packet of pills flew from the opened hands of a Swiss-cheesed corpse. Apparently, a "guns and ammo" store and the local police headquarters had provided the killers here with more than enough ammunition to settle such arguments.

Jen watched the NB run to the victim, grab the pills and then bound behind a nearby house. She thought of the lifetime struggle the NB would always face, and she shook her head. She knew the drugs eased the pain caused by the poor surgery the cyborgs, bionic freaks or street bionuts suffered from. They needed the substances, since it was the only way their minds could function properly—function so that they could seek out quick wealth, prestige and, ultimately, her hate.

Would she ever feel pity for those suffering from such addictions again? She rubbed Max's head again. He was snoring.

"Jen, are you done packing yet?" A familiar voice came from upstairs.

"Yeah, Mom," she said but without sounding irritated, even though her mom obviously had forgotten that she'd packed Jen's things last night. "But there's still no sign of Dad."

"Patience, Jen. Your father will be here soon enough. I'm sure he'll be running through the door at any second."

"I hope so," she sighed, noticing two men in tattered clothes pointing in her house's direction. She checked the power reserves on the Hi-Ball's battery again; laid the weapon back down with her hand still gripped around it; and closed her eyes and tried to take a nap. She was sure that the alarms would go off if those men tried to cross the perimeter.

"And God help them then." She smiled bitterly, even when the smell of ozone returned.

Her mother shouted, "Jen, your dad's—"

CRACK-BOOM!

Her house, her very life seemed to explode in her face. The world shook, she shuddered. Max howled and jumped off the couch. Her palm squeezed hard composite, she blinked out any disorientation, and her eyes sought for a red dot that she'd use to end the life of anyone seeking to harm her family.

Her eyes scanned the walls and quickly saw the dot near the family entryway. It then cut through the smoke and dust, created by the apparent explosion. Her trigger finger squeezed—

"What are you doing?" A scream seemed to shatter glass over her heartbeats. "Splicin' McNeil, Jen, it's your father for Christ's sake!"

"Hmm?" *Really?* She holstered the pistol and ran to the edge of the billowing cloud of dust and steam. She saw a shadow come out of a dark cargo hold, and then jumped into her father's arms when he finally got close. She hugged tightly, happy to see him.

"I wasn't gone that long, was I?" he joked, but she felt his hand gently caressing her shoulder. It made her feel safe, safe enough.

"Sorry. I know you wanted to leave sooner. It just took longer than I thought to get the van. But it'll be over soon, Noogy Monster."

She closed her eyes and hugged him more tightly. Usually, she hated that nickname. But today, like back when she was nine, she was proud to have been such a terror around the neighborhood. "I'm just glad you're home."

"I know." Even though her face was buried into his shoulder, she could tell he was smiling.

"David, thank God." Jen heard her mother running down the stairs, a strap of a suitcase hitting each step. "I thought you'd never get here."

Did she fall into her father's arms before or after her mother had come down the stairs? David Hendricksen was soon hugging them both.

A whine came from somewhere in the living room. Jen turned and saw Max pull himself out from beneath the coffee table. Her mother reached down and picked up the four-month-old pup, cooing him softly.

"Are you guys ready?" Her father looked her way and then at her mother. Jen only auto-bobbed her head. She threw a gaze at her three suitcases and ammo box, which had almost been obliterated by a twelve-ton transport. Obviously not taking anything to chance, her father had simply plowed the van's rear end right into the house. Jennifer doubted the insurance company would be happy.

"I need some more help," her mother said. She was pointing in the same direction she had come, and was pleading with amber-green eyes. She passed Max over to Jen.

"OK, Theia," her father groaned, apparently already exhausted. He had gotten no sleep at all. But, really, none of them had. "Jen, get Max into the van. We'll be down soon."

She watched them run upstairs and out of sight. She looked at the empty stairwell. Then a hiss from one of the van's landing jets caused Max to shake and give a frightened whine.

"OK, OK," she conceded and took the pup into the cockpit of the van, managing to somehow strap him into one of the seats. It only took a couple minutes for her to get her bags, put them into the cargo hold, and then belt herself into one of the three remaining cockpit seats.

"Odd, auto-defensive systems still work, along with the 30mm cannons," she whispered, looking at the cockpit surrounding her. She wondered where her dad had managed to pick up this monstrosity that was still armed. It was over thirty feet long, ten feet high, and nine feet wide. It could have taken down most of the house when it had landed. It was old by its markings, probably about five decades, but still.

Whimpering entered her ears again. She looked beside her, seeing Max with his snout pressed up against one of the windows.

"What is it?" she asked, nudging forward, as much as the seatbelt would give. "A nightboy? something else?" She couldn't see anyone nearby, although there were people gathering across the street, but only in curiosity it seemed. Were they looking at her?

"Mom, Dad?" she shouted.

She didn't hear an answer, but her parents were probably still packing.

"Stay here, Max," she said, about to hit the strap release on her belts; however, the cub wailed and bit at his belts.

"What?" She looked out the window again in frustration.

There was a flash and the people across the street disappeared. She thought she heard—

KA-CRACK!

An explosion, loud, blinding and ground shaking—the van jerked and tipped and the tail end ripped out from the house.

Alarms rang in her ears, and her hands grabbed onto her seat. Max howled and screamed. Jennifer did too.

KA-CRACK. KA-BOOM. KA-CRACK!

Another series of explosions seemed to shake the whole

world, and then the van lurched and spun hard with centripetal force.

"Daddy! Mommy!" she screamed, fearing the worst. Then there was another flash, another explosion, another lurch, and another howl before—

Darkness.

CHAPTER FOUR

Patriotism is the last refuge of a scoundrel.
(Letters to the Earl of Chesterfield)
**—Samuel Johnson, English
Lexicographer (1775 A.D.)**

A single, large metal wall stood in a huge chamber. Its light-gray surface, a metallic/ceramic material, reflected some of the bright calimar lighting above. It was taller than any man. It was wider than a car and thick as a battleship's hull. Nearly hard as diamond, it reflected sounds off its irresistible face.

Then—*Bang!*—it was gone. Pieces flew everywhere—shards of shrapnel and dust to be sent to the recyclers.

"How was that?" Jim sheathed his blades, rubbed his knuckles where they had rung from the powerful hit. He turned toward the rear corner of the training center. A round station jetted out from there. Windows encased the entire protrusion, which provided a panoramic view of the entire area.

"Hmm, could you have made a little more noise?" Arthor's voice echoed irascibly in Jim's helmet.

"Well, you know, I just thought you were falling asleep up there. Maybe you shouldn't have stayed up so late last night."

"Right, you were the one who brought that movie over to begin with. I don't know how you and Rebecca are able do that to me. Why didn't you two just bother Logan?"

"Pish-posh," Jim laughed, even though Arthor couldn't see the grin behind his mask. "He just doesn't seem to have an appreciation for ancient American cinema like you do."

"Yeah, funny, it's not like he doesn't have a collection of shit like that," Arthor Jones grunted acrimoniously. Everyone knew that Logan was known for staying up late, watching some of the worst Old World and Panterian World movies. Subsequently, the ex-CIA man often joked that this was the reason why he showed little compassion for his prey.

"You know, I got a lot of equipment up here that I have to monitor without you pestering me," Jones finally said. "I can't let Ecie take all the credit."

"Yeah," the computer joked too.

"Well, I guess so." Jim made a quick glance at the other Executioners around him. Some of the things they were now capable of astonished even him. About a year ago, he had turned the job of combat training over to the Crytonian, and Arthor had to be commended for his guidance.

Yeah, he told himself, *they've become accomplished killers, just like they wanted.* Despite his feelings about the matter, Jim knew that Arthor had to train the Crystalians—had to train them if they were to survive a fight.

"All right, Arthor," Jim sighed then threw a quick glance toward Rebecca, who was currently dodging a series of laser attacks. Today her long, blonde hair was bound tight, and her bodysuit looked like it was painted on.

St. John chided himself, bit his lower lip as punishment, and then looked back up at the observation platform. "OK, Arthor," he said, remembering the movie last night and deciding to quote one of its awful lines. "Let's do dis tang."

Rebecca heard a war call and turned her head in the direction of its tenor pitch. She looked at the man that had talked her into watching an old movie, a horrible movie he had gotten from Ecie the night before. Now, though, she didn't see the boyish grin and handsome features she considered so attractive. She only saw the monster, the demon, the very beast he said that he kept dormant inside him.

Behind him, a forcefield flashed periodically when something massive hit him, thereby protecting those around him. Awestruck, she shook her head in disbelief. She'd once thought she'd seen nearly everything that the AOM had created. However, because Arthor had managed to actually set up a somewhat taxing training session for him, a program without any safety controls, she knew she had been wrong. She watched Jim's talons slash through titanium, his fists pound through heavy, round metal targets and his arms knock aside hundred-ton beams as if they were made of Styrofoam.

She had seen Old World movies that had heroes with blades like his and with powers that rivaled anything of the beasts today. Still, she knew those were simply fantasies and she knew that there was—

No other like him, she thought, but, just as quickly, shook it out. *A friend, nothing more, can't be*—

"Shit!" Something hit her side, and she buckled to the floor. Her body shuddered again, but this time from temporary pain. She was only human, and her lungs pushed out a scream.

"Artemis." She heard her nickname even though her ears were ringing. "Ye knoweth better than dat." Verengoshian echoed, too. The language sounded so much like neo-classic—not entirely like how Anderson used to speak it but close enough. "What were you thinking?" Arthor asked. "Medium Cyber-lasers don't get confused when their targets stop moving."

"I know, Art." She waited for her breath to come back. This would be the first and last time she would be hit by one of Arthor's Cybernetic laser imitations. "I was just thrown off balance from the last attack. I should have pivoted with my left foot instead. I wasn't thinking."

"I see." She heard his fingers drum on a control panel, knowing he was looking at the replay of her defensive posture, and saw her wild card. He didn't call it out though: "Well, I guess last night hit us all pretty hard, except for Jim. How long did you two stay up and watch that thing anyway?"

"We watched all of it. I don't know why. I don't know how. But he's human," she laughed. "I caught him off-duty once sleeping in his chair."

"Great, I'll remember that the next time he talks to me about —What?"—the Crytonian was pulled from their conversation —"No, she's all right, just got caught off guard, that's all."

Rebecca wondered who asked, and she felt herself gulp—*a gulp?* She was still on her knees, and her abdomen was still tight, since her body was still trembling from the beam. She raised her head up and discovered exactly what she had feared—seeing St. John staring in her direction.

Rebecca saw her own reflection in the oval mask he wore, and she wondered what he was thinking, what he thought of—

She turned away. *Can't let him see me like this, or at least have me see him see me this way,* she told herself. She felt giddy from the beam, and she damned the realness of the training laser. *But that's why I didn't go to him after killing Eric. We're friends. That's all.*

Feeling silly for such a childish response, however, she looked back his way, but found him already on another level of his training program. She felt sick—obviously still from the beam.

"Rebecca?"

"Yah?"

"That was Jim. He knew it was the first time you were hit by the laser, and he said to squeeze your abdomen muscles tightly and breathe deeply to rid yourself of the numbness.

"Pretty simple, but according to others—since he's unaffected by electromagnetic attacks—he said it's quicker that way. But of course, you can always consider my suggestion."

"And that is?" She was looking at Jim train while she flexed her abdominal muscles.

"Continue on with your level."

"Right." She stood up and turned to face the weapon she had been hit by. She took another deep breath, feeling the rest of the numbness ease away, and then thought of pain and what the sight of it often did to friendships.

I can't have that. He won't have that. She looked up into Arthor's direction. "OK, Art," she said, crouched down and pulled out her twelve-inch-long Deflonalé knife.

The Cybernetic laser moved to aim. She jumped aside before it fired, threw the knife perfectly into its targeting array and ended the level barely after Arthor yelled, "Go!"

Logan's suit registered a nearly blurring number of hard recoils, each slamming into the Panzer's armored palm. But he could distinguish every electromagnetic kick, every shot fired at a stack of sandbags fifty yards from him.

The targets were at the end of a firing lane, one of several hundred. A counter was elevated before him, but he ignored it, preferring to holster each weapon after being fired. And he fired with relentless precision, emptying each gun, and quickly replacing it with another. In all, he wore ten weapons. Most couldn't be fired without the suit, since the recoils of the pistols alone could shatter the arm of an average Joe.

Something impressive to think about, he considered. He, however, was thinking about the other day in the *Blade*. It was a moment of weakness, which caused him to tremble, a moment of weakness that got the better of him.

"Don't see my hands shaking now," he mumbled and cursed to himself, directing his comment to no one in particular, or at least no one he could be sure of.

"Come and get me. Come and get me. Try it." He continued his onslaught on the bags. Sand covered the floor all around. Then, throwing caution to the wind, Logan pulled out his antimatter rifle, his primary sniper weapon, and set it on a low proton group. He eyed a sandbag that hadn't yet been hit. He aimed and fired. The chamber flashed and rocked with a low-yield explosion. And he detonated another four proton groups and obliterated any evidence that the sandbags ever existed.

He cursed again. Despite the biofeedback he was getting from his suit, McMillian was breathing heavy. Despite the environmental controls to prevent such, he was sweating. Despite everything he tried, his hands were indeed shaking.

Logan gritted his teeth and set the antimatter rifle aside. He grabbed a canister housed in the armor's thigh and another weapon in a case above the armor's waist. He locked the two together, and grinned. "Nid Hog will feast on your broiled bones." He triggered the weapon, and flame and plasma engulfed—

"Logan, stop. Stop!" Ecie shouted. "Put the flame thrower down. Please. Snap out of it."

McMillian released the trigger. Glass glistened over the floor of the firing range, with flames burning on most of it. He shuddered within the armor and crumbled to its knees, dropped the weapon to the ground before he popped the suit's seams. He needed some sleep badly.

"Logan, are you all right? Do you want me to get Dr. Kyle? I'm sure he'll be able to help—"

"No, Ecie." Logan pulled out of the suit, pulled off the drive helmet and wiped the perspiration from his face. "Please don't tell anyone. They're my own demons. Don't tell anyone, please."

"All right." The computer seemed to hesitate this time. "I will do as you ask. The mess won't even appear on the logs."

"Thank you, again." Logan squeezed back into the armor and then unhooked the fuel cylinder from his flamethrower. He got back up to the armor's feet and looked over the mess he had created. He knew Jim wouldn't have been upset about the mess, especially if the Crystalian Leader knew what was going on.

He frowned.

Shit, like I know?

"Rebecca, wait up." She turned, hoping it was someone else. But sure enough, Jim came running toward her.

She sighed, somewhat defeated. She hadn't made it out soon enough. She should have skipped the shower since she hadn't really worked up a sweat.

With a few strides, he was by her side. He held a welcoming smile, one similar to the one she'd seen about five months ago. Not long before he'd asked her to join the Executioners.

"Can I ask you something?" Jim said then quickly nodded to a young soldier walking toward the training center.

"About?" She nodded. Rebecca watched him fasten another button on his shirt, showing the rush he had made in getting dressed too. She hoped he wouldn't bring up the laser.

"Do you have any new projections on the trade?"

The Drug Trade. She wondered why she gave a silent sigh. "Oh, I haven't gotten much new."

"It's just," he said, while he stared down the hallway immersed in thought. "I was looking at your last report, and then from our latest inforun. It looks like the old drugs aren't even being touched."

"Uh, hmm." She made a mental check for anything else to help him. The news hadn't surprised either of them, even though Logan wasn't all that happy about it.

"That new drug, nirv, the one we found after the cleanup of Hillmount, lots of reports on that. We're still running tests on it." Jim frowned, puzzled for the same reasons as she was. "I don't know. Maybe it's addictive if it's used under prolonged circumstances? Otherwise, how can it be preferred over coca, let alone disperal?

"Of course no one's willing to try it amongst us. Sake of science or not," Jim half joked, scratched the back of his head and then grew somewhat solemn. "Besides, Logan would have a tizzy, and I don't care to play the guinea pig anymore."

Rebecca didn't say anything, knowing Jim would take the drug himself if he had to. She needed to talk to Dad later to see if he knew anything about it. Needless to say it probably wouldn't do anything at all in Jim's system. Nothing—including poisons, biochemical weapons, toxic gases, even bullets—seemed to affect his metabolism and regenerative powers. Some things had, like those designed by the FGGO; however, despite everything the

FGGO had done to prevent such, Jim's body had developed inhibitors to those behavior-controlling, artificial hormones as well.

They walked the hallway slowly. She realized they'd tested the new drug with a variety of different human compounds, seeing if there were any reactions. Molecularly, the substance itself— sold as a light pink powder—didn't share any forms that were often abused. In fact, Crystal Mountain's Central Lab had identified it simply as a steroidal derivative.

Reports from the street suggested nirv was a hallucinogen, and it had quickly substituted what the Panzer had helped reduce weeks before. To date, however, best simulations suggested that nirv slightly increased activity in the Frontal Lobe; however, it was only a slight increase. Its structure resembled a few known drugs that helped patients suffering from schizophrenia and other mental illnesses, so it could be a street version of those.

But that's where the research stopped. Like Jim said, no one in Crystal Mountain would risk taking nirv. Most of the designer drugs developed within the last century created immediate addiction—the very reason the Executioners had planned to eliminate disperal and other such drugs in the first place.

Rebecca figured the next step would seek out a user in the field and take medical scans. Then, in turn, take the junky to a detox clinic, since they didn't like the idea of enabling users to see its affects.

"In any case," Jim said, fixing his collar. "I can't really force myself to pursue this matter much further."

"What?" Rebecca stopped. Not this again. "You've got to be kidding me, right, of all the people? How can you let this stuff go on? Weren't you controlled by one during your time at the Agency? Don't you remember what it did to you?

"Clearly you do," she said, her hands shaking. "You've told

me every time you think about the Battle of Henderson. The weapons encased in your arms. The death of Lisa."

"It wasn't entirely the drug," Jim sighed, shrugged, and looked away. Was he thinking of the woman Rebecca had just named? The woman he still loved? "The hormones they used to manipulate me were in everything—in my food, drink and medicine. But it's not the same with the general public. Out there people do it by their own free will. Who are we to judge?"

"But the Panterian Guard seems to condone it, and shouldn't that be enough? You say it might not be addictive, but what does the drug actually do in the body? Remember, it's not a natural substance." She felt as though she was giving Logan's argument all over again, but her own initial years in Infiltration were her motivation.

Silence. They started walking again. "You're right." Jim finally nodded, but still seemed skeptical. They all knew the whole scope of this plan lacked real direction.

Who will really benefit, besides those seeking such ends? Rebecca conceded despite herself. She knew that St. John really needed to get more involved. Otherwise Logan was going to get them into a lot of trouble, since that man wanted all drugs gone. And that wouldn't do anyone any good.

"I guess," Jim seemed to think out loud, "that I am tired of seeing people getting rich off of others' vices, and watching children die from a substance they don't really understand. Maybe there will be something positive that will come out of this in the long run. I hope so."

He looked her way while they moved down the corridor. She smiled reassuringly. Because of the lighting here, a few shadows rested on his cheeks, under his nose and lips, and under his chin; however, somehow, this particular part of the hallway seemed brighter today.

Rebecca returned his gaze and looked deeply into his dark amber eyes. She thought about his convictions and compulsions.

I love his energy, his smile—

Immediately, she buried such thoughts and forced herself to look down the corridor, just in time to nod at a technician walking past them, and then at a squad jogging toward the Training Center. Finding that she was tongue-tied, she didn't have much more to say on the subject at hand. But she really didn't want to leave either. Rebecca figured that she really needed to say something soon or—

"Breakfast? I'm cooking." He grinned quickly to lighten the mood. "Let's give this a rest. Besides, I have some new plants that I'd like to show you back at my place. They're blueberries from South America, and they're producing too."

"Sure, I could use some pancakes. Can I have blueberries in mine?" she laughed. He knew, as well as she did, many problems were never solved if they were continuously brooded over. Even Executioners had to forget their business every once in a while.

"Absolutely, young lady." Jim winked. What's more, Jim could cook one helluva breakfast.

"The sky once again took on its characteristics of sunset. Sol seemed to burn its last breath. And the chariot, steaming from the chase, fell slowly behind the Rocky Mountains, beautiful ever so." John looked around in the cabin of his hovercar, after reciting some of Rebecca's prose. He'd never written anything he— or anyone—would ever say was from his heart. Possibly his search for the wizard would never end.

He grimaced then at that shitty cliché. Evidently he could fake feeling sorry for himself extremely well.

"Still sleepy?" he asked, trying to think of something else. His right hand slid from the controls and rested on his passenger. John brushed the cat's head and cheek. The liger kept his eyes tightly closed, even though John could see how he moved closer to his hand. His new friend didn't like heights.

Couldn't tigers climb trees if they wanted to? "Don't worry. We're almost there, Scythe." His hand moved to the back of the animal's head, between the ears, prompting a left leg to shake.

Anyone else would have smiled, would have laughed at the sight. Instead John tried to keep from thinking about how he didn't do either. His friends, obviously, would probably question his choice of names, even though the liger's claws had simply reminded him of the old reaping tool. They, however, would probably say something about how he hated Infiltration more than he let on. Sure, it had been three years since he'd left home, three years since he'd set out to find the people responsible for dishonoring his parents.

"FEMET," he whispered quietly, not wanting to disturb his new charge. His mother and father also had been recruited for the Fetal Manipulation Experiments. But, unlike Rebecca, his parents had managed to escape from the FGGO. And in their search for freedom, they had sought out sanctuary in Japan.

After the Fall of the World and its own financial collapse, the nation developed advanced martial arts facilities for the armies of surrounding city states. Undoubtedly in its own best interest, Japan had been the driving force behind such treaties as the *Ecological Preservation Agreements* and the *Henry-Kilaraki Disarmament Talks*, which helped eliminate the global use of nuclear weapons and thereby protect precious ecosystems. Therefore, throughout the Apocalypse, Japan had become a well-respected and valuable training center for almost every other government.

"ETA for Crystal Mountain in five minutes," the car's

onboard computer said without sounding too perky.

"Thanks," John said and sneered at the AI's best efforts at sparing his feelings. He lowered the thrust on his repulsars and began a landing sequence, while thinking about his hometown of Moki.

The town, essentially, was a safe haven created in 2875, when the Panterian Guard had suspected that Japan's Grand Masters were instructing rebel armies and began to imprison them. Luckily, thanks to the *Spiritual Enlightenment Act of 2865 A.D.*, the right to create spiritual communities to help the world cope with the Unification, thousands of settlements began springing up around the world. That of course had made it difficult for the newly formed Panteria to keep accurate counts of who all lived at such places. Moki, being one of these communities, provided a home for several refugees from the old training centers.

By the time John was born, six decedents of such Masters lived in the village. One, Jupa Tomolota, a teacher of Aikido, had noticed a six year old John running along the top of a narrow fence. Impressed by the young boy's balance, the Grand Master asked John's parents if he could begin instruction.

Ironically, his parents had thought this good for their son, which was something physical, cultural and something to lure him out of his shell. They readily agreed.

"They blamed themselves." John remembered how his mom had cried when he'd left to find the FGGO three years ago. She didn't understand that they couldn't have stopped his training anyway. It had been the only time he'd truly felt alive.

"Cliché," he said quietly, but thought about his mom, dad, teachers and friends. He had no real attachments to any of them. No admiration. No feelings of joy. No love. Only an overwhelming sense of honor, which made John wonder if his parents ever feared him. Especially when they'd set him down one day and told him about the FEMET for the first time.

"Had they feared their emotionless, fifteen year old son?" he whispered to himself. "Did they fear the boy that had become a black belt in Ninjitsu, a green belt in Tara-Dow, and a Master of both Aikido and Kendo-Samurai?"

He glanced at Scythe, finding the cat wasn't even listening. "But did it go back farther than that?" he asked. "Had they even feared the little boy who'd never whimpered in the night or screamed from his nightmares?

"I don't know. Maybe they hadn't feared me," he conceded. "If so they probably would have never told me about FEMET."

Back then, he hadn't even argued about his Fate. He'd simply sat in front of them, sat and experienced the worst feeling of dread anyone could have ever felt. He remembered even crying very briefly with his mom holding him tightly. Then, no other emotion ever flowed from him again.

Three years later, he, after learning everything from his masters, told his parents that he would seek out the FGGO and find a way to destroy it. His family's honor would be avenged.

I was terribly naïve. John flipped a switch on the car's control panel, and a green grid formed inside the Heads-Up-Display being projected on the car's windshield. Concurrently, a red bull's-eye moved within the new grid, searching for a target on the ground. It moved side to side, but eventually rested on a single spot. It grew larger as the craft approached Crystal Mountain.

"ETA in two minutes," the car's OBC said, attempting a monotone voice this time. It was getting better too, since it almost sounded like John's own pitch.

"Yeah, I guess it didn't help when I turned sixteen and my voice change to this monotone." He yawned. "But, that changed when I turned eighteen."

He then wondered what his parents really thought when their

fully trained son had developed his own fighting technique; and, subsequently, had defeated all six masters simultaneously when sparring against them.

"He is unearthly." He remembered what Jupa had told his parents just before he'd walked in on them unexpectedly. To this day, John wasn't sure if *that* comment had been praise or concern.

Would it have mattered? Powers knew he wasn't supernatural. But he was surprised, more or less, that his parents hadn't argued much about his quest, simply providing him with as many credits as they could spare. And although the HC he'd inherited from Grand Master Kemta had been pretty small, he'd managed to pack a considerable arsenal.

"The oldest masters, Kemta and Jupa, hadn't been happy. They had voiced their concerns and anger even with their last breaths." They'd died a week before he'd begun to pack. And even though he had actually spent more time with them than his own parents, he hadn't ever felt any connection with them. Well, at least, not like in the sappy Master-Apprentice type of relationships in some of Logan's shitty and inaccurate "Avenging Ninja" movies.

"Executioner Hangar Bay Two is ready to accept you. Enter through Door Three." John slowed the hovercar to a full stop above the appropriate doors. While lowering the craft, he wondered if he would have left Moki even if he'd never been told the truth. He'd always had felt the wanderlust. It only subsided once he had accepted the offer of joining the Executioners.

"Low-level optical and security fields breached." His car passed through the holograms, and he soon found himself gazing into HBII. There were four levels below the landing deck, which held most of the light and heavy hover vehicles that were used for inforuns, transport, geological sweeps or assassinations.

But when would he eventually go after the FGGO … or Infiltration, as it was now called? But how could he even consider it possible without the help from the Executioners?

He wondered if he even should. With Eric van Anderson dead, wasn't his family's honor avenged? Wasn't it time to go back home to visit? Even though he'd never experienced homesickness, John had been away from his family for a long time.

Well, his other family. He tried another smile. About a year ago and while helping the local Extermination Office, John had bumped into Logan on a crowded street corner in Medley.

"Hangar doors sealed and lights engaged. The car's skids have been deployed. Prepare for landing. Welcome back home, John."

I better get Ecie to reprogram the car's computer. It might start getting smug, he joked, realizing that the car's own OBC seemed to have greeted him back with more emotion than he would ever be able to.

He looked out the windshield, and saw four of his best friends waiting a few yards away. Despite not being able to get excited about being home, John was more or less glad to see his friends after such a long vacation. He took a breath, woke up Scythe and opened the door.

"John, nice to have you back." The Crystalian Governor waved as John approached.

"Good to be back, Jim," he replied the best he could in excitement, but the odd tone from his voice made the greeting sound anything but appreciative. "Always good to be home."

John took a brief look behind him at the HC, another, and then walked up to his friends. He tried to smile too, but he felt an odd sneer take hold when he shook Jim's hand.

"Honestly, it's good to be home," he said again, making sure Jim knew he meant it. He also erased his misshapen grin before nodding to the others. Logan, always the goofball, made him shake both hands. Arthor, obviously caught up in the spirit of things, had him shake all four.

Rebecca chuckled at the men's antics and then welcomed John home with a quick hug. Overall, she seemed to be a mixed bag of anxiety and relief. For whatever his perception was worth.

"Great," Logan cut in, just as John was about to tell them what hotel he'd stayed at. "But what do you keep looking at?"

Powers hadn't thought anyone noticed his frequent but subtle glances toward the car. Obviously, he was mistaken when the other three asked him too. He knew his gazes were of curiosity and nothing else. Would the liger accept this place as his new home?

"I brou—Logan, you may not want to do that." John watched his best friend, without hearing any explanation, move toward the HC.

"Hey, what's in here?" McMillian joked, knowing his friends saw the same thing. "Got a new rug, eh? Come on, John, you'll never get a woman with such bad taste—Hey, I was just kidding, little guy. Hold it!"

Oh, crap. John grimaced and watched Scythe pounce and knock McMillian onto his back. Luckily for Logan, however, Scythe just plopped down on Logan's chest, and mumbled happy liger talk while rubbing his wet whiskers across the guy's face.

"Hey, come on. Get off. Yuck." Logan squirmed and pleaded and began to laugh uncontrollably. Eventually he just gave up and surrendered to Scythe's relentless assault. Making matters worse, he kept rubbing the cat behind the ears.

"Great diplomacy, Logan," Jim said. He, Rebecca and Arthor started laughing too and didn't provide nor offer any assistance.

John moved closer with them to the scene of the attack. "Oh, Logan, meet Scythe," he said. "I guess you two pretty much know each other … now." The group giggled by his joke, even though his face and voice prevented the actual comical sarcasm.

"Nice to meet you, Scythe," Logan added quickly. "I guess you've found your Welcome Mat."

Other laughs echoed in the hangar too. The rest of the Executioners were around them now, adding to the apparent excitement with gasps of joy and "AWs".

Although there were quite a few animals in Crystal Mountain, many were descendants of guard dogs, cats and other animals that people had sneaked in before the Ter-rex explosions. No one had ever seen a great cat with so much energy, since the ones in cloning zoos seemed to only patronize nature. And until these recent events, John had thought such cats had been wiped out during the Neo-Holocaust.

But Scythe could have been born in a special cloning zoo.

"This is great, John." Julie Anders, one of the regular technicians in the hangar, smiled at him after petting the cub. She then moved aside to let someone else in. He'd seen her a number of—

"So, he's named Scythe, eh? Interesting," Rebecca said and grinned too, and then elbowed Jim in the ribs for no apparent reason.

"Yeah, I guess you hate Infiltration more than you could have figured." The Governor soon winked John's way.

"I guess so." John tried to smile again. If he had a dollar for every time one of his friends tried to attribute emotions.

"Now didn't I always tell you that," Logan reassured him. The man was still beneath Scythe. Rebecca and some of the other women petted Logan too.

"And I'm supposed to believe you?"

Others laughed again, knowing the weapons specialist never seemed to take anything seriously. McMillian chuckled as well, obviously not hurt by the jest, and then continued to pet Scythe.

"Beautiful. Reminds me of the shartal," Arthor whispered,

before shutting up, as the Crytonian got an arm in too. He soon commented on how soft the cat's coat was.

John, in fact, heard how everyone around him would love to see the cat walking around the base, looking for and getting attention, and finding new friends around every corner. And it appeared as though everyone expected to enjoy Scythe's company, and treat him like, well, even like a person.

But such enthusiasm is impossible for me, genetically impossible, John thought, remembering what his parents had confessed to him long ago. The FGGO, in hopes of providing the war with remorseless killers, had done an excellent job.

As far as John was concerned, Infiltration would pay for the sins of its father.

A giant moved and kicked—

"You little motherfucker, come back here!"

Max howled and ran back across the length of the restaurant. Once safe behind his owner, the young cub growled and bared his teeth, trying to bring fear into the person he'd just bitten.

Five figures turned her way, but their full appearances were distorted by an air full of smoke. Their voices, four of them talking to Max's victim, were also concealed by the noise of the restaurant. Then, with the vents turning on again, the smoke cleared—

You've got to be kiddin' me. What type of mods has this guy gone through? Jennifer gawked at the thing Max had decided to ostracize. Mostly ape now, the man's size and motion toward her made her cringe. Max, full of venom, still continued his howls, determined to see justice prevail.

"Thinks, bud," she whispered, succeeding in pushing him

under a nearby table. Then she groaned and took a quick glance around this bar & grill set near the Coloradan Forest. To her right, a familiar man with gray and green teeth, continued to stare in her direction. He stroked his wild beard with a calm hand. His cheeks tightened. His lips spread—

You've GOT to be kiddin' me! She scowled and turned away just as he threw another nasty, decaying smile at her. Adding to her ire, her eyes were beginning to itch from the smoke of tobacco and indistinguishable drugs—once again overwhelming the ventilation system. Even worse, prostitutes were dealing with their clients, with some doing business on the spot and only partially hidden by table covers.

Jen shuddered and decided to witness a prettier sight, so she eyed the Gorilla-Man, the monster that Max had bit. The monster that was walking her way.

"Shit. Shit. Shit." Hendricksen backed up when she realized that he hadn't been standing on the high platform by the bar. The ceiling was about 12 feet high and the top of his head was only a couple feet from it. Then, as he got closer, she took another step back when she saw that he indeed had glowing red eyes.

"Dat yer dawg." A powerful statement, rather than a question, came from the guy's lips and was carried by a particular accent she never heard before. Jen thought her family had had a large selection of different dialects on file. Her mother had been a philatelist and a good one.

Despite Jen's moment of distraction, the restaurant began to smell different than before, a familiar scent—Ozone?

"Yes." Calming herself, she reached into her overcoat, as though searching for an itch. She figured this was the best time to release the safety on her Eliminator pistol. And in case his pace quickened, she kept her left hand within the coat, letting her fingers reach to her shoulder and tug on the strap of her holster too. She smiled when she thought of the green-toothed man, who was probably disappointed that she was wearing a bra.

"Yeah, he's my dog, umm, Mister? Trouble?" She blinked her eyes, painfully aware of how vitriolic her voice sounded.

"Well, I'd say so. It just bit a chunk outta me." The man-beast moved closer, while his accent seemed less obvious now. He was still a fair distance across the room, and with his boisterous comments had gathered everyone's attention.

"Maybe"—her lips moved before her mind could stop them —"you shouldn't have kicked him then. Valnder's animal rights laws are specific on—"

"Well, well, smarty pants," the gorilla said and took another few steps, a grin etching his lips. "I believe Valnder also mentioned the owner's responsibilities."

Tables, on automated platforms, moved to give the beast some room, thereby allowing everyone to enjoy their meals or business without being bumped by the monster walking toward her. Right now, regardless of the furniture arrangement, everyone's eyes and attention were on a girl in her late teens being confronted by Goliath.

"What do you mean?" She moved back another step and pointed to his leg anyway. "Mister, your leg looks fine to me."

"But that's not the issue here, is it?" The beast was only steps from her. "You know, you coming in here without proper restraints for a violent animal, and allowing the little bastard to bite a total stranger."

"But—"

The beast stopped twelve feet in front of her. She almost had drawn her pistol. "So, I figure that the animal needs a little extra guidance. Therefore I claim it under animal codes 48 and 64, citing improper training and inadequate supervision."

Max whined as if he could understand the conversation.

"And under said code 48, I suggest that since I lost some of mine"—he gestured almost theatrically—"Should I continue?"

The entire establishment roared with laughter, either the people agreed with that bastard or they'd enjoy the outcome. Jen shuddered from both.

The gorilla took another step, and—

Her hand was quick, quicker than the eyes of those around her? Even her own?

One saw it—

Now you see me! Jen felt her finger squeezing the trigger, a red dot glowed on his chest and she proceeded to empty her magazine. Thirty slugs slammed into their target, causing the behemoth to slump and eventually collapse. Almost an instant later, the pistol's green RE-LOAD light blinked at her, but she covered it with her right thumb. *Now you don't.*

"Go, Max!" Not turning, she yelled at the cub, but he was already out the door and running toward their armored van. Despite Max's excited yelps outside, Jen continued to stare at her victim and watched the gorilla-man's four rat-like companions gather around him.

One with an eye patch seemed to question himself—Attack? But Jen's magnum pistol—menacing but empty—kept them at bay. Naturally, she did her best from not shaking, knowing the rest of her magazines were currently in the van. And she backed out of the restaurant.

"Nobody move!" She made quick glances all around, making sure no one tried to jump her. And after reaching the exit, she sprinted toward her AIM-90 hovervan in the parking lot.

"Great, just fuckin' great," she cursed, then said a quick prayer. She hoped the van's reactor core had had time to cool.

Tarf moved to his boss's side and looked at the gray-eyed girl with long black hair, who had shot about thirty hot piercing slugs into his Commanding Officer. Personally, with his one eye, he had counted twenty-eight recoils from the pistol. Figuring that there were only two shots left in the Hi-ball Eliminator the girl held, he knew his people would have taken the blunt of the defense if he had ordered a retaliatory strike. Instead, he allowed the girl to walk away, letting his squad picture the stunned face of their boss, Captain Tillian Gridlock.

"Is he goin' t'be ok?" a soft voice asked.

"Sure," he smirked, turning around, suddenly eye level with breasts barely contained in lace. They were big, but with only one eye he couldn't quite tell.

"The loss of depth perception will be the most immediate effect," a doctor had once said, and Tarf suddenly regretted losing it in the accident, blaming his recklessness. But taking risks were part of his job.

Besides, he'd pay quite a penny to touch those beauties soon enough. He grinned, somewhat conscious of the drool about to drop from his mouth. "Sure, sure," he groaned, shook himself out of his trance and swallowed back possible embarrassment. "He'll be just peachy."

Tarf then lowered his voice and said, "The bastard isn't even bleeding."

Someone touched his arm, bringing his attention from the prostitute's sweet chest to the hideous face of his commanding officer, who was still staring up at the ceiling. Many of the bar's other customers had already gotten back to their drinks and meals, hoping to get out of here before the local patrol—probably an Extermination Officer—came by.

He shuddered despite himself. Even though EOs tended not to have a "shoot first" policy, Tarf didn't want to talk with one of those freak killers either. Considering, this bar was bordering one of the worst red zones.

I am a mutated rat for fuck's sake, he laughed and took another look around the restaurant. The smoke and stench of the place was as strong as ever, and mostly everyone had turned away, trying to finish their meals. The EO would be here soon enough.

"Spineless, friggin' stems," he uttered softly while wondering if the EOs out here took the job of protecting the people a little too seriously. Indeed, they were uncontrollable at times, often disobeying their superiors, enforcing codes of conduct and honor that rivaled the best fiction.

In the scheme of things, it made no difference. The organization Tarf worked for didn't answer to them anyway. Nor did he care about such politics as long as he was allowed to do his job, which was to hunt.

Tarf's hand reached into his pocket and pulled out a small med kit. In it, he found a large tablet. He smiled then frowned when his fingers latched onto something. He'd left his comlink, along with the internal camera, in the fighter.

Perish the thought, he scoffed. Gridlock wouldn't be pleased if such a picture was ever found. Besides, when Tarf gazed at the lace-covered breasts, he wanted to see those again.

Even through the one eye, he mused. He placed the tiny capsule under his captain's nose, but paused to take in another brief glance at the woman beside him. He sighed at missed opportunities and then squeezed the capsule between his fingers. Then he felt a fist hammer him in the jaw.

Gridlock cursed at the sting of smelling salts and humiliation. His chest, neck and head still throbbed from the attack. He coughed too, but the sharp assault from the renewed stench of burning tobacco and other drugs soon lost their bite.

He had misjudged the girl—the girl! "Where'd she go?" He eyed his team with scrutiny.

They did not or possibly chose not to answer him. His lieutenant, basically a mutated rat-man, lay unconscious in the arms of a young prostitute. Gridlock was astonished to see that the scantily clad vixen held the man gently, making sure he was OK. No prejudice—

"She escaped," a muskrat, his second lieutenant, answered when no one else did. "She ran out the door before we could get a clear shot. But, sir, good thing you had your plating on. She sure knocked you on your ass."

The ape quickly latched around a skinny neck. Gridlock had noticed the weapons his troop now held in their hands, which were fingers and thumbs. Either he had been out longer than he thought—contrary to what the bar's clock said—or his squad was just a group of conniving rats.

"Who needs armor, you little shit?" The Captain tore open his jacket and shirt, exposing a chest of black matted hair. A rainfall of light metal thuds hit the artificial wood floor.

He looked down and eyed the inch-wide welts spanning over a hand-sized area on his chest and upper abdomen. Each of the fleshy mounds barely poked through the thick hair, and many were already beginning to diminish in size. Then he felt the stray that had caught him on the right side of his neck, which still burned and subsequently fueled his anger.

"Now, where'd she go?" he repeated.

But the second lieutenant could only gasp for air—

Another voice, artificial, the powering-up of a reactor core, averted his attention from the shrugs of the other soldiers.

"There." He flung his subordinate down, kicked the lieutenant to consciousness, and pointed out the main door with his monstrous left arm. "Outside, get to your vehicles. Bring the girl and the animal down.

He growled, giving them each a long stare. "And I want them alive."

The power coil whined with exertion at full throttle, and Jennifer hit the hover button, sending the six-ton carrier into the air. Her stomach reacted a little to the Gs created by the ascent, but her G-rated jumpsuit countered the effects so that she could concentrate on the task of leveling the craft for flight. She soon noticed that the energy boost was peaking at eighty-three percent, and Max was whimpering as much as the emergency lift-off systems.

"It'll have to do." Her left hand throttled the repulsars. The van shot out from over the parking lot, kicking her back into her seat.

"Yikes," she cursed and immediately wrenched up on the controls, barley missing the trees near the eastern section of Milton's Garage and Bar & Grill.

She took a calming breath once the van was aloft and away, and then held it as she looked at the control panels. The reactor core whined. It was still hot, but she spread out the lower shields and opened the coolant systems a bit more, sending a greater amount of air and liquid into the compression chambers. Soon the forest was the only thing beneath her.

"Proximity alert," an electronic voice sounded, followed by a Siren-blast and flashing red lights in the cockpit.

"What now?" she asked, flipping the rear viewer on, and discovered three HCs pursuing her own craft.

She magnified the images and saw the vehicles were of the same make—black, streamlined and deadly. Not normal hovercars at all but—

"Fighters." She uttered a prayer soon after, knowing the birds she saw, even though the van's onboard computer couldn't identify their make.

It's an old van, she told herself while looking at Max. "How'd those guys get a hold of a *Nighthawk?* Let alone three?" she questioned and soon felt vibrations from the cockpit, causing her hand to automatically ease down a bit on the throttle. "Max, the government's opposed to using Nagis, right?"

The dog was either too scared or didn't know the answer. If those were Nagis, she'd never seen the like before. They were probably just bionuts who had too many genetic alterations done, right? Shaking her head, Jennifer began to jerk the steering yoke side to side. It was the only action available to her, since the reactor was straining at the van's 830 mph max, and the AIM-90's weapons and defenses against the SR-M Nighthawks were about as much use to her as the empty Eliminator in her shoulder holster.

True, the whipping motion of the van was a feeble gesture, but she had to try something, anything to avoid the targeting sights of those terrible fighters. She was not ignorant of military vehicles. When the reports on the news had come on about the wars with the Rebels, and Boeing-Lockheed-Randlson's SR-M Nighthawks had been the forerunner for many anti-terrorist campaigns.

The black and red markings on the pursuing craft were not Panterian Military, though, and she could only guess the most obvious and the most possible conclusion. The people behind her were probably mercenary or could be part of a Rebel team itself.

"Whoa!" She slammed down hard on the airbrakes and tugged on the control stick, causing the van to buck-up like a startled horse. Eight Gs pulled hard on the vehicle's occupants, and Jennifer heard Max whine a mournful howl.

"Dammit, where'd you come from?" Another hovercar had sprung out at her. Black and dark green markings riddled its sides—almost a blur, a mesh, when it slid just under the van's rear deflector near the starboard repulsar jet. Even now, the AIM-90's radar did not pick it up.

Leveling off, she looked down on the rear viewer and saw all three of her chasers dodge the same craft successfully. The Nighthawks leveled their own paths off and accelerated toward her. They still did not fire.

Her hand was still twisting on the controls, but she soon stopped the frenzied jerks, allowing the van to fly on a single heading. She had finally concluded her actions were hopeless, and her mind filled with the most rational thing left at her disposal: let the Nighthawks get closer.

The rear viewer showed her that one had taken the bait. It accelerated to get alongside the AIM-90, velocities soon matching. Jennifer looked out her side window, perhaps trying to see her next victim—

Fear, her heart pounded in her ears, when she saw that face. Dark and merciless, his thoughts were so transparent.

She shuddered and her cheeks tightened, but the fruitfulness of that pilot brought on a new sense of frustration and renewed energy. Better judgment told her to wait and tried to force her hand to pause and let the others come closer, but the red eyes through two plates of shield glass glared into hers again.

So she did the last thing she could do. Her left hand slammed onto the electromagnetic field generator's override system, forcing the forcefields to burst up by three hundred percent and fail within seconds. Her other hand jerked left on the yoke, banking the armored transport into the fortified war-bird.

Max gave out another canine scream.

Sirens sang and the control panel lit up like a thousand tiny red stars.

His eyes snapped open with an emotion he hardly felt, and Gridlock drew in a sharp breath, unable to do anything else. His hair stood on end from his lower back to the base of his neck. He watched the AIM-90 bank into his fighter and saw the metal-mesh from his canopy slide up to act as another shield.

He felt the jolt, thankful that the shields had held to protect against the initial assault, thereby keeping the van from crushing into his lap. He should be all right.

The alarm sounded again. "What the fuck?" His eyes read the scanning equipment, showing the van had overloaded its force-field generators and created a massive electromagnetic pulse. He howled in disbelief—his reactions useless, tapping pointlessly on the offending button. Most of his fighter's systems were rebooting or knocked out.

A spark burst in his face, then another, telling him he no longer had his shielding. He tried to move from the AIM-90. But the warning systems screamed at him again as the van crashed into him, this time tearing out the primary starboard repulsars. His hand groped for the secondary systems—

Too low, too late. The tanks spiraled down, tearing through the forest growth, into a clearing, pasture, barn and darkness.

Jen did her best to try and stabilize the van, but the controls were frozen and didn't respond, since the EMP had taken out many of her own systems. It would take a few seconds for them to come back on line. "Hold on, Max, we're going down."

Forest streamed past the windshield, branches and needles doing their best to gain access into the craft. A clearing followed, a pasture on the outskirts of a growth zone but a forest taking back what it once owned. The van twirled down. Secondary crash shields were operational, but Jen still clenched her jaw from the suspected landing. She hit the forward retros, pulled up on the stick, activated the airbrakes, anything to try and slow the craft, and somehow managed to tighten the strap on her harness as well.

An abandoned farmhouse rushed up on her. The ground zoomed beneath the craft. An old steel-wire fence zipped by almost unnoticed. The windshield blackened, her straps held and she did not have time to even blink.

The van dropped, creaked and shuddered. She hoped the crash shields—

They stopped, motion ceased. A prayer finally escaped from Jen's lips, but the catastrophe was already over.

Immediately, her nose took hold of ozone, a product from the burned-out control panel. She thought of a man covered by bionic armor and a half-cut helmet. But she shook out the image, realizing it was only a memory.

"Max, are you ok?" They were about twenty degrees catawampus to starboard and inclined five. She reached over to her fateful companion. Due to Jen's quick strap job, he was twisted into his harness like a fork spun into spaghetti. He whined on his back, with his legs spread out in disarray, and his blue-green eyes stared at her with plate-like awareness. She hit his strap release, and he tumbled off the seat, landing onto the rubber deck of the hovervan. He growled but he was fine.

Jen sprung her own seatbelt, eased herself to her feet and moved to the rear of the cabin. Her right hand unlocked the door to the cargo bay while her fist punched the button for the van's side door. Some rubble from the farmhouse slid into the cockpit and structural moans echoed from beyond.

"Out, Max." The animal resisted at first, but a spark rang out from the control panel, and Max hopped out. Caution moved him, since he knew the space he jumped into wasn't much safer. There was no fire, but many of the primary support beams contributing to the structure's stability were cracked and breaking. He howled and whimpered again.

"I'll be out in a sec," Jen yelled over the steam being thrown from the cracked repulsars, and the moans from within the vehicle itself. She grabbed some nutrition bars and a couple bottles of water from the center console.

She then ran into the cargo bay, bypassed her luggage and opened a locker near the door of the cockpit. Two rifles lined the inside, along with a number of magazines and a long slender bag in the corner of the cabinet. She grabbed a bunch of magazines for her pistol. She squeezed as many as she could into her coat's pockets, and then more into a survival pack she'd pulled from the bottom of the cabinet. She also yanked free a packet of batteries for the weapons she was about to carry, and took hold of the rifle concealed in the long slender bag. She strapped it to the backpack and then pulled both onto her shoulders—neither weight would impede her flight. All those survival games her dad put her through paying off. Ready, she stood up and hit the door release, and—

"Great," she swore and then punched the emergency cargo-door charges when the exit failed to open the first time. The bay shuddered and exploded, opening a clean pathway out of the craft. Max peeked around the corner of the new opening and yelped.

"I know." She jumped out of the downed van and ran from the rubble, making sure to get out of the house as soon as she could. Max was already out of the building.

She exited the place the same way the van entered, through a giant hole, torn through plastic and aluminum materials of a home built sometime during the Neo-Holocaust, over eight hundred years ago. A cool wind hit her face, and a late afternoon sun glimmered in the sky, over a tremendous forest where Max was heading.

Jen took one last look at the hovervan, her home for the past four days. Only the sound of the Nighthawks, landing in the background near a barn two hundred yards away, kept her from pausing too long to think of why she was here, of what led to her crash into an old abandoned farm fifteen hundred miles from her former home, and what she was really doing.

"Running," she told herself, sprinting off toward the forest to catch up with her pup. Maybe the answer was single-minded, but she couldn't think of anything else.

This was the second time the girl had made him look like a damn biotech in front of his crew. He was definitely angry with her now, and Gridlock realized he was going to kill her. The animal he would keep, a wonderful symbol, a mascot, for his squad.

But the girl had to die … after he took care of his own needs of course. Two months in occupied territory was a long time, and he had no intention of bedding a prostitute. The thought, in fact, sickened him, despite what he had planned for the girl. For a moment, he wondered if someone human would have thought differently. Therefore, he'd make sure not to include such actions in any of his reports...

They keep reminding us that we're not human... Tillian grinned, thinking of the girl's athletic body, full tits, long jet-black hair, her dazzling gray eyes and her sharp wit.

A pity, he mused, *but she must die!* He figured that she was a mercenary or more possibly a stig. Her actions, her movements were so quick, spontaneous, and organized. In another second, he had convinced himself she was a stig, thereby giving him more right to do what he intended. A prisoner labeled an *Instigator* had no rights. The Torson Traitor Codes were specific, and he would follow them to the letter. Even though he'd make sure his crew didn't know what he was going to do to her ... nor, again, report any of it. Maybe he'd even extend her torture for a couple days or longer?

Then his grin faded, a thought causing him to grimace. *The girl must die,* he told himself again. If she had any opportunity, his head would be on a plaque in whatever rebel stronghold she lived.

Killed by a little girl? Never! he cursed and ripped the composite, metal-mesh canopy from the Nighthawk's hinges. His crew was outside and he looked at them. They all held astonished faces, two of them also carrying Zielman plasma cutters. And worst of all, they froze.

Gridlock could only shake his head in disgust. *But they're still new,* he reminded himself, figuring he'd been in charge of this unit for only six weeks. They'd wanted to be self-autonomous, rouge, set on living by their own terms. He, Captain Tillion Gridlock, had ended such foolishness from the start; however, the team was still unorganized. It didn't function as a single entity and he wondered if it ever would.

They will learn the methods of superior recon, even if it kills them, he thought. He had been retraining them, teaching them the skills of subterfuge, showing them more practical techniques than the cursory lessons they'd learned at the University.

McNeil be proud, he mused. *They have to become aware of their potential and strive to be more than simple security guards.* He looked at the ignited cutters and groaned again. Too bad a Bicdové soldier had more smarts.

Faster than expected, though, the one-eyed lieutenant over-came his shock of his CO's strength, motioned his team to drop the cutters to the ground, and then pointed out the gaping hole in the barn, which Gridlock's SR-M had crashed into. "She went that way, toward the woods."

"Well, then go get her, you ass-rat."

"Aye, Captain." His crew saluted him and ran out the large hole in the barn's west side.

The girl was, by now, a couple miles away. He knew they liked the thrill of the hunt, something he enjoyed himself. He didn't question their motives when they skipped past their own vehicles, relying on their own feet to capture her.

He gazed at them for a moment, and then finally stretched his neck, which was a bit kinked from the rough landing. He undoubtedly had broken a few ribs from the crash too. But, never wanting to show such weakness, he simply growled and ran after his team.

<><><><><><><>

She was running as fast as she could, but she still couldn't keep up with the pup. He was sprinting ahead of her and was almost hidden in the tall field grass.

"Max, wait up. You might get lost."

What the hell? Her logic questioned the statement, realizing the both of them were as lost as they could get, with no immediate chance of being rescued. She had no food, except for the nutrition bars and the two bottles of water. And she didn't know exactly where she was, since the flight from the mutants had caused her to run wild. It would be nearly impossible to find her way back to that bar and grill.

But there's no need for us to be separated. "Max, slow down," Jen said and glanced over her shoulder. Five beasts ran after her. Right now they were only tiny specks in the distance, but they were quickly gaining on her, and she shuddered from the incredible speed they were moving, thereby reinforcing the fact that they weren't human. No, they had to be just genetically modified people. Just like the biomech-freaks, there were also people who genetically modified *themselves.*

For whatever reason, that gave her some comfort, even while she tried to run faster. But the woods were farther away than she had first thought, making her wonder how tall they really were.

Oh crap! She dropped to her knees. The extent of her travel finally hit her and she gasped for air. Until now, she'd been heading to California—after, of course, the length of time that she couldn't motivate herself to leave Hillmount ... or what was left of it. She was still pissed that the "cleanup crews" hadn't even made it to her old house. She finally just left, defeated.

Doubt of her current path suddenly surfaced, doubt her Uncle was still living on the West Coast and doubt that he was still even alive. However, for decades, the region had been a hotbed of civil unrest, instigated by rebel forces in the area. Ultimately, the sector's boarders had been closed and martial law imposed. Jeremiah Tidleman was most likely dead. Jen's mother hadn't heard from her brother in years. The Hendricksens had sent letters, had tried to visit, but the government had prevented any trips into the area. California's borders had been closed for years.

Jennifer had had no choice. She figured she would have found some way in. If smugglers could get in, she figured she had, at least, a small chance. Uncle Jeremy was the only family she had left; and even though she should have just stayed with friends, she had just wanted to see him regardless of the difficulties. She had to find him. She had to tell him about Mom and Dad!

Jen fought back tears, now realizing that she sat face-to-face with the Coloradan Forest. Her only means of transport, no longer operational, was under a collapsing farm house. And her pet was sprinting toward those six-hundred-foot-tall trees as fast as he could.

She had only an idea of what those assholes behind her would do to her and Max if they caught them, but it didn't matter. She was just tired of running.

"Max," she shouted. He stopped, looked her way and then ran back. At the same time, she looked over her shoulder again, seeing that those monsters were still a half mile away. Max, soon by her side, whined and tried to nudge her forward.

"It's no use," Jen said, then unzipped the long slender bag she'd been carrying, and pulled her dad's slinger from the soft case. She grabbed its 6in-long by 12in-deep magazine from the survival pack and slammed it home, powered up the rifle, and loaded a round into the chamber. She gave her pup one last scruff behind the ears, before pulling him to her side and out of the way. Then she leveled the rifle, peered through the scope and began to squeeze the trigger.

"Max, our fight is here."

Gridlock laughed triumphantly when he saw the girl stop and fall to her knees. Because he was sprinting as fast as a cloned cheetah, he would be upon her in less than a minute.

"The girl is mine," he barked, reminding his troops. "Touch her, and you will be sorry. Make sure you get the pet."

In the distance, he saw a flash. Half a second later, his second lieutenant screamed and turned into ground beef. Seeing that, the other members of the team flopped to their bellies, knowing full well what type of weapon the girl had. They didn't move a muscle.

"On your feet, you slimy worms."

"But, Captn', she has a slinger. A big one!" his first lieutenant shrieked in terror. "And our powersuits are in the Nighthawks."

Another flash came from the crouched figure in the grass. Gridlock immediately jumped thirty feet ahead and then threw a quick arm before him. He deflected the bolt into the ground before the proximity fuse had had time to fragment.

"Child's toy," he laughed, even though being hit by the slinger would sting like hell. But the pain would be worth it when he finally caught up with the girl. She was only making her situation worse. He gave her the finger.

He continued laughing, even kicking the grass playfully. Then his troops yelped and hollered and took places behind him when he began to move forward again. Adding insult to injury and protecting his people behind him, he now walked instead of ran, allowing the girl time to wonder what he'd do to her. He smiled broadly again, knowing she could see his face.

Apparently as her rebuttal, Gridlock saw another flash of her rifle, and his sergeant screamed out of existence.

"Holy Fuck!" A shout echoed behind him. The girl was a good shot.

His 1st lieutenant and private suddenly took better positions behind him and stopped the cat-calls. That suited Gridlock just fine, since he had been about to shut them up anyway.

Three of those bastards were left—two rats using the horrible gorilla as a shield. The slinger's scope told her that they were only four hundred yards from her. They'd be on her in seconds if they chose to run, and she figured she'd only get one of them that way.

Cursing then, she overrode the slinger's normal power settings and prayed. Her finger twitched eight more times regardless of the terrible recoils slamming her shoulder, which would be bruised terribly later. If she lived through this.

Her eyes watered, but she blinked out the tears and watched the space she aimed at become a blur—swallowed by a dull grayish red cloud of blood and mess and dirt and bits of grass.

The light wind cleared the area fast, and she saw that the high grass was gone, reduced to dirt and particles. The rats were gone too, disintegrated, but Jen couldn't breathe any relief, since the gorilla was still standing.

He had lost his smile and he didn't look at all happy. He was bleeding, but not enough. The needles from the slinger hadn't done much.

She threw down the empty slinger and looked up into the clear blue sky, then sank to her rump. The field grass rose to her neck, and the breeze felt comforting.

Max helped too. No longer whining, he sat by her side, laid his head on her right thigh and shut his eyes. She stroked his head while she watched the monster approach her.

The wind, cooler now, hit her face when she looked down at her pup. With her free hand, she tried to close her coat a bit.

"I'm cold, Max. I'm really cold."

She brought her eyes up to see where the monster was. He was running now, faster than before. He was only a hundred yards from her. His sight didn't make her look away though. If she was meant to die here, this very spot—

"What do you want?" the beast screamed in rage. Blood caked his chest and shoulders, bits of flesh were missing from him, thousands of tiny shards had impaled his hairless black skin, and only bits of a bodysuit concealed his modesty.

"An inquiry." Behind her, a voice, a rolling tenor, answered before Jen could shrug her shoulders and ask the gorilla the same thing.

She spun around and a silhouette entered her eyes, a giant figure of a man, blocking the late afternoon sun. He walked near her, out of the glare. A comforting smile etched the man's lips when he looked her way. His eyes were concealed by a pair of ruby visors, but the rest of his face kept her from fearing him. She sat in silence and watched this mountain—dressed in nondescript black fatigues, gray coat and black boots—stand in front of her to confront the gorilla-man.

"About what?" the monster growled. "Step away. I call 'Right of Vengeance' upon this girl."

"What?" The man raised his arms, as though shrugging off a mistake. "You must be joking, this girl? What did she do, call you cute and throw you a quarter?" The insult hung a moment. "Oh, sorry, an ancient analogy, but you still look like a sideshow. So where's your little piano and leash?"

"Get out of my way. This girl killed my people. Her hostilities cannot go unpunished. She is stig trash."

Jen didn't move, but she questioned what the beast said. *What, is he mercenary then?*

She stared at the back of her—temporary?—protector. His

dark hair was cut short, tapered around the back and sides. He was a giant too, not as tall as the gorilla, but appeared stronger, heavier and more adapted at killing?

"You mean this girl slaughtered your people?" A giant arm motioned toward her, sarcasm thick in her protector's speech. "I think your memory is starting to resemble your looks. I only see you here, and, besides, what gives you such a sacred right to vent your frustrations on a helpless girl?"

"Helpless? This bitch wiped out my entire crew, a squad of skilled soldiers. Revenge is mine. This girl will pay in flesh. Move out of the way!"

"I only ask that you leave the girl alone. Be thankful you lost only that worthless bunch." The man stepped forward. His arms hung by his sides, hands appearing to hang an inch or two lower than normal.

"Worthless?" The ape grinned, exposing sharp teeth—*Filed?* "Perhaps you're right, but they were my people. I will avenge their deaths. Leave the girl to me. I won't ask again."

"Very well," the big man conceded, but did not give ground. "I see words will not bring Peace, but what of violence?"

"Do not bring about my wrath, villain." The gorilla grinned, almost in anticipation. "This isn't your fight."

"And what authorization justifies your actions now?"

"Shit, so be it!" The gorilla stepped to his right, then his left. Then his voice changed, but held the odd accent. "I'm Tillian Gridlock, Capt'n y squad leader of Infiltration's elite surveillance and reconnaissance division, Black Panther. Our team es highly secretive and any-un dat discovours oos, mus'die.

"Few knoweth of de true government, and ye shall regret hearing dis truth, but thee brought dis upon thyself, m'friend. De Congress es jus'a shoo, de President a virtual puppet. The Pante-rian Guard es de Leader and Infiltration acts as one of its swords. Remember, I tried to avoid dis confrontation, but thy death shall ne sicken me."

What? Jen could only pet Max on the head and try to fully grasp what Gridlock was saying, and how he had said it. Her protector didn't move. He was a giant cast in bronze with no fear.

"Ye askth me to giv'er life to thee by a sacred blood right, a component of honor, a ter'r like you could never compass?" the large man said in a gravelly voice, and a dialect much like the monster now spoke. His right fist clenched tightly. "Listen t'me, fiend. Leave now. I warrant dis girl's protection. Do nay cross."

"Ah, Neo-Classic, eh? No matter, traitor. Thy puny form makes those words trifle," the beast growled, still pacing.

"Pity, perhaps you thought learning a dead dialect—albeit, poorly—would bring you prestige in Infiltration." The man's speech returned to normal. "But I remember that your kinds' projects were just starting when I left. Mutated dogs, boars, alligators, or whatever he could feed into those tanks.

"Anderson was a conceited nut job and it seems his arrogance somehow flooded into your psyche as well, considering how your eyes now judge me with such contempt.

"But are you prepared to start combat with a man you have never met, a foe you've never seen in battle? Heed my words, ape. You will only discover my name upon your last breath." The Protector stepped to his right and bowed when Gridlock smirked out loud.

The man sighed, "Alas then, take your words of vengeance. Try and force your way upon this girl. Come forward if your arrogance wields you so. But I swear to God that you will never reach her. But it's fitting. Infilt-Guards make terrific trophies."

"Damn you," Gridlock screamed and lunged. Jennifer almost shrieked, but the action was a blur and happened before her lips could move.

The Protector lunged too, grabbed his opponent by the neck, and slammed Gridlock hard to the ground. Gasps, many, soon followed—the ape concealed by the high field grass.

The man was on one knee. His visors were still on his face. A grin tugged his cheeks, and he even laughed. A second later, he pulled up as he stood and rose up into the air—floating!—and his left hand was drawn tightly around Gridlock's throat.

Suspended in the air, the gorilla pawed at the man's hand, the vice, but couldn't pull free. He even tried to scratch at the man's face, but couldn't even knock off the man's ruby shades.

"Now, fucktard," the Protector spoke thunderously, while holding the monster in the air. "My name is Jim St. John, and I hate everything Infiltration stands for. You might have been commissioned long after my employment, but your training emphasizes the identities of FGGO traitors. Therefore think back, Scab. Search your memory. Think of what type of person would allow himself to be 'Re-forged.' Maybe then you'll find honor from being slaughtered by me."

Jennifer shuddered, suddenly feeling more anger toward the gorilla than ever. What if he had gotten a hold of her? Who or what would have saved her life if Jim hadn't shown up? She nearly reached for her pistol, not caring if the weapon couldn't penetrate Gridlock's tuff skin.

The gorilla choked and his eyes popped open. His struggling stopped. "Jim St. John"—he tried to bring in a quickened breath but failed—"the Beast, t-th-the MUTILATOR!"

Gridlock's torn bodysuit began to drip of urine. He continued his struggle against the hand around his throat, but he began to scream as well, howling in a high pitched wail. "No, no leave m'be, stayth those horrid blades. Spare me. Take the girl. Get away, demon, DEMON!"

Jennifer watched Jim's head spin toward her. She knew the face of pity, but was it from the words Gridlock spoke, or from the man's own thoughts, his own doubts?

The arm lowered, but the hand still stayed. Gridlock stopped his pleads, but continued to struggle. Childlike breaths, as though a young boy was trying to free his jacket from a sharp fence, came from the gorilla's form. The monster's feet scraped the grass-covered ground. Exertion and fear caused tears to fall from the beast's face.

What are you doing? she asked, but not voicing the words. *He can't live, he just can't.*

His eyes on her, Jim's lips straightened into an apathetic line, and he nodded in her direction, no longer showing any sympathy toward the creature he held.

She blinked. Jim turned, let go, and swung with his other arm and then became a blur. Jen saw one flash in the sun and then another, another, another—hundreds more!

Then … calm. The wind twirled Jennifer's hair softly. Jim still had his back to her. She couldn't tell if he was breathing any harder from his attack, couldn't picture what expression his lips now held. She just looked at him and wondered.

Short dark hair blew in the breeze. His face gazed skyward, Jen noticing only a few clouds in the sky before the man nodded as though completing a prayer.

Who is he? she asked again, but she sat in silence, petting Max softly on the head.

"I'm sorry, Lisa," Jim whispered then pulled his gaze from the sky. Despite how many the Executioners had performed because of him, this was the first person he'd killed in nearly six years. But his heart raced with satisfaction, pleasure, damnation —he couldn't be sure. "B-but Infiltration will not find our Lair. I'll be damned first."

He turned to face the girl he had saved. She sat motionless in the high field grass. Her puppy rested his head on her lap, and she petted the pup behind the ears and under his neck. She only stared at him. A question seemed to cross her lips, but nothing came.

He moved cautiously toward her, fearing she might try to run, but she did not.

Who are you? he asked, though only to himself, but realized she probably had the same question.

I know. I should have tried to help you sooner, he chastised himself. Obviously, he had tried to lure the Nighthawks away from her by allowing the Infilt-Guards to see his unmarked vehicle. But why had he allowed the crash to occur, or the chase? The Beast within had wanted the chance to slay, to use its blades earlier, but he had resisted.

Why? The promise to Lisa, he knew. But it had almost gotten this girl killed. How much torture had Gridlock planned?

She still sat in front of him, petting her little friend, who rested and whimpered by her side. Her gray eyes continued to stare in his direction, up to his face, seeking. The summer breeze tugged on her hair a bit—causing a jet-black tangle over her dark gray overcoat—and her face and full red lips couldn't utter the question she held.

"My name is Jim St. John," he said again, but this time to her. "Don't be afraid. I'm here to help you."

Jim knelt down on his right knee. He gently petted the puppy that shrank back at first but soon stopped whining. Then he eased the girl into one of his arms, while picking up her slinger with the other. "I know a place where you can rest and regain your strength, maybe even stay."

She didn't resist—trust or fear? He stood up to his feet, and took a moment to gaze at the Coloradan Forest before he decided it was time to go.

Her pet followed him to the HC, which was invisible. Jim had left the vehicle's cloaking field on to surprise the gorilla.

Jim smirked, wondering if it would ever be possible to really "pop out of thin air." He knew that EuroAmerica had pursued it, along with a number of different methods of high speed transport.

St. John thought, then, about that old forgotten city-state, which had been based in Toldeclevchikee. *They wanted so much to evacuate this planet. But did they know what they were doing when they destroyed all their records before Panteria took over? Did they know what they did?*

The Crystalian Governor looked up into the sky for a moment and wondered briefly about what those people had tried to do, and what they had tried to accomplish. Only to have all of their research deleted before the Unification, when the city-state of Panteria finally took over the world, almost one hundred fifty years ago.

Too bad really, Jim figured, because there had been two methods of teleportation that would have made modern travel so much easier: The beam method, regardless of being impractical and unpredictable, would have been very cool. The other, a more practical series of tele-disks, would have been more convenient than a hoverbus or taxi.

Jim frowned. He knew that matter-energy conversion created considerable anomalies in DNA restructuring. However, with today's superconductors, he knew the problem could have been solved, could have been.

Alas, had the Old World really been more innocent and cultured? St.

John shook his head and thought about all the technical knowledge that had been lost when EuroAmerica had all its R&D tech centers format their databases. Naturally, Old World Science Fiction had loved the concept of instantaneous transport. However, in the thirty-first century and after nearly five hundred years of war, people never gave it much thought. After all, who cared, besides, of course, Jim and others who liked the Old World's fiction?

Jim realized he was just trying to think of something else—something other than him having sliced Gridlock into mist.

"Cloaking off," he said, and the HC popped into the view. It was about the size of an Old World SUV, and painted in *Executioner* Charcoal. He opened the passenger-side door. He eased in, set the girl in the passenger seat and then put her slinger and backpack in the cargo area.

He noticed a slight grin on the girl's lips when he buckled her into her safety harness. It was a bit sooner than expected, but he'd always had a way with people.

Yeah right. He suddenly thought about his blades, his harder-than-diamond bones and the thousands of people he had killed in his early career. He grinned at the adorable sight of the girl's puppy jumping into her lap and propping his head on her left arm. But then his lips straightened as he closed her door and walked over to the driver's side. *Yeah, I've got a great way with people.*

Jim St. John got in and closed his own door, warmed up the car's repulsar and engaged the hover controls. Once he'd reached an appropriate altitude, he opened a direct-line communiqué to Crystal Mountain, thereby bypassing their cloaked satellites.

"Delta Six, this is HC Twenty-three dash A. I have a situation here requiring an immediate body sweep and equipment pick up.

"There are two craft needing to be flown back to base, along with two others that are salvageable. The coordinates are located on my current signal, but are spread over four grids. A team needs to get here immediately, and the area should be cleaned up within the hour."

A response came immediately. "Acknowledged. A team has been alerted and will be at those coordinates in five minutes. Will you be able to assist?"

"Negative, I have a couple of passengers here that I'm taking back now. Arrangements must be taken care of."

"Very well. Out." The line was closed quickly, even though the chances of intercepting a direct-line communiqué were nearly impossible.

Impossible, impossible, he reassured himself. Ecie monitored all transmissions. Any anomaly would cause him to terminate a signal. At the same time, a spontaneous threat-status check would be logged and any risk would be dealt with accordingly. Thankfully, to this date, the Mountain's Protector hadn't needed to take such precautions, even though Logan wondered when he'd be selected for such a turkey shoot.

Jim smiled, realizing Crystal Mountain was full of quite an eclectic group of people. And he knew every one of them by name. Taking off his sunglasses, he looked at his passenger and kept smiling. He realized there was another name he would have to learn. The breathing on her lap reminded him that there were actually two.

He turned away and looked out his side window. They were just beyond Ecie's *Wasteland* and he couldn't take any chances. Begrudgingly, Jim flipped a special switch, which darkened all the windows and distorted any devices capable of giving away their location.

"It's just a security precaution," he reassured his passenger, and then he took a moment to think about trust and if there was actually enough of it in the world.

Frickin' clichés, he sighed, and then wondered if the confrontation with the Infilt-Guard could have gone differently. Oddly enough, he had considered letting the poor bastard go.

But my blades fed anyway. He nodded and thought about the body he had left behind for the cleanup crews. *I had no other choice. The Crystalians are more important than a single life, especially when it's just that of a Kurgon Beast.*

CHAPTER FIVE

Words are, of course, the most powerful drug used by mankind.

(Speech)
—Rudyard Kipling, British poet (1923 A.D.)

L ogan stood on an open plain. The grass was yellow and as short as Astroturf. There were trees in the distance, grouped in clumps on several of the nearby hills.

He looked up, seeing a foreboding red sky and black, wispy clouds that were violently swirling from horizon to horizon. The moon too was bloody red, prophesying a Ragnarok that was to come. The prairie he stood upon was quiet though. And, despite the dark, bloody moon, the plain was well lit because of the special implants in his eyes.

The wind wasn't cold. He actually felt quite comfortable, even with only wearing a T-shirt and a pair of shorts. He laughed to himself, figuring he had fallen asleep with less. But he was a modest person, never really one for exhibition, even in his dreams.

"Logan?" asked a familiar, but also disparate, voice. "Logan, is that you?"

He turned and was shocked to see four of his old friends standing several yards away. The Commander, Miles, Brent, and Kevin waved.

"Hey, guys," he yelled and began walking their way, but soon stopped short. They shouldn't be here.

"Logan, what's the matter?" his commanding officer, Craig Kirk, asked. Puzzled looks also appeared on the faces of his other friends.

"What are you doing here? What do you want?" Logan actually began to back away from them. He tried to avoid their gazes too.

"Logan, what's gotten into you?" Kevin asked.

"I don't trust you. I can't trust you."

"Come on, Logan, we're your friends," Craig said. "It's been ages. What's gotten into you? Come—"

Lightning flashed before Logan's eyes, enveloped the entire group in front of him and incinerated the area. It had been quick. No screams.

Smoke soon cleared, the calm returned, but his friends were gone. The sky still burned red. The prairie was so damned quiet.

"Why didn't I go to them?" he asked himself, wanting to move to the spot where they had been, but still could not. "No, I didn't trust them. How could I?"

Groans entered his ears. Pain seemed to be voiced in a terrible melody. He turned completely around and took a backward step. His eyes were deceiving him. They had to be. Was this a new dream or just a replay of the same one?

Four armored demons stumbled toward him. Scales, golden and triangular, lined the parts of skin not covered by medieval-like armor. Protruding faces and tails were also covered in plating, and armored boots propelled the monsters forward.

"Logan"—the Commander's voice resonated through his ears again, but this time it came from the creature before him—"look what you did to us. Why didn't you come? Why did you let this happen? Why did you leave?" Hisses followed many words.

"I had to."

"No, there was another way." The one with Kevin's voice moved up beside Craig. They all stopped and held their arms out to him, as if pleading to him.

"Logan, come now," the Commander said, dropped his hands and moved another step forward. "We foresaw greatness in you the moment you began attending Briar Mount University. Seeing such drive and enthusiasm from you at only sixteen, we knew your determination would have benefited us. That's why we came to you after your eighteenth birthday, to help us."

They all grimaced and pointed to themselves. "But look at what you did," they cried.

An old memory flashed through his mind. He shouted back, "Right, you tricked me into joining your organization in the first place."

"Tricked?" His former commander shook his head. "Didn't we give you everything you wanted and everything we promised you?"

An empty armored hand implored to him now. "You wanted a change, Logan. Don't you remember? You were tired of the monotonous school schedule, the same old thing. You wanted to make a difference in the world and make the guilty suffer for the crimes they committed. Didn't we change that? Didn't we bend over backward to keep you entertained?"

The leader shrugged and turned his head as though thinking of something else. "Oh yeah, and didn't we help you with your proposal for the suit in the first place? Wasn't the Director afraid of the antimatter generator and collider being practically in the same space?

"But we did, and we promised that we'd get it done. Didn't your friends help you accomplish all this for our precious and dear Company?"

"But what good was the Company?" Logan snorted in disgust. "It was based on an ancient agency that collected Intel on other countries, other nations. We're a one world government. Who did we have to spy on?"

"Rebels, terrorists, rouge mercs—History repeats."

He conceded, "Fine, but did that have to include the assassinations of all those government officials in the Puppet Government? A fake government that none of us were told about? Were those people really that bad?" He raised his hands while he shouted, trying to make his point clear, to make them understand. "Craig, look into these implants, talk into these modified eardrums and tell an assassin it was all necessary."

"It was." They resumed their steps closer toward him. Their silver armor reflected the images of the red sky, and Kelson blades—electromagnetically reinforced zip-wire swords—glimmered as though they were emitting their own light.

He continued his slow backward flight, knowing he wasn't prepared for battle.

Ka-crack. There was a flash and he suddenly gaped in horror when a nickel-sized stick materialized into his right hand.

"Great, thanks!" He gritted his teeth and motioned a middle finger up at the sky. The blades his former friends carried would cut through that stick like it was warm butter. Then they would cut him apart like a tofu turkey.

"Soy-gobble, soy-gobble," he said, defensive mechanism.

"Rejoin us, Logan," his commander actually pleaded with him, and the demon's shimmering alloy armor merged well with the turbulent fire in the sky. "If you come back now, nothing will happen to you. We can forgive and forget."

"No, that's why I left. I no longer had a future with the Company. It was all an illusion. Deceit and murder were the only truths. Rejoin? Never, never again."

"Are you sure, Logan?" Kelson blades were pointed his way. "Think of what you're doing."

"Yes, death would always be a better alternative." He raised the wooden foil against them, and he felt a surge of wind behind him, forcing his voice to become stronger. "The Executioners are my future, an organization created to eliminate the evils you now me remind of."

The creatures looked at each other, and then nodded simultaneously. The Commander was the only one to speak, and said, "Very well, friend, very well, it is true. Your beliefs no longer coincide with our own. We regret the actions we now must take, and this we are sorry for."

They still vectored toward him. "But, alas, we'll see this fight as a noble one, despite your delusion ..." Craig paused, coughed and cleared his throat. "Prepare to die."

The Commander attacked first, barely missing Logan with that terrible blade. Logan then lunged with his stick, forcing the helmet off Craig's head.

"Ah, the years inside the suit haven't slowed you down at all," the leader of the quartet said in almost applause. "I trust you can still kill without a weapon."

They lunged again. Logan moved once more, and his stick managed to pry off another piece of armor, and then another. And soon the battlefield was littered with several pieces—arm guards, kneepads, chest plates, anything the stick could be forced into and be wrenched free.

"Very good, friend." Praise continued to echo across the

landscape. "Your memory and reflexes are excellent. Try this." The troop spread out and attacked from all sides. Logan ducked to his knees, rolled onto his back and flipped onto his feet. He turned and avoided another slicing blow from a blade, then brought his right hand up into a chop. It contacted with one of his deformed adversaries.

"Log—" An empty gasping entered the calm atmosphere. A demon fell to his knees, clawing for air. However, it never pleaded for mercy. Such would destroy the image of the Company's strength.

Formally, it had been strong, McMillian thought of the CIA. But, after he had left, the Guard and its minions had moved in and had wiped out the entire organization. No one had been left alive, or so Logan had thought. *Damn the Guard.*

"Poor Miles." A triad looked at their fallen friend and could do nothing for the monster except watch him die.

"I would worry about yourselves," Logan yelled, his confidence now at peak, proud of his speed and resourcefulness. The armor he had pried off from his enemy now rested on his own sturdy frame, and the dead demon's sword hummed in his hand.

"Hmm?" The monsters gazed over into his direction, and then gave him toothy grins. "Ah, Miles would have been so proud. You decided to join us after all."

"What?" Suddenly his skin began to burn. He dropped the sword and began to tear at the armor surrounding him.

He fell to his knees in pain, finally grabbing hold of his right glove and tore it free and looked—"No, it can't be!"

He gazed at his forearms and hands. He held them up against the blood-red sky. Before his eyes, they seemed to change and his fingers lengthened. His arms grew skinny but kept their strength. And smooth tanned skin soon yielded and formed into thick, triangular scales which were colored by a hint of bronze on a grayish green. "Bastards, what have you done to me?"

"Nothing, Logan," all the demons laughed this time. "You knew you were a part of the team. We just had to remind you of your loyalty to your government and to your friends. Never forget that you were and are part of the CIA, part of the family. Don't you understand? You must. Welcome home."

"Lights on," Logan shouted. The lights came on, and he looked at his hands. They were fine but were shaking uncontrollably. *Nightmares* … "They're getting worse."

He looked around the bedroom. Everything seemed in place, undisturbed. None of the paintings on the walls were misplaced or upset, and the potted plants sat quietly.

Logan groaned, finding himself upright on his bed. He was shaken up pretty badly, so he sat there a minute, trying to think of something pleasant so that he could get at least another hour's rest.

He failed. "Fine," he swore, tossing aside the damp sheets and jumping to his feet. "I've slept enough. An hour of nightmares ought'a be worth eight hours of regular sleep, eh?" Of course no one answered him. He'd also asked Ecie for privacy about three weeks ago, no use having the computer worry.

Logan showered and then moved to the closet and put on some working attire, which consisted of a dark blue jumper and a utility belt. Both were military issue and thereby displayed the small logo of the Executioners, which was a silhouette of an executioner's hood facing forward with a double-bladed axe blocking the left eye.

He eyed the emblem for a moment, wondering what Jim really thought about the fierceness it portrayed. He shrugged, clipped on an empty holster and entered his armory. Several rifles entered his eyes, lining an entire wall. He ignored them and went to a wide central cabinet and pulled open the top drawer. A loaded handgun sat there with seven full magazines around it, all in soft foam. He grabbed hold of the weapon, a forty-five caliber electromagnetic pistol, and pulled back and released the loader. A caseless bullet was slammed into position, and the laser sight sent out a red dot when he pulled the trigger half way.

The dot hit the electronic calendar, quickly alerting him of an anniversary he'd never forget. He engaged the safety and spun the weapon on his finger, twirling it like a gunslinger, before holstering it.

Forget about it. Your life has been killing. What else would you have done? he asked himself, recalling that he had joined the Company when he'd only been eighteen. Like most eighteen year olds, he thought he knew everything, especially old enough to make life and death decisions. Naturally, he had been simply brash with youth and easily manipulated.

Some genius. Logan brooded then grabbed a couple of magazines for his pistol before he closed the drawer, walked out of the room and left his apartment. Checking his watch, he noted that the street lamps were on and that the simulated night of Crystal Mountain was timed nearly perfectly with the outside world.

He smirked. The distraction did little to lighten his mood, since today was the anniversary of his first kill for the CIA. Guilt helped make his mood worse, because he still considered the first one justified. That man, after all, had been supplying explosives to madmen for years, and a government raid would have cost several lives.

Over the years, however, Logan had begun to question the intelligence reports about some of his targets. Eventually his suspicions had grown so much that he had hired a private eye to investigate one of them.

During his tenure with the CIA, Logan had designed hundreds of weapons and had pulled hundreds of triggers. He'd killed so many people because he'd been told they were corrupt, evil, wicked and beyond redemption. Truthfully, his hate—hatred for all the monsters that'd terrorized him as a child—had made him prejudice.

"I had to leave before I killed Carla Franco. She would have been just another innocent victim," he reassured himself. She had simply been some governor's daughter, who hadn't known she was dating a rebel's niece. Hell, even the niece hadn't known her uncle's identity.

"But God damn, why did my life have to play out like a cheap Soap Opera?" His life had changed so much. Obviously, he still killed high profile targets for the Executioners, but it was always a last resort.

Well mostly, he added. He had a sadistic sense of humor. Always did. But he knew the line. "At least I tell myself that I do," he joked too, even though he knew he wouldn't be living here if he ever crossed it.

He took a moment to eye the faux moon beginning to set at the edge of the huge Tunnel Plex, *Denver-Springs Cavern*, where he lived. Despite being buried for over eight hundred years, the Crystalians had advanced their technology considerably well— more so than what the ex-CIA man would have expected.

"Liked I'd know," Logan said and then took a short bypass tube, just to the right off of Headley Ave. At its end, he entered a white room. The bright color seemed out of place, especially considering the black walls of the tube, but all elevators and turbo lifts were white inside.

He chuckled for no reason, while red doors closed in front of him. Ecie immediately greeted him, "Wot destinacion dothe ye wish, Mr. Pan-zuer?"

"Ecie, you're overly cheerful today, eh?" Logan tugged on the front of his jumper, making sure there weren't any wrinkles. He only wished that he'd had the opportunity to make the initial voice programming for the E.C.C., if that had been even possible.

"Who? Me?" Ecie often used a mixture of Verengoshian and English in the presence of Arthor's close friends. It had struck a chord when Logan had first joined, but after a year he was getting used to it. As if he had a choice.

"Oh, never mind. Take me to the third observation deck, near Obstower Eight." Logan never admitted to anyone that the computer's use of Arthor's home language annoyed the shit out of him. The last thing he wanted was the Verengoshian man to be offended if it ever was brought up accidentally. However, to McMillian, the Verengoshian language wasn't much different from the revival of the archaic British dialect, Neo-Classic, which the Panterian Guard had adopted over two centuries ago for subversive reasons.

The FGGO had adopted it too of course. Actually it was responsible for its creation a century before. By the time Jim had been recruited, new members were taught it simply to understand the older AOM generations. Therefore Logan knew even Rebecca understood it and could even speak it if need be; however, he'd never once heard her utter a single word.

Good for her. The weapon specialist smiled and remembered when an obscure CIA Black Ops division had taught its personnel Neo-Classic. Logan found this out only because he'd had to train some of them on new anti-tank weapons he'd developed. Back then he couldn't understand why they'd been taught it and never got a satisfactory answer, especially since the guy who'd let it slip hadn't gone into detail. Knowing what Logan knew now, it was certainly obsequious nonsense, especially since Jim said that the Guard no longer spoke it either. What really grated Logan was how much the CIA had kept from him, and all the while they'd demanded his absolute loyalty. Such as it was for super-secret agencies.

"Looks like I got you here in one piece," Ecie said, interrupting Logan's thoughts.

"Thanks, Ecie." He waited but the door didn't open. "What is it?"

"Logan, is everything OK?" The computer was a marvel of computer science. Logan could have never imagined the complexity of an organic frame nor dreamed of such a unique personality. "You can always talk to me."

"No, I'm fine," he lied, shrugged and tried to avoid the scanner equipment placed in the turbo lift. "Just couldn't sleep—too much late-night coffee this time, no need to worry."

"Oh, in that case, can you say 'yaloh' to Arthor for me then?" Ecie said while the doors opened, revealing another black tube.

"I will." He began to walk out, but paused a second. "Ah, Ecie, thanks for asking. I really do appreciate it, knowing that you care. Anyway, Tirson told me a joked the other day, pretty funny. I'll tell it to you a little later."

"Fine," the computer said, bemusement obvious in the disembodied voice. Logan was just thankful that Ecie was quite adept at dealing with various social interactions, especially knowing when not to push for an argument. "I found a file of Old World jokes. I thought you might like to hear them?"

"Good, friend, good," Logan chuckled nervously walking away. "Talk to ya then."

He followed the bypass tube into a relatively short, quarter-mile-long passageway, which was short, considering some stretched from one end of the Mountain to the other. There were over a thousand miles of transit corridors running throughout the Lair. Light rail, express carts and turbo lifts—obviously named after the show—handled most of the business traffic when people were in a rush or didn't feel like hoofing it. Logan usually preferred to do the latter, since walking tended to keep him awake.

McMillian reached the end of the corridor and then unlocked a door, which led to a spiral staircase. Ignoring the freight elevator to the left, he took a deep breath and then initiated the six-hundred-twenty-foot climb up those corkscrewed steps.

"Ecie, I can't believe these people lived for over eight hundred years underneath this rock," he said, feeling like talking again. To top it off, these people hadn't seen a murder or other violent crime during most of those years.

"With a perfunctory glance, a Communist would claim that we live in his ideal state," the computer commented. "However, we have private ownership. We have a Capitalistic economy."

"But it's not like anyone's left to fend for himself," Logan countered. "Also, when was the last time you saw a shop go out of business? Here, people do things they love and enjoy, and their friends and family are their best clients. It's not the real world."

"Touché," Ecie went quiet for a moment then continued. "My experience with people has been bias, I admit. What I've read and seen on Panteria's news, it's disconcerting."

Logan soon reached the top of the stairwell and found himself behind the transparent walls of a little room in the middle of a main observation tower, which was slightly larger than a common obstower. This MOT was located near the top of the Mountain's southeast ridge. Its blast plates were currently up, so he could see that the sun was not nearly ready to rise.

Like always, he tried to listen for a hum of some sort, but couldn't pick up anything. Although imperceptible to all forms of detection, the electromagnetic shields and holograms surrounding OTs were operating at full force and could survive several direct hits from large antimatter detonations. Also, the surrounding shields acted as view screens, showing and identifying and labeling all objects that could pose a threat to the base. Obviously, Jim never took a chance when it came to the safety of his people, and that man understood the outside world better than anyone.

"Disconcerting? Nice choice of euphemism, Ecie," McMillian said, realizing he himself had another word for Human nature. "Hey, let's talk about this later, OK? Jim told me that Arthor's been in the dumps lately. Give us some privacy, OK?"

"Sure. Have a good one," Ecie said and signed off.

Logan opened and walked through the door of the entry way. Except for the information on the inside of the holograms, OTs didn't have any lights in them and it would have been pretty dark if not for Logan's cornea implants. He quickly found Arthor near the western part of the deck. The Crytonian sat at one of the workstations, while he also checked some information on his PDL. His second pair of hands twiddled thumbs.

"How's it going, Arthor?" Logan asked. He found himself whispering, realizing Jim's paranoia of the Mountain ever being discovered was more infectious to Logan up here.

"Dastel-es, Logan," the Verengoshian said quietly. He didn't turn around. Then he said in English, "You're up early."

"Yeah, I couldn't sleep." Logan stretched his back. "I figured you might want some company, since you've pulled this watch about six days in a row." He moved to the Crytonian's side and looked over the vast forest surrounding the Lair. He picked out an owl as it flew from a tree. Then the electromagnetic screen, following the direction of his eyes, magnified the image and even told him what type of owl it was. "How are you doing, Arthor?"

"I'm fine, Logan." Arthor twisted around in the chair, and McMillian noticed a smile or at least a good try at one. "I wasn't expecting anyone tonight. I was just talking with Ecie too. Oddly enough, he didn't mention you were coming."

"Yeah, he's quite the character," Logan said, realizing the computer had an odd sense of humor. "By the way, he told me to pass a 'yaloh' to you."

"Even though he was already talking with me?" That brought an authentic smile to Arthor's lips. "I would have never guessed someone like him could be so full of life. Just before you arrived, we were comparing the differences between Panteria and my world. Truthfully, I was thinking more of the latter, of my true home, of my own time."

Logan nodded. He understood homesickness. He knew that the Verengoshian couldn't help but feel the most alien though. The man wasn't human, per-se. Hmm, wasn't *that* an odd sentence?

"You know, Arthor, over a year's gone by since I joined this outfit, and I don't even know how you got here. I've never asked anyone," Logan said, tapping his fingers nervously on a thigh. "Anyhoo, I'm probably sticking my nose where it shouldn't belong, but you know I'm good at that, so what in the hell happened?"

The Crytonian said nothing. Logan followed the man's eyes as he looked east and west, at his PDL, and over at the large defensive gun and nazer rocket emplacements on the roof of the OT. Finally, Arthor took a breath, and let out a long sigh. "OK, I'll tell you."

Arthor collected himself. He thought back to a time when he hadn't been imprisoned on a planet populated by an entirely different type of man and woman.

He threw another glance in Logan's direction, and tried to remember how Aenglan, his old teacher and father's royal bodyguard, used to relay stories to a young Arthor Jones.

He smiled uneasily, blinked his eyes and began to tap his foot. "About six of your years ago, I was a Duke's son," he said. "However I wasn't your average youth. Obviously, I wasn't human. I had wings, a tail, four arms and a dark green skin.

"My father was Jacobson Jones, the Duke of Verengosha, which was a province of Crytonia, which, in turn, was a country on the world of Deliplain. I lived with my father, mother and our many paid servants in our family's castle.

"I won't go into detail about the social structure of our country. To be brief, unlike the cruel feudal system of ancient Panteria, our 'Peasants' had rights, owned property and were essential for providing the cities and villages with food, water and life. And it was our job, our duty and our honor as Nobles and Knights and Krastieks to protect them."

CHAPTER SIX

A knight's tie with God is his promise and
oath to protect his people and country.
(Regarding the Return, Compliled by his Disci-
ples)
—Yali, Savior (0 Ayve Yan
[After Yali's Rebirth]

I sat in our family's study, a huge library packed with thousands of volumes. Built generations ago, it held a millennium of Crytonian prose and poetry, including several
accounts of battles with terrible creatures.

Today I was reading about the Demons of the McCaslitor
Hills. They had once plundered the outlying villages of Tyland's
principle city, Tyngeld. Coincidentally, it was only after the
McCaslitor Demons were wiped out when Tyland, once known
for its unwavering independence, petitioned for annexation into
Verengosha and ultimately Crytonia.

I was surprised about how large and agile the creatures could
be. The book also spoke of amazing tactics the monsters knew,
practically sentient when it came to hunting. And during a fight

they were like Torvianishan Berserks, terrible and blood thirsty. In fact, hundreds of Verengoshian citizens and knights had suffered by the hands of those predators, which preferred hunts on a moonless gloom.

My father, Duke Jacobson Jones of Verengosha, had led the assault at Floker's Plateau, a small village about twelve miles south of Tyngeld, to eradicate them nearly a century before I was born. Even my father felt the genocide had been an unpleasant necessity, but the McCaslitor Demons had begun to prefer typhon flesh. Only a miracle could explain how they had eliminated the fifteen-foot-tall, half-ton creatures.

Although they were extinct, I studied them anyway, wondering if I could incorporate any of their attributes to my own fighting style.

I turned a page while I daydreamed of knights and battling with monsters not yet known. My Comicíon, the ceremony in which I'd pledge my oath of knighthood, couldn't be far away. I'd completed all my great quests. Sure, my Shartal Hunt twenty-five Deliplainan years ago had been a bit unorthodox, but I'd been praised for my valor.

"I'm not sure what else I can do as a squire," I said to myself. "Lately, all I seem to be doing is 'keeping busy.'"

I smirked uneasily. I knew a knight had to be patient and also humble. I'd never called these last stages a waste of time. Certainly Aenglan, my teacher, said it often enough.

Perhaps too often.

"Arthor, son, are you here?" My mother, the Duchess Amanda Clarkson Jones, cracked open the door to the library. I knew she had just started looking for me, since she always started a search with this room first. I wondered if I was becoming too predictable.

"Yes, Mother." I looked from behind a bookcase, tilting my

chair so I could see her. "What can I do for you?"

She walked in. Her white gown clung loosely around her white skin and jewelry hung around her neck, wrists and fingers. Earrings sparkled from the light of the enclosed oil lamps placed throughout the library. Her gray-green eyes flickered too from the burning wicks. "Your father wants you dressed in your colors with a Fytoker's speed. Then take your sword and stripes to the Great Hall."

"My sword?" I suddenly got a bit giddy. I didn't need a practice sword for some ceremony for the Great Harvest, which had been going on for the last week and the reason so many people had been in town. "Did the Duke tell you what he wants?"

"No, my little one," she said as she always did in private, even though I now towered over her. "But don't keep him waiting. Make sure you dress appropriately."

"Chetok," I agreed and quickly jumped from my seat; however, before I ran out of the library, I gave my mom a quick peck on the cheek.

"Taqik? What was that for?" she asked with an amused grin, as if she didn't know.

I laughed, too excited to answer.

Twenty minutes later, I was running to the Great Hall. My squire stripes hung from my upper shoulders, and my upper right and lower left hands tightly held onto a sheathed practice sword. The steel sword was long and double-tapered, and normally it required two hands to wield. However, I'd worked hard so that I could wield it with one hand, thereby leaving my others free for a chain-link battle axe and shield.

I turned a corner and took a right into a narrow hallway, which was illuminated by several lanterns. As I did so, I brushed against the wall, and the sheathed sword tapped the dark gray blocks in a rhythmic bump and scrape.

The sound reminded me of when I'd gained this practice sword. It was long ago, on my Second Quest, but I still remembered the two days of riddles and orienteering through the Royal Garden. I'd traversed some 12 jolds, about 9 miles, by the time I'd reached my last clue. After climbing up the Northeast Tower, I'd had to wrestle an opponent for the prize.

My upper-right hand gripped the weapon a little more tightly. I'd won the sword on my first try, despite the menacing opponent—a Gray Knight—I'd had to wrestle. The Gray Knight, however, had limited himself to a third-level fighting style—not realizing Aenglan, my teacher and Father's Royal Bodyguard, had been teaching me how to fight and wrestle since I was a child. In an instant, the knight—underestimating my drive, strength and skill—had gone down. Therefore the Gray Knight's wings fell flat on the tower's floor, and the armored servant could do nothing except yield.

I turned another corner and ran down a flight of stairs. At that moment, I daydreamed of flying down them; however, despite being able to move their wings gracefully, typhons couldn't fly, since years of evolution had taken their toll. But, naturally, I was good at running up and down flights of stairs. Being a squire had made the action a trait.

Because of too many errands, I joked and ran the last length of hallway into the Great Hall. I saw a man at the middle of the cathedral and ran to him. Excitement, not exhaustion, was making me breathe heavily.

Father smiled when I approached and held his upper hands out to me. I grabbed them with my own then dropped to my right knee to say a prayer.

I'd been quite young when I'd asked Father if I could become a knight. Even to this day I remembered his face of disappointment; however, never once in all these years had he discouraged me.

"Nice dat ye'athe fin'lee graced us wid thy presence, Arthor," he joked. The Duke spoke an older dialect of the province Verengosha.

"Sorry, m'Duke, but I came as fast as I could." Despite previous reservations, I didn't mind being my father's squire, when he'd created such a position for me to fill. Although it was not normal and I felt some guilt by it, I'd learned so much and gained so many skills in weapons and diplomacy, which some knights had to learn on the job. But had Father believed that it wouldn't have been fair if I'd been someone else's squire?

No, no matter what the situation, I knew I would have—

I blinked, letting something else soak in. Father grinned and stepped back.

"Us?" I finally took a good look around the hall. There were many more people sitting in the pews than I'd originally thought. It looked like the whole town was here. Also, tapestries flowed down between lanterns and columns. In above archways opened for the event, flags of every province blew in the wind. Decorative shields, spears and swords lined the chamber.

Polished armor flickered from the lights of the lanterns. There were hundreds of knights in various colors of armor standing behind Father. To the knights' right and across a long red carpet, Verengoshia's Krastieks, female typhons who had taken up weapons to protect the country, stood proudly. In the stands, the highest ranking of knights and Krastieks sat in places of honor beside the statue of Yali, Messenger of God. Over so many lifetimes, the fight against monsters had bestowed honor on many.

But will Crytonia one day not need us? I shuddered and looked back toward Father and the rear of the Great Hall.

A large figure walked out of the shadows and was surrounded

by guards. The armored warriors gave the man they protected room to breathe, but made sure no threat would come to him. Of course if anyone could be so dishonorable, they had no soul.

Everyone in the cathedral was quiet. Clumps of Magner's flesh fell upon my skin. *This has to be it,* I told myself, *my Comicion.* The day was always kept hidden from the prospective knight; mainly, because his reaction and composure had a lot to do with his initial rank.

Out of the corner of my right eye I saw Mother. She smiled at me from behind her ladies in waiting. I nodded, quickly smiled too and dropped to my knee when the group of men stopped in front of me.

"Your Majesty." I pressed my lower hands onto the hard brick floor. My wings spread out to a full span and my tail made no motion. I closed my eyes and waited, wondering what the King would say.

"Knightly apprentice," a tenor broke the air, flowing throughout the chamber. The King spoke universal Crytonian, a dialect understood by all provinces.

I looked up and saw the King reaching out. I clasped hold of the monarch's hands and brought them to my forehead. Surprised, I marveled at the strength yet in those hands. "It's an honor, M'Ku-rex."

King Thegrison was over six centuries old. Scars stretched across his brow, cheeks and neck. His wings showed several accounts of battles. The Crytonian leader, like my father and me, had been born into royalty. He was not a knight, but he was brave and trustworthy and had endured tremendous tortures while protecting his people. To me and anyone, this man was the pinnacle of nobility and honor, and I was almost afraid to make eye contact with him.

"Arthor, are you ready for the rite which now falls upon you?"

Thegrison asked, his strong tenor practically resonating in the spears, swords and shields on the walls—seemingly even in the armor surrounding each knight and Krastiek.

"Yes, Sire." Langrid moths seemed to be hatching in my belly. I had to force those words out so they sounded normal. I also managed to keep my teeth from chattering and my tail from shaking too. This was it.

Finally!

"Very well, give me your sword." I pulled the weapon from its sheath, raised it up parallel to the floor, and passed it to the King's opened hand.

"Yes, it is a great instrument," Thegrison spoke when he grabbed hold of the weapon, one hand also wielding the practice sword. "Its weight seems heavy, but comfortable. The Verengoshian Duke says you wield it like no other. Many other knights say the same. I look at you, and I am not surprised."

"Thank you, M'Ku-rex," I said. That nearly floored me, such praise from the King.

The old ruler grinned, looked past me and uttered a request in Tylandnese, Aenglan's language: "Gras mi d'flactor."

"Bring me the long sword," I translated silently, a common practice I'd gained with Aenglan as my teacher. The bodyguard knew as many languages as I did, probably more considering his age and experience. Needless to say, he had often taught me proverbs and tales in the old language. The only complaint I could think of was that the translations often used more Verengoshian words.

Small price to pay for knowledge, I reminded myself of a little bit of witticism. Even after seventy-five Deliplainan years of trying to master self-discipline, it took me another four breaths to calm down. Come on! at one-hundred-and-three-years-old, I was a young man and eager to protect my people. I was fucking excited!

My sword, a knight's tool, his symbol of strength, his vessel of honor. I tried not to look for it, kept my head forward, but my peripheral vision scanned for the object that symbolized the Chival Codes. Each edged instrument was forged for a specific person, and many considered their weapons as their personal ties with God. For a knight this was the rule.

"Fellow Crytonians," the King began, taking a breath while a younger squire walked toward us. The boy carried something wrapped in silk covers, but I knew what it was, since an impression of a hilt and pommel poked through the cloth.

A drum slowly began to beat, and the young sword-bearer marched along with it. The audience was still quiet, although many, who I could see anyway, moved impatiently in their seats, wanting to do something other than just watch.

I waited in artificial calm, doing my best to conceal my impatience. *Let's get this started already!* I whined to myself. I just wanted to give my oath to my Lord, my King, my country and my people. But I stayed rigidly still, constantly reminding myself that one of a knight's best attributes is patience, even in spite of unbearable and purposely lengthy ceremonies.

Thegrison looked at me and smiled, obviously knowing what I was thinking. I know he was taking guilty pleasure in this.

"I wish this happened every day," he said. "But all knightly candidates must be patient. They must learn their skills well, honor the Chival Codes that they are taught and be ready to protect us."

I gazed up at the King and nodded. Then I noticed the colorful garb of a very young squire named Lance beside him.

Lance was breathing deeply, and his tail swayed in an anxious irregular motion—back, up, down, side to side.

The audience was still quiet.

"Yes, every knight trains for this day, the Comicíon," Thegrison continued. "He who is deemed ready is initiated as an Armored Servant.

"He, for the Krastieks have their own sets of Codes ..." Thegrison paused and nodded thoughtfully to the women warriors. As one, they hammered their shields once in salute. To coin a Panterian phrase: they were "badass."

"For as long as there has been a Crytonia, a knight is given his first rank upon this initiation," the King said. "This rank is a color symbolizing the Code he best personifies. Red for 'Ferocity' in battle, Blue for 'Confidence,' White for 'Integrity,' Green for 'Humbleness' or 'Perseverance,' Black for 'Stealth' or 'Cunning.' Truthfully, the list goes on and on, for there is a color for every knight.

"Then, over time, a single color can no longer identify the man he has become. At this point, he either gains another color upon his armor, or he may obtain a mix that can blend into a Bronze, Brass, Iron, Steel and finally Silver."

The crowd's awe filled the giant room. There were only a handful of knights that had reached the rank of Steel. To this date, no single knight had ever reached the rank of Silver. There were a few instances in which a group of knights gained the rank as a single entity, but only in posthumous celebration.

"It is time. Please give me the blade, Lance." The King nodded to the young squire. Naturally, Lance tried his best of not freezing up and not succumbing to the enormity of this spectacle; however, his wings and tail shook nervously.

"Y-y-yes, Your Majesty," the boy managed to choke out. Thegrison laughed and patted the boy on the shoulder. Lance smiled had gave the shrouded weapon to the King, while Thegrison handed my old practice sword to the younger squire. As one, the crowd let out a single "Ahhhhhh" when some of the shiny black blade peaked through the silk as the King took the new weapon.

"Arthor, have you completed all your quests?" the Ku-rex asked, smiled and tossed aside the silk wrap, while Lance moved behind the monarch's bodyguards.

"Yes, Sire."

"Have you taken the Codes of Chivalry to heart and promise to obey them throughout your life?"

"I have, Your Majesty."

"Then tell me, knightly candidate, what Code has guided your training the most, which one symbolizes Arthor Jones?"

"No single one." I bowed my head and spoke with my heart. I'd idolized Knighthood ever since I'd watched Tinold take on four Krazter gremils, which had managed to get into the perimeter of the castle. They had nearly gotten Mother when she had pulled me away from terrible claws. Tinold had killed two of them before the rest of the guards killed the others. I had been just a little kid—maybe around your equivalent of five or six—but Father had been away in the next province. Of course, he had gotten an earful of how amazing Tinold had been.

A week later, we all witnessed the ceremony of Tinold's elevation to the Iron rank.

I got chills. Thinking about that day and how it was as nearly as exciting as this one.

"They all are dear and equal to me," I said, having started reading about knights and their Code of Honor the very day Tinold had saved us.

"I see ..." the King trailed off, as though smiling. "Such enthusiasm, common for the Initiation, but yours is different, sincere."

"It is, King Thegrison." A hard, hammer-sounding voice, as though such a tool had been struck against an anvil, echoed in the hall.

That voice had come from Tinold, who was the greatest knight Verengosha had seen in half a millennium. Tinold had been the first knight ever to be initiated with the rank of three colors. Eventually, the red, green and purple had been replaced by a beautiful Bronze. Iron enshrouded his plating, covered by the marks from many battles. It was inevitable that he'd achieve the rank of Steel soon.

"Ah, Sir Tinold Harker, why have you spoken for this lad?" the King asked.

"He claims the truth, Your Majesty. During his training, I've seen such qualities, over and over again. I swear that I've never seen such a squire before. He is confident, deductive, skilled and humble. Although I wish to see one again …" Sir Tinold trailed off and gazed to the benches below him and the other honored knights and Krastieks.

Nathan, Tinold's squire, sat there with other attendants. The boy had been the Iron Knight's apprentice since my Shartal twenty-five Deliplainan years ago. Of course, there wasn't any doubt in my mind that what the man asked would come to pass.

I, however, wondered why Tinold spoke for me now. I'd thought our relationship had dwindled after the Shartal, in which I'd chosen a route no other squire had considered. Since then, Tinold had grown somewhat detached. Honestly, I'd wondered if he'd thought that I no longer took this all that seriously. Had he thought that a Duke's son was just playing a convoluted game of knights and monsters? If so, what was Tinold doing now?

"What I've heard is true then." Thegrison took a step back for a reason I couldn't fathom. Then the King threw his arms up into the air—hoisting the sword up and gesturing to the crowd —and whispered in a language I'd never heard: "Le'Jocal tola de flanir sa." Then louder: "Is it true?"

"Yes, it is true," another knight spoke, then another, and soon all their swords were banging on their shields while they yelled, giving their full support t-to me! I'd never seen this pandemonium at any other Comicíon.

The audience in the Great Hall screamed as well. Had they ever seen or been a part of such a spectacle? Maybe they wanted to be a part of it, and, for a brief second, to experience what it was like to be an Armored Servant? As a consequence, the hall actually shook with excitement.

Eventually, they stopped and quieted down. The King's arms fell back to his sides, except for the two holding the new sword. "I am speechless," Thegrison choked. "I have never seen such support for a squire, and even the bravest of knights have never gained the cheers like I have just heard.

"My people, I have been your king for four and half centuries, and I've never seen the likes of this. Your compassion for this young candidate moves me, and it would be an injustice to not allow this squire to gain his final honor.

"Therefore, young man"—the sword came down, and I felt it upon my left shoulder—"under God and by the laws of Crytonia, I bestow Knighthood upon you." The blade then moved to my right shoulder and then was lifted away.

"Rise, Sir Arthor Jones," the King bellowed, as though excitement was getting the best of him. "Take your sword, *Omniemnan*, into your grip and exclaim your feelings to your people and God. Honor us with your words, Silver Knight."

What? My eyes flew open, and I looked up to the King in shock, excitement and wonder. The Langrid moths in my belly seemed to be breeding like grobons, and my wings and tail nearly flapped out of control. I rose to my feet in restraint, even though it took all of my energy to keep from jumping into the air and yelping incoherently.

I again looked at Thegrison, who now had to look up instead

of down. The monarch's golden eyes and face seemed to hold admiration and even jealousy in them. Suggesting, despite everything he had done for Crytonia, even he wished to be blessed with the honor a knight embodied.

"Thank you, King Thegrison." I, now Knight of Crytonia and the Province of Verengosha, was the first regal to gain such an honor, and I took hold of my sword.

Omniemnan's black, dual-tapered blade shimmered in the light. It was a product of the Verengoshian Blacksmiths who kept their profession a carefully guarded secret, a secret that allowed the material to cut through the hardest steel and never need sharpening. And even though *Omniemnan* was made of different materials and took several years to complete, I wasn't too surprised that it had the same shape and weight of my former practice sword.

I held the sword up and read the inscription on the blade: THE SWORD *OMNIEMNAN*, CONSTITUENT OF SIR ARTHOR JONES. PROTECTOR OF VERENGOSHA AND GOD'S ARMORED SERVANT.

This made my heart pound so hard that I thought it would leap out of my chest, and I almost found it hard to breathe.

I looked at the audience, who sat in awe. I looked at my mother, who was smiling, while tears fell over her white cheeks. She'd been as important as anyone in my education, since she had taught me about the Arts and Sciences and the fine art of negotiation.

Aenglan stood proudly too, with light armor under a guardian's robe. The bodyguard had given his all in my training, and I saluted the man.

Then I looked at Father. The Duke's wings were spread out, his tail swaying back and forth. His lower arms were crossed. His upper fingers were laced and were held out about six inches from his chin, thereby presenting his praise.

I gazed at Father and time escaped me. Ever since the Shartal Hunt, I'd felt more comfortable in the man's presence. I never understood why this had been the case, but I'd appreciated the better relationship. And oddly enough, I noticed that the Duke smiled the same way as when I had finished that hunt. But … but was there something missing and different?

But the magnificent blade soon regained my attention. Then I nodded to the King and turned to face the audience. I took a deep breath and calmed myself.

"My people," I started, happy that I even had a voice. "I have trained for this moment nearly all my life. This honor you have placed upon me is great, but I shall never let you down. I will never fail you."

I knelt down and bowed before them, holding *Omniemnan* tip down. "By this sword I pledge myself to your service. My life is subject to my people and country and any innocent that needs my protection. My blood flows with the Chivalrous Codes, and never will I toss these aside if sadness, fear or rage tempt me. I am a knight, and your lives and safety mean more to me than my very life. This I promise."

I rose and suddenly felt a great vibration beneath my feet. Everyone hummed a specific key. The Great Hall trembled, and I now had to shout, "My People, I am ecstatic. I am your new armored servant, sworn to protect you. God, watch us all!"

The humming rose to a thunder. I kissed the *Blessing* made by the hilt of the sword, and then I held the sword aloft and cried out, "Long life for Crytonia. May its presence always to be united on the grounds of Deliplain."

The cathedral then thundered with everyone's cheers. The sword seemed to vibrate in my hand, and I suddenly realized the gravity of the rank I'd just received. Shocked and bewildered, I shook out the uncertainties, the doubts and the fears. And even though the sword seemed heavier in my grip, I straightened my arm and held *Omniemnan* high.

I was such a damned fool!

I'll be in a battle soon enough and they'll be proud, I told myself for justification and trying not to think of myself as egotistical. But I had to repeat that several times so that the sword no longer felt so heavy. And I kept repeating it so that the armor, the Silver armor that was being brought before me, didn't seem so blinding.

Deliplain spun ten more times around its sun, Flafir, after my Comicíon. During this time I did my best to settle matters concerning domestic squabbles, which was a job Father had requested of me when he wasn't able to reside over them. Mostly, these disputes amongst the people were civil crimes caused by miscommunication, and there were about twenty or so a week.

I dealt with them quickly, always leaving the matters settled, and as fair as possible. It's funny. My decisions were never questioned, even if some of them might not have been so good. Still, I put a lot of thought into them and knew most were reasonable, since there hadn't been any battles to distract me. Therefore, I tried to make sure both sides came out ahead whenever possible —adhering to Crytonian law, of course.

When not playing judge, I focused the rest of my energy on training. I'd developed several new tactics for the battlefield and developed new fighting styles. I loved training others—In fact, during this time, I'd set up a specialized school of warfare for squires, knights, mercenaries, and even the Krastieks. Hundreds came to train at the school.

One day between court appearances and training classes, I sparred with both Aenglan and Tinold. The Bodyguard and Iron Knight took both flanks against me, each of their swords clashing about mine.

Omniemnan sang with a bell-like melody, a chorus when combined with the voices of the other blades. I kept my wings tight in fists and danced on the courtyard we battled on. It was a war dance, a movement of twists, turns and even somersaults. Today, I performed them without armor, mainly to add to my quickness. Later I'd have to cover myself with plating to make sure I didn't grow clumsy with the extra weight.

Omniemnan rang again and again, keeping my attackers at a sword-and-a-half length away at all times. There was no way I could win but I was doing what I could to simply keep them away from me. I howled with joy and exertion, careful not to be too aggressive, thereby allowing me to keep this stalemate going as long as I wished. Well, until I got tired, which I was.

Aenglan and Tinold shouted too. Smiles were on their faces, but a sign of frustration showed as well. The music from their swords continued to echo within the castle's walls.

"Vlo'lee," I finally cheered, raising my lower hands and clapping them. "I submit"—tugging the braid of my shoulder length hair—"It looks better unbound."

Aenglan and Tinold laughed, sheathing their swords. Soon both men began to clap and speak to each other. "Finally, the boy listens to reason," Aenglan bellowed.

"Lebo," Tinold agreed, taking Aenglan's hand then searching for mine. "If he was yet a squire, we'd still be playing our blades. His Honor has made him wise."

"Ne-tok." Aenglan nodded and gave his hand to me. The three of us made a triangle. "But is he getting soft?"

I looked at my comrades and waited for the mutual gesture, realizing my rank should initiate it. "Tas ve leot, God, a glotic. 'Praise our Lord, thank you for our strength.'"

Tinold and Aenglan uttered the prayer too, but both still grinned and stared oddly in my direction.

"No," I answered Aenglan's question. "My blood boils for a battle as always." I raised my sword. "Here, let us continue."

And another two blades slid out again from their sheaths.

"Flectni!" Both the Iron Knight and the bodyguard joined in my war call. They readied their swords. Their wings too were clenched in fists.

"Arthor"—a powerful voice rang into the courtyard before I could attack—"Tinold? Aenglan?"

"Chetok? M'Lord," I said, while the others bowed and acknowledged our Duke. Their swords were sheathed instantly.

I approached Father and grabbed his upper hands. I bowed my head. The highest-ranking knight, as a sign of honor to respected dignitaries, was always the first to offer salutations to someone who greeted or sought dialog with a swarm of knights. "What can we do for you, m'Duke?"

"I have troubling news," he said uneasily. I released his hands and walked with him as he moved toward Aenglan and the Iron Knight. "A messenger came in today, almost ran the legs dead off his malix."

We gathered round. The voice of Duke Jacobson Jones was grave, almost strained. "It is a sad day. The Emperor of the next kingdom has broken off ties with our King Thegrison and is mounting troops as we speak. A large force already has begun to gather in Sadolo, near Melborn. It is expected to reach four thousand within the next week. They will stage an assault against Verengosha first."

I looked at my feet. "So, we now fight against each other,

over the land we once shared."

"It was only a matter of time," Aenglan added. "The dark creatures that used to plague us are fewer in number. Now we find conflict amongst ourselves once more. Yali curse us."

The Iron Knight said nothing. He was from Verengosha but some of his family had moved to Melborn a couple of centuries ago. I wondered if Tinold was picturing who he would have to fight if a battle arose. I tried my best to empathize, even though none of my family lived there.

Eventually, Sir Tinold Harker took a deep breath and then looked into the eyes of those around him, letting his amber globes rest for a long time on the Duke's before he opened his mouth, and shook his head. "So it begins."

I poised myself for battle; readied my great sword within its sheath; and checked the company of knights, archers and light sword- and spears-men behind me. There were one hundred and fifty people in my group, adding to the two thousand armored and lightly armored men inevitably under the Duke's command.

I looked at the surrounding soldiers. Fifty heavily armored knights road on their malix, and their magnificent swords seemed to shake in their sheaths, thirsty for battle. The rest of the men making up my Company checked their bows, chain mail, half-plating, spear tips and other tools of war.

Many of these men were from the peasantry, the Varlou, and would be relatively inexperienced in battle. Worry was on many of their faces, and I did my best to re-enforce their bravery and the idea that they would survive the defensive.

I saw familiar faces, the same people, whom I'd helped settle disputes over the years. I was proud that they had requested to stay and fight. Hell, much of this army was voluntary. I nodded to as many people as I could, although my visor shielded my smile of encouragement.

At the moment, the morale was good, and each person nodded back. However, I knew that the battle would have to be within the next ten days. Any longer and the army would have to move to find new foraging plains, which would be another fifty jolds to the Northeast and much closer to the enemy's stronghold. And although typhons were good at conserving their strength and rationing food, this army was still consuming twelve thousand keldis, about six point two tons, of food a day, and the seven hundred and fifty malix were eating fifteen thousand keldis of daily fodder. Naturally, I tried to picture what the charburis-covered plain would look like at the end of the tenth day, and I realized the moon wouldn't look much more barren.

I shook my head and looked toward the Northeast, where the opposing army was to come. A giant mountain entered my eyes. Varnasha towered into the heavens, twenty thousand delbits, about twenty-seven thousand feet, high. It stood within the Mons'de Yali, a mountain range which defined the Verengoshian/Melbora boarder.

There were few Crytonians who'd ever traveled or climbed those peaks, let alone Varnasha itself. Only a handful more from Melborn had ever succeeded.

Can there be an army capable of crossing such an obstruction? I asked. There were no travel routes over the mountain range. All the old trade routes between Melborn and Verengosha had been along the rivers Logath and Tumis, which were two hundred jolds to the Northwest of here.

Taken aback by the hazardous terrain, I immediately wondered if King Thegrison would have ever made his troops cross such a land. However, I twisted my tail knowingly, realizing that such was not the case.

I squinted at the jagged peaks in the distance, their sides start-ing to show a growing orange from a setting sun. I'd never met the Arc-Emperor Culom Flacokr, the leader of the Tolsejies Empire, which encompassed the large provinces of Melborn, Sadolo, Tarnir, Ivatr, Klopir, and a host of smaller Prince and Duke-domes. I'd heard a great deal about him. He was a Regal whom others once respected for his techniques in combat. He was also responsible for eliminating the Yal'owers from his empire. Those had been large burrowing snakes that had grown content with living beneath the homes of typhons and preying on them while they slept.

Honestly, in that empire, there were still plenty of creatures who liked the taste of typhon meat—preferred it rather than anything else. *Why then,* I wondered, *why has the man sent such a large force to do battle with his own kind? We'd never had any disputes in the past.*

I gazed at Verengosha's highest peak. Near Varnasha a large flock of birds flew. It had been years since I'd seen such a group, and it made me feel jealous for not being able to fly.

Shrugging, I looked away from the birds. I was riding along a fairly wide trail. The Crytonian Army—Thegrison had also sent additional soldiers and supply wagons to Verengosha—took up most of the path. Some of its members sang war hymns, others prayed and some looked at the scenery. Others either chatted or simply kept to themselves.

I nodded to a middle-age farmer, who carried a great hammer on his back. The mercenary was singing the triumphs the ham-mer had once rout.

I grimaced and wondered if the man truly looked forward to engaging other typhons in battle, or if he was simply singing to distract himself. I shook my head and let my eyes scan up ahead, soon catching a glimpse of a shining gold figure.

"Lofta," I shouted and nudged the sides of the malix a bit, prompting it to increase its hop-jump motion. Eventually, the quiet double-taps from its two-toed feet were spread out to a slower but heavier rhythm, as the distance the malix jumped increased and gained speed.

I passed soldiers, men-at-arms, mercenaries and volunteers— waved while doing so—and then brought my malix back to its slower hop-jump trot when I reached the head of the army and where Father was.

"Ah, Sir Jones, how do things look?" The Duke turned his golden helmet around to see who had rode up from behind.

"M'Duke, many of the men are getting hungry and tired."

I also nodded to Aenglan, who rode alongside Father. The bodyguard wore a dark green armor, appearing as an emerald in the sun. I knew that Tyland, once a country unto itself, awarded its knights differently than the rest of Crytonia. And although Tyland had been incorporated two centuries ago, it had never completely merged with the rest of the country, even after what had happened to the last Tyland king. At any rate, I was positive the green plating on Aenglan's body represented more than one rank; however, the old knight had become the bodyguard of Duke Jones long before I was born, and had never reminisced about his days as a knight.

"Chetok-se," Jacobson Jones conceded to my warning, regaining my attention. "The battlefield is only a short distance from here anyway, and the enemy will be visible from far off. We should be able to meet up with them in the morning if they come over the range at dawn."

The Duke turned and nodded to a Purple Knight. "Alert the troops. Stop the march. We'll set up camp here. Hoist up the wagons and begin dispersing the rations. Everyone gets equal, size-proportionate shares."

"Yes, Sire." A blur of purple spun with an armored malix. Shouts immediately followed, preceded by others. Soon enough the great army stopped and began to set up for the night.

"Did Tinold have anything to say?" the Regal asked and looked back into my direction.

"No, m'Duke, Sir Harker has said little to me since we left Martoluf." I frowned and shook my head. The very idea of having to kill a cousin or an uncle sickened me. "And I don't want to push him. Iron Knight or not, he's still a man, although I'm sure he'll fight regardless."

"Yes, I know." The Duke nodded. "When we fought the McCaslitor Demons together, he killed two, despite having a spear rammed into his side. I don't know how he survived or even recovered. But later, he did wear the new Bronze armor well."

"He will be OK as long as he does not hesitate." A sharp voice came from beside the Duke. Aenglan moved forward so that I could see him too. "I have known Tinold a long time now, my Lord, Sir Jones. The Iron Knight won't endanger his people. A knight's own personal grief comes second to those around him."

I nodded, knowing what Aenglan said was true. As horrible as it sounded, I would have gone to war even if my own father had been on the enemy's side.

"Yes, Tinold will," I conceded, but the very thought of killing typhons brought on a terrible weltschmerz, especially when they would die just like the beasts our people had once slain. "But will others? The town's peo—"

"What are those? Birds?" someone asked in the background, making me wonder if the flock had left Varnasha completely.

Odd, usually large birds such as those stayed near the cliffs during their mating season. They seldom flew over prairies. We all looked up in surprise.

"No, 'tis the Zarmbats," a shriek came from an aging villager, whose tongue sounded Landish. "Dey haf'com for owr'sols. We mus'flee, owr'Lor, o perish in ta depths o El."

"What's a zarmbat?" I thought back to all the books I'd read and all my teachers' lectures about dangerous beasts.

Father shook his head. "I thought their description had been lost with time. Boogiemen, nothing more ..." his voice trailed off. Then the Duke pulled free his one-armed sword, *Operus Magne*, while grabbing a shield with another hand; another two held tightly to the reins. "Be brave, my countrymen. Fight hard. And, Arthor, when you fight these vial beasts, do not let them grab a hold of you. They'll suck the life out of you for sure."

Then the army regrouped, and most formalities were lost. Aenglan shouted the Duke's name and not the title. Many of the other knights got off their malix, and stood in front of the voluntary soldiers.

Not all formality was discarded: "But, Sire, why have they come to our country, and what of the army we were to face?"

The Duke broke off from his orders long enough to pause and look at me. "I'm afraid this might be it. The Arc-Emperor's heart is colder than we thought. This Regal has no morals. He might have saved his people, but he's made a pact with demons instead."

I gripped my reins tightly. Just as I was about to return to my Company, I gazed up into the sky and noticed the forms coming toward us. Their bodies were awkward, skinny and wide-winged, and their long tails ended in large trapezoids. Big heads gazed back at me, teeth shining in the sun nearly a half-jold away, and I wondered when I'd hear their screams. What would they sound like?

Enough! My people need me, I told myself, preparing to protect my comrades. But before I nudged my malix's sides, I saw a flash —almost like a bolt of lightning—blaze from one of the creatures. It burned the ground where it hit and the grass immediately smoldered and blackened.

"What was that?" I shouted, turning back toward Father, who was busy issuing orders and who was facing a different direction.

Perplexed, I looked back at the scorched ground. Apparently, the flying demon—

Something clicked, and my heart began to race. My eyes popped wide open, not believing such sorcery. I turned back toward Father and screamed, "Dear God, Fa—"

"I see," Logan mumbled after Jones had finished the first verse of his tale. He still couldn't understand why the Crytonian never mentioned that he'd been a knight in Crytonia, or why he never wore his armor in Crystal Mountain. He had once heard Arthor say that a mysterious flash had brought him to Panteria, and he could only guess that the Verengoshian stopped his story at that particular moment. But what guilt tortured the Silver Knight now? What caused him to forsake his rank?

"Arthor …" Logan paused a moment, not really knowing what to say or where he was going with this. "Your people must've thought you were killed. They couldn't have believed you were transported to a different world. The weapons the zarmbats were carrying must have—"

"I know that it somehow blasted me here," Arthor interrupted him. "I know that the EuroAmerican 27th Century Transport Experiments tore up our dimension pretty well and was probably responsible in some way. Regardless, I wish that I'd had an opportunity to fight alongside my men and my father and my friends. Or, at the very least, I wish I hadn't made it to this world alive."

That said, the Crytonian frowned, turned and looked over the far horizon, which was being painted a golden, reddish blaze by the approaching dawn.

"What are you talking about?" McMillian shook his head and couldn't fathom Arthor—of all people—saying something so negative. "How can you say that? Don't you know how much everyone appreciates you here? Don't you realize the impact you've had on every single one of us? Fuck, Arthor, what the hell?"

The winged man sighed and cleared his throat. His wings and tail swayed in erratic motions. "I don't know. There are just so many things I did wrong when I first came here. There have been so many things that have happened, and I have no means to expiate myself."

Logan shook his head, ignoring Arthor's nonverbal requests to stop. "Oh, give me break. You can always—"

"Please, Logan, just give it a rest." Arthor's cheeks flushed red and his teeth showed his irritation.

"Come on, Arthor." Logan frowned. "It can't be that bad. It's not like you—"

"Bastik!" Arthor hit his lower right hand on the composite bench they were sitting on. He didn't break it, despite the tension in his voice.

"All right, you want to know?" the Crytonian yelled. "Fine, I killed a child!" The Knight's body shook suddenly, his wings collapsed and his voice softened again. "I killed an innocent, little boy.

"What?" Arthor said derisively, obviously seeing the shock on Logan's face. "Surprised? Do you think it is so easy now?"

What the fuck? McMillian tried not to allow a deathly silence to enshroud them, but he couldn't help it. He tried not to think of what horrors Arthor might have done. Still, he reminded himself of the pain the knight had been dealing with over the years. He imagined the most macabre thoughts, which made even a well-trained assassin shudder.

"What happened?" the ex-CIA man finally choked out. "I couldn't imagine it happened intentionally."

"No, I didn't do it on purpose," Arthor sighed plaintively. "Of course that doesn't make it right and actually sickens me even more." Black-green cheeks held tight, keeping back three years' worth of guilt. Four hands rested without any type of motion. The HVAC system in the obstower blew air through blond hair, making it flutter in a simulated wind. Blue eyes were left in trance. Water collected around the orbs, but couldn't escape.

"It was a few days before Jim and his inforun crew found me," Jones continued. "I had just escaped from a laboratory that must have found me unconscious after I was zapped here. I was starving, confused, weak and had no idea where I was going.

"I had no idea how far I had flown, but I smelled food from a nearby house and decided to land.

"A family was having a BBQ behind their house. No one was around, so I figured I could sneak something."

Logan cocked an eyebrow.

"Don't ask me how I knew what a modern BBQ looked like. We had another word for it"—Arthor shrugged—"For some reason, when I woke up in that lab, I just knew what things here were, and how to speak and understand your languages. All of them."

"That's odd, very odd," McMillian said while maintaining his puzzled look. "It's frightening even. Do you think the lab did some type of flash memory on you? Any reason—"

"Who knows?" Jones shook his head. "Jim thinks it was an Infiltration lab. Their search squads are always combing the Growth Zones for animals to put through their experiments. I must have been quite a find. Who knows what they were eventually going to do with me."

"I care not to guess, but if they spent the time to flash your memory—"

"Yeah, but do you want to talk about this or about …?"

"Right, sorry."

Jones smiled meekly. "I looked around, didn't see anybody, so I walked behind the house and found the cooker. I was so hungry, and I just needed a few seconds …" Arthor paused and took some breaths. Logan noticed the man's hands were shaking. "I actually made it to the lid—"

"And the kid saw you."

"He was only four. Since I was so tired I didn't hear him sneak up behind me. He knew I was going to steal the food, so he spooked me with a RED ZONE panic horn."

Logan's eyes widened in understanding, and asked, "And you thought—"

"Chetok, I thought the lab's soldiers had found me. I reacted without thinking and caught the kid square in the chest with the point of my, my tail—

"And you know the worst of it?" the Knight stammered. "I didn't even try to stop the bleeding. I didn't even try to help him. Shocked, I just shot up into the sky." Jones lowered his head in shame. "Later, after I had a chance to investigate what happened, I found out that the boy survived but I could have killed him and nearly did. My God, how could I have ignored his mother's cries for help? What type of honor did I hold dear? I essentially killed him."

Logan was sitting on one of the benches located in the obstower. How could he say what happened was simply an accident without belittling the whole thing? Didn't the Knight already know this? And did such matter when honor came into play? Concomitantly, Logan was somewhat envious and a little put off. As bad as what had happened, Arthor's compunctions so far didn't nearly equate to anything Logan himself—let alone the things Jim or Rebecca—had done.

Fuck! Logan kept himself from sneering. *The kid didn't die? Why does Arthor say he killed him?*

Thankfully, there was a beep from the Crytonian's comlink, and the Crytonian snapped a finger on it before the second beep. "Chetok, good morning. No, it's been pretty quiet here. All right, see you in a few minutes. It's chilly, so you better bring a sweater."

A joke? Hmm, what we do to try to keep others from worrying, Logan thought to himself, and then to the Knight: "Arthor, they'll be up here soon. Can we continue this later?"

The sun rose above the horizon. Logan noticed the sunlight, simulated by the holograms around them, glistening in the Verengoshian's eyes, as though a fire was cast in a turbulent sea. "Chetok," Arthor agreed and rose to his feet. "Later."

Logan got up too, stretched his legs and actually forced out a most convincing smile. "Great, let's eat. Have ya gotten used to the synthesized eggs yet?"

"Chetok," Arthor let out a groan. He was obviously still circumspect of their ingredients and how they managed to taste like real eggs, even though Deliplain's version of "chickens" gave Logan a future set of nightmares, if he could ever get over the current one that kept him up at nights. However, since Panteria's chickens had been wiped out nearly a thousand years ago by a genetically modified plague, Logan had no frame of reference for either.

"Good, Ecie told me he found a new recipe for an omelet." McMillian heard himself smirk. "Maybe he'll leave the shells out of mine this time." That had become an ongoing joke.

"I don't know," Arthor countered. "Computers can hold a grudge for a long time, and he's never really forgiven you for the first prank you pulled on him. He's organic but still a living computer. Time might be more forgiving than he is."

"Yeah, I figured as much."

"Well, don't worry. He won't be able to do anything with your bones after you die." Arthor made a hissing sound, mimicking the unique cremation system the Executioners used.

"Right, he'll still probably send me off with red and yellow shoes."

Arthor stopped him. "No, Jim and I will."

Logan gave one last grunt and led his friend to the elevator of the obstower, preparing to meet the members of the next shift. He looked down at his feet and then back at Arthor, who was smiling. The man's pain was now clearly masked.

The ex-CIA man concocted a frown, realizing this day was going to be a long one. "Thanks, just as long as no one forgot."

"Father?" Arthor blinked and was suddenly blinded by what seemed like a dozen suns. Had he fallen to the ground and hit his head? Had he been knocked unconscious?

He reached up to remove his helmet, but armor-less fingers soon pressed against his bare forehead instead.

"He's awake." Arthor heard someone whisper but was immediately hushed. He opened his eyes just a little, seeing an empty white room with a dozen lights in the ceiling. He gathered that he was on some type of an examination table?

He closed his eyes again to calm himself. His mind, however, suddenly swirled with images, sounds and names that he couldn't quite place or remember where he'd seen them.

The Devil's work! He tried to fight these thoughts by thinking of Crytonia, his armor and his sword. Thankfully, the images began to slow and finally stop.

Arthor took some additional calming breaths and looked up. A ceiling, white and sterile, appeared above him. Walls of a material he'd never seen before were eighteen *feet* wide one way, and ten in the other. An odd smell entered his nose too, and he wondered if they cleaned the room with *bleach*.

He shook his head, trying to shake out the new words that simply were there. Looking for a distraction, he got off the table and walked over to one of the white walls. His back was sore, but he stretched his shoulders and took a breath to ease the discomfort some. He had no clothes, taken earlier no doubt, so he covered himself with his right wing.

A viewing laboratory? His head began to ache again from a sudden rush of information. However, he began to use the information to his advantage. If that was what this room was, then there might be a hidden window nearby.

Someone said something, he remembered, *and it sounded like a woman.* He traced his fingers over the surface of the walls. Nothing was felt and there didn't seem to be any one-way glass around. Maybe there was a *camera*?

"What do you want?" he asked the emptiness. "Why have you locked me in this room? Speak now. You're in the presence of Nobility. Where are my clothes, my armor and my sword? And why do you treat me like this?"

No response.

"I know someone is in the next room. I heard you and I can

still hear you breathing," he said, playing a bluff. It didn't work. His wings and tail began to sway in frustration.

"Alweighs muse ye be calm." Old advice from Aenglan rang warningly in his ears when anger began to surge through him. A bit surprised by this uncharacteristic behavior, Arthor immediately tried to suppress the rage, but he began pounding his fists against the wall anyway.

He heard a door slide open. He turned his head. A troop of semi-armored men walked into the room. They held black-metal *rifles* in their hands. The very presence of those weapons immediately made him more agitated, but one of the men raised a hand in a way Arthor believed as proffering PEACE.

"Al'right now," the man said soothingly. "No one's going to hurt you." Arthor nodded and stepped closer to the apparent leader of the squad, but the other's hand suddenly twitched. Then the man barked, "Hold it!"

The Silver Knight growled when he saw weapons rise up in distrust. *They dishonor a knight who has engaged in diplomacy?* he cursed, then saw that one of them was squeezing a trigger finger, about to fire on an unarmed—

Arthor spun and hammered the group with his tail. Hard metallic armor popped and gave way, blood sprayed the walls, and the men collapsed.

What in God's name? What's happened to me? He clenched his fists, feeling strength in them he couldn't understand. He shook his head in disbelief and looked at what he'd done to the soldiers. In the corner of his eye, he noticed something—

He jumped. The door slid shut. His body crashed into the door, denting it outward some. He ran into it again, then again, but it no longer gave way.

Arthor turned around in frustration and calmed himself. He realized it had taken much longer than it should have, but he blamed his circumstances.

The Knight grimaced and moved over to the dead soldiers. He searched one of them, then fiddled with some of the *electronics* and other items the man had on him. He found nothing useful.

Well, at least, let's see what they were going to shoot me with, he told himself and then took one of the rifles. He pointed the *barrel* at the would-be attacker and looked it over. The weapon seemed much like the new crossbows his people had recently invented, but it lacked the tension blade and drawstring. He aimed and pulled the trigger.

"Tash'et," he swore when he saw a small dart stick into one of the bodies. He pulled it out and examined it. Naturally, he tried to justify himself by thinking it was poisoned, but he knew the obvious and he began to feel a little sick.

"You could have told me that this wouldn't have killed me," he said disgusted, holding it up for whoever was looking at him.

Arthor threw the dart down but kept the rifle. He moved to another soldier and then the next, trying to see if any of the *gadgets* on them would be of any use. As he did so, images and memories—he never remembered experiencing—flashed in his head and helped him sort through the *devices*.

He soon gave up the search; however, feeling the cool air of the room, he reluctantly cut swatches of their clothing to cover himself.

Before he could contemplate on what he had just done, an acidic stench suddenly began to fill the room. His tail jerked in reflex. He felt his ears perk, and he listened for the direction of the *gas jets*, but he couldn't find their location. He shook his head and dropped to his knees in utter frustration and felt the return of that horrible anger.

The Silver Knight looked at the door, outlined by the color of a Tulian rose. He closed his eyes, wondering how quickly the gas would overcome him. His heart beat anxiously. He thought of the door again, the barrier—

Arthor Jones screamed. His wings flapped open. His tail straightened. His body shook. Then he heard a hiss, a sound of extreme heat and spontaneous steam. He opened his eyes.

Amazement! Fear! But he didn't have time to question fate. His legs were already moving, even though he could no longer see them. His arms, his wings, his body were all gone!

No time to think about it now. Arthor curled his lip and reached the end of his newly created tunnel. He looked out into the openness before him. He felt the wind on his skin, which had been turned invisible by some demon's craft.

Sirens screamed behind him. He heard shouts and calls for help. His wings spread out with reassurance, but Jones hesitated, despite footsteps and voices running toward him. He looked over the edge, seeing nearly a hundred-foot fall; however, regardless of a sudden, once-justifiable fear, he took a deep breath, said a prayer and jumped.

His wings held firm, but they did little to keep him aloft. He was levitating!

A great forest spanned out beneath him, and he shot forward without thinking. In seconds he was a hundred *miles* from the lab he'd just escaped.

"Tash'et," he cursed, not daring to look back nor returning to claim what they had taken from him. Fear of where he was and the new images flashing through his mind forced him farther away.

"What am I going to do? What can I do?" He knew a knight couldn't let fear and emotions rule his actions. But he remembered the anger he'd experienced earlier, remembered the unjustifiable slaughter he'd unleashed, and remembered desecrating those who'd died.

"And I've lost my armor. I've lost my sword! What will you have me do now?" he asked, but since he was so far away from home he wondered if God could even hear him.

Five days later, his wings ached, and Arthor dared not think about the boy he might have killed. He couldn't imagine how his life had taken such a shitty turn.

"Bastik," he swore a Verengoshian word instead of hundreds of crass expressions he now knew. A valiant knight supposedly never cries, but Arthor's eyes no longer could produce anymore tears—from dehydration or overuse he was not sure. He missed his home, his life, his family.

His vision finally blurred out and his wings followed suit. He dropped and spun downward in a long concentric path. He felt himself slam into what felt like tables and chairs and finally slide to a stop on hard *pavement*.

The people screamed and ran. He hadn't the energy to calm them but he didn't think they would have listened anyway. The screams continued and finally faded into the distance.

"Well, well, seems we have an unexpected guest," a tenor voice said. "Take him to the hovervan and power up the DNA degenerators. We'll give Walter a break today."

"Aye, Jim," someone else said. Then Arthor felt hands upon him, but he didn't have the strength to break free. He just let them carry him away. Despite his fears, the rocking motion eased him to sleep.

"Father?" Arthor woke up, but kept his eyes closed because of the morning sun. He remembered a dream and was thankful that it was finally over. He ran his arms beneath soft sheets, and he enjoyed the warmth and the sudden ease they brought him.

Jones moved his head on the pillow and stretched his wings on the enormous bed. He yawned, blinked and opened his eyes.

His heart sank when he saw that the surrounding room was not his own. Then the thousands of images he'd thought were imaginary once again blasted in his mind when he noticed objects that never existed on Deliplain. Adding to his disappointment, his stomach still growled from hunger and his muscles still ached from overuse.

Obviously a different group of people held him this time, but he remembered little of how he had been brought here, vaguely remembering some orders and a ride in a *hovervan*.

He waited for the nausea caused by the sudden flash of images to ease. When it did, he got up to check his surroundings. He took a deep breath, opened and walked through the first door without any trouble.

It's only a bedroom, he told himself, thereby downplaying any surprise. *Even if it's a bit more than what a grawbit gets in a cage.*

Connected to the bedroom he found a large living room. It was close to the same size as his accommodations at home, although it lacked the decorations he'd grown accustomed to in Verengosha. Overall, the room seemed comfortable; however, was it yet a prison?

He moved to a door, which appeared to be the main entrance. He examined it from top to bottom, moving his hands over every inch, and finally found what he was searching for.

The Castle of Verengosha had many secret rooms and hallways throughout its walls. All anyone had to do was press a well-placed stone or pull an unnoticeable lever and a door leading to safety or mischief—the latter, his mom often joked she'd found him in—would present itself.

Arthor thought he'd found such a stone. He knew it was only a regular doorknob; however, the way it was shaped, just a large red dot, made his memories surface and forced him to take a sudden, relaxing breath.

True, he reminded himself, *this is no longer home.*

The circle entered his eyes once more. It was eight *inches* in diameter, rested four inches from the right side of the door, and stood a *yard* from the soft carpeted floor. He pressed his lower right hand on it with caution but didn't believe it would really budge.

It did. He cracked the door open, peeked out and saw a pair of amber-green eyes staring back up at him. He grunted, but to himself, and soon smelled a pleasing fragrance.

A *human* female was standing outside the door. She had long brown hair, a round jaw and a button nose. She had shapely hips and other nice curves he tried not to notice. One thing he immediately saw, however, was that her hands held a tray loaded with items of those delightful aromas. Was this his breakfast?

She didn't seem afraid, and he noticed that she was even smiling. He didn't know very many people—including knights—who would calmly step up to someone who was two heads taller than themselves. This immediately impressed him.

But, a knight's first actions would still have been those of diplomacy, he reminded himself. *What type of honor do these creatures really know?*

His eyes followed hers and watched them move downward, lower and lower—until they closed and she jerked her head to the right. Her smile broadened and her cheeks turned bright red.

Peculiar reaction, he mused, questioning the emotional stability of these humans, amongst other things.

Wait a second? He frowned, feeling a draft.

He blushed—his wings suddenly wrapping around him. He back-pedaled into the bedroom, beginning to wonder how many times he was going to wake up naked on this world.

"Excuse me," he whispered and raised an index finger in her direction, hoping she would understand what he meant. He turned his head slightly to look for something, discovering his tail had already speared what he was looking for.

An opposable tail? He didn't bother shaking his head this time, somehow numb to the ever-increasing changes he was finding. "This has to be a dream," he whispered to himself. *A nightmare? Hell itself?*

He brought the blanket around him and walked back to the woman who had entered his apartment and was looking at the bare walls of his living room. He waved, getting her attention.

She smiled and walked his way. She stared at him, but he couldn't tell if it was from curiosity or prejudice. Quickly enough, he discarded the latter.

"Hello," he broke the silence. He'd missed the sound of voices. Anything would do.

"Hi," she said with little reluctance, nodding her head as though she had done this before. "Did you sleep well?"

He eyed her, doing his best to study the ever-increasing number of typhon-like lines in her face. "Yes, the bed was very comfortable. I haven't slept on one for days."

She pointed behind him, giving him another familiar grin. "Well, you slept on that one for nearly two. I was alerted that you woke up, and I came to see how you were doing."

He rubbed his chin, trying to ignore the ache coming from his bladder. *So, am I a prisoner after all?*

"Anyhoo, I wanted to get here before you started banging on your door, and broke it," she added, obviously aware of his newly acquired strength. "It was locked until I got here. We wanted to talk to you before you started roaming around the halls, and before you got yourself into trouble." She smiled again, and he knew their caution was justified.

She tapped her fingers on the bottom of the tray she was holding. "So, I brought you some breakfast. My name is Anna, Anna Murphey. I'm here to assist you during your stay."

The dialect she spoke was initially difficult to understand. Again, it was the odd, twisted version of Crytonian Standard he'd heard since his first arrival to this world. His intellect and thrill of science, and the recent *download* of information he'd seemed to acquire, labeled her speech as English, even though it held many similarities to his own Verengoshian.

"My stay?" he inquired. "I hope it's on a voluntary basis?" He also wondered how well Anna understood him.

"Of course," she said, answering both questions. "But I'm sure you'll stay with us. It's a wonderful place to live now. There's everything you could possibly want here: parks, recreation, entertainment, education and work." She sidestepped and shrugged her shoulders, but Arthor hadn't noticed her apparent rambling. "Ah, yeah, after you meet Jim ... well, you'll stay. I guarantee it!"

Arthor winced by her choice of words and her smile of confidence.

"And speaking of Jim." Her words sounded a bit stressed, as if followed by a sigh? "He wanted to speak to you as soon as you were ready. And, despite my great physique, my arms are getting tired," she smirked, but Arthor guessed she was considered very attractive by human men.

"Oh, by all means." He motioned her from the middle of the living room and into the dining area, where a table and chair were waiting.

She nodded and then giggled when she walked by. It was a dangerous thing to do when opening diplomacy with a new person, but she managed to pull it off. It even comforted him some. A little, but not entirely.

Anna set the tray down on the table, and then laid out dishes, a fork, spoon, knife, a cup and a kettle. The scent of herbal tea hit his senses, and he stepped away from the doorway of his bedroom to gain a better view of his meal. It smelled good, a lot like the meals in Verengosha, but a sweeter fragrance seemed to hang in the air.

"Will I get served like this every morning?" he joked and sat down on the chair behind the place Anna had set for him.

She poured him some tea. "Only if you're good, and you say, 'please.'" She dropped three lumps of sugar into his cup without even asking. He raised an eyebrow, but didn't protest. He'd always put three spoons of sweetener into his tea, even though Aenglan never quite got used to Arthor's desecration of such a good drink.

"Are you going to join me?" He held his lower right hand out, offering her a chair. He did it only out of courtesy, immediately wondering how these creatures ate. They had mouths but—

"No," she said, shaking her head, while he kept in a sigh of relief. "I already ate, but go ahead. Enjoy." She turned a knob on one of the food containers, while stirring something that looked like gravy. Then she poured it over some *potatoes*, which were on a side dish. That done, she looked at him intently, smiled and soon bobbed her head a bit, while throwing a number of glances between him and the food on his plates.

He pursed his lips, picked up a fork and chopped off a small segment of what looked like joal-cake, which was covered with an unusual kind of syrup.

Oh, just a small sample. He restrained his growling stomach. He just needed a taste.

Satisfaction! With five days of famish eating at his guts, he dug into the elaborate breakfast as quickly as his manners would let him. Every taste seemed to swirl in his mouth, and he soon heard his fork scraping on empty plates. He took a breath, wondering if he'd done so during the meal.

He laughed at that before looking up. Anna's eyes gazed upon him in what looked like pure astonishment. Had he eaten too fast, too slow? He thought she had left but should have figured differently. She'd been ordered to do more than just feed him.

He wiped his mouth with a napkin. "Oh, pardon my manners, Ms. Murphey, but I haven't eaten for some time. Yet that is no excuse. My name is Arthor, son of Duke Jacobson Alexander Jones of Verengosha. I am a citizen of Crytonia and former inhabitant of Deliplain." He had obviously left out one of his titles, but he felt too ashamed to proclaim it now.

"Nice to finally know your name," she said. The human fluffed her hair with a single right hand, tilting her head with a raised brow. "It's good that this man before me actually has one, but Jim's waiting and don't you think it's time to change into some clothes?"

A man in her eyes? "Chetok?" he asked and gave her an expression of inquiry and then consent, realizing he was still dressed in a bedspread. "Is there anything for me?"

Anna nodded and pointed to the bedroom. "Back there, in the closet."

After quickly being shown how to use one of their bathrooms, he moved back to the sleeping chamber and searched for the closet she was talking about. It was exactly that, nothing different than what he had in Verengosha, and he opened its door. Normally, he'd take a bath before putting on his clothes, and he was excited to use the *shower*, but his guests had apparently washed him before putting him to bed.

He looked in the closet and pulled out a suit of tight flexible material. It was like silk but different to the touch—thicker and insulating? He found an opening in the back, and stepped into the dark gray *bodysuit*.

It stretched and he pulled it up to his waist. His four arms searched and found other holes, forcing the material over his head and around his shoulders. The material gave way and moved around his wings, making a tight but comfortable fit around the aerial limbs, and the rest of his frame.

Once in, he looked down. There was a decorative trapezoidal flap—narrow-end down—attached to the front of the suit. He tugged on the ends and connected the top corner with the cloth on his upper right shoulder, where it stayed due to the scruffy round patch sewn into the fabric there. He pulled at it and he heard a tear. He cursed, wondering where the rip was.

"Finally introduced to Velcro?" Anna's voice sounded very close to him.

He turned around and found her within the room, apparently interested in his bedroom walls. Her cheeks were red again.

"Um, yes, peculiar invention." Ignoring the fact that a pinkish green tint was obviously on his own cheeks, he attached the front flap to his shoulder for a second time, discovering it was just an aid in dressing. It was something like a button.

"It's an old one." She nodded and looked him over. She also pulled down a flap of material that ran between his wings to Velcro patches near his lower set of shoulders. "I think a thousand or more years past? I forget the person who created it. Georges de, someone, Mestral?" She shook her head in uncertainty and came closer and tugged a wrinkle out of the front. "Don't ask me how I know that much. Anyway, it fits well on you."

"Thank you, but how?" He looked down, finding the suit did feel comfortable. It had four sleeves and there was even a hole for his tail.

"Ecie, our computer, synthesized them after he took your measurements." She smiled and pulled one last crease from one of his sleeves. Then she handed him some *cargo pants*, which he quickly put on. After that she asked, "Are you ready to go?"

He only nodded his head, knowing the noun *computer* even though there were no Crytonian equivalents.

"Good." She grabbed and tugged on his upper right hand, which dwarfed her own. Then she led him out of the apartment, which was temporarily his for the visit.

"Holy hell!" he shouted in English as soon as he walked out the door. A giant expanse opened up before him, in which an artificial sun and sky blazed high above, and hundreds of people walked here and there. Various potted trees were in front of dozens upon dozens of apartments, and a nearby park echoed the voices of children.

Immediately, he tried to grasp some understanding, some bearing of where he was and what he was doing, and how he knew so much about this world.

Government or Resistance? He kept that inquiry to himself.

"All right, all right," Logan interrupted Arthor's story. The Crytonian looked at the man's raised hands while eating some pancakes.

"What is it?" Arthor asked, wondering why his friend stopped him.

<><><><><><><><>

"I know this part," Logan said, reminding his friend. "You told it to me the week after my arrival here. I'm familiar with how you and Jim were introduced, and how you decided to stay here in Crystal Mountain.

"But how can you think you've been dishonored? I can't say the things that happened to you aren't bad or not your fault—hell, in some cases, they're justifiable. But they are matters of circumstance and you obviously feel guilty because of them. Shit, our knights of old did a hell of a lot worse and didn't seem to care."

Arthor looked up. His eyes narrowed a bit. "Jim has said that to me many times." Then the Crytonian's lips drew tight around humanlike teeth, obviously holding something else back. "Logan, we can find few mistakes with our good friends."

"You're speaking to the Choir here, man. I'm just saying … relatively speaking …" Logan scanned the blue eyes of his friend and bit back his last words. He wondered if he should try and push this any farther. He looked down at his eggs and pushed them around on his plate instead.

"May we join you?" a powerful tenor asked. Just as well, Logan had nothing to say.

"Sure, Jim." He looked up and slid down on the bench, nodded and waved to his friends. All of them had been on an extended swing shift. "I'm always partial to company. John, Rebecca, have a seat too.

"Did Jen join you?" He searched for the girl Jim had rescued recently.

"We decided to let her sleep in. She's still at the hospital." St. John looked at Logan and then at Rebecca. "The shock hasn't lifted from her yet, and she hasn't had a chance to really grieve for her family. She's still full of a lot of anxiety, and she hasn't said much. Dr. Kyle says the amount of stress she experienced was considerable. She still might withdrawal into herself, but Becca's trying to prevent that. They might look for an apartment soon." Jim smiled at the ex-Infiltrator, and she did the same. Like other times, they said little else but they stared at each other long enough.

God, I think it's obvious to everyone but them. Logan just shrugged off an old cliché. He also thought about Dr. Kyle, and wondered if he should tell him about his dreams. *No.*

"Hey guys, I hope we weren't interrupting anything," the ex-Infiltrator whispered loudly, scooting next to Logan. She gave him a wink and a smile. A nice one.

"I, well, shit," he stammered, looked at the Dishonored Knight and then at Jim. He suddenly realized that the typhon and human had been debating this for nearly three years.

Logan nodded, not wishing to double-team the Crytonian today. "Arthor and I were just discussing the special night we had together." He crossed his arms, caressed his own shoulders and puckered his lips at Jones.

Arthor immediately blew him back a kiss. Laughter burst out around the table, even though Logan's smile suddenly faded when he noticed that somebody hadn't laughed.

John Henry Powers appeared as though he had wanted to try. And despite displaying a perfect smile, he appeared to be left out as usual.

Fuck it, not sure if I can deal with all this shit today. McMillian looked at his watch, reading zero six hundred. To his own chagrin, and despite what he'd kept telling himself, he knew this was going to be a very long day. So, he immediately flagged down a server and, to the surprise of his friends, ordered a mimosa. Then he made it a double.

Uncomfortable silence followed. Each of his friends looked at his or her watch, made 'tisk, tisk' sounds, and then laughed and then ordered some too.

Logan laughed hard at that, especially when John joined in

the fun regardless of his handicap.

And, just like that, McMillian's sour mood quickly dissolved. Regardless of their various and nefarious pasts, they had become family.

Family. Hell. That was the real strength behind the Executioners, and Logan wondered if he should feel guilty for whomever they faced in battle.

Poor bastards won't have a chance, he thought. *Tough shit!*

EPILOGUE

Only a Christ could have conceived a Christ.

(Ecce Deus)
—Joseph Parker, British Preacher (1868 A.D.)

"You know that the Executioners are looking into the prevalence of nirv on the street?" Frugal asked matter-of-factly.

"Yes." Henry nodded, even though the mercenary on the other end of the comlink couldn't see. "One of your people told me that they were probably responsible for killing the disperal and tokom czars in South America. You think they'll come after us?"

Harvardson looked out the window as he talked. It was storming out. He stood in awe of it as bolts webbed across the dark sky. A storm was unusual for this time of year, but it was beautiful.

"I don't know. Be careful. You might try to establish some type of truce through the underground before anything happens.

Nirv isn't really that bad."

"You think it will matter?" Henry asked. "I've seen their like before. Rationality often doesn't equate. People like them ruined California. And I have people I need to keep safe. Reaching out to those bastards might lead them to us."

"True enough, but I still stress caution. We don't need … complications."

"I understand," Henry agreed. Frugal wasn't someone he wanted to upset. The man was a mercenary but kept a low profile. His group didn't even have a name, which actually comforted Harvardson some, since *that* underlined the necessity of privacy. "But we will protect ourselves."

"I understand," Frugal sighed. He, after all, had provided Henry with the weapons and means for defense. "Again. Just be careful. I will do what I can to help. But business, as of late, has been demanding."

"OK." The storm outside flashed and thundered and began to rain buckets. *Or cats and dogs,* Henry mused and imagined poor little animals falling from the sky. *How is* that *even a phrase? What sick fuck thought of that?*

"Thank you," Frugal smirked. "I would prefer not to kill off another rebel group right now. It upsets the balance some, and it's always … messy."

Silence … Henry at a bit loss for words.

"Right," he finally said.

The connection was cut and Henry just looked out the window. He didn't have any love for rebels or terrorists. Less so, for the government. President Lyly didn't know what the fuck he was doing in California, and things kept getting worse.

Well, he thought. *God help the Executioners if Frugal gets involved.*

—<><><>---

Please visit **PageBacon.com**

for more exciting titles

www.ingramcontent.com/pod-product-compliance
Lightning Source LLC
Chambersburg PA
CBHW071253170626
46809CB00001B/199